'Julian Bonser is a world-acclaimed writer whose literary brilliance has graced stage, screen and television. He has won the coveted Booker Prize five times and has just been appointed by Bill Clinton as his official biographer. His worldwide book sales now exceed twenty five million'.

Well someday, perhaps. But for now, this is my first full length novel to be published.

Like so many people, I've been fortunate to have enjoyed an interesting and eventful life. And to have worked my way through several careers, all of which had a strong creative thread. In addition I've been able to travel extensively and absorb an immense variety of culture and ethnicity.

And like so many people, as the autumn of life approaches, I've taken stock of the experiences I've accrued, the skills I've learned – many of them having no use in a today's world, and the general pot of trivia rattling around at the back of my head, and pondered what use it now has. It seems ironic that when our brains have reached their zenith in knowledge and experience there's often very little facility to transfer this into the heads of others.

But there is one highly effective means of recycling all those treasures, which, of course, is to write a book. I would even go so far to say that there should be a law to extract that one book from everyone in the realm.

Every one except perhaps David Jenner, who at 59, and aimless and unproductive, has little to offer of a cerebral nature. But then he…

Well, I'll leave you to read on.

If, having read the book you have comments or feedback, please feel free to express these using the following email address: LI5D@julianBonser.co.uk

Julian Bonser

Love in Five Dimensions

Matador
9 De Montfort Mews
Leicester LE1 7FW, UK
Tel: (+44) 116 255 9311 / 9312
Email: books@troubador.co.uk
Web: www.troubador.co.uk/matador

ISBN 13: 978-1905886-852

Typeset in 11pt Bembo by Troubador Publishing Ltd, Leicester, UK
Printed in the UK by The Cromwell Press Ltd, Trowbridge, Wilts, UK

Matador is an imprint of Troubador Publishing Ltd

This book is dedicated to my wife, Adeline.

Without her encouragement this story would have remained little more than a notional idea rattling around at the back of my mind.

Contents

1. Another Year ... 1

2. Some Cracks Appear ... 6

3. The Autumn of Life ... 10

4. From Bad to Worse ... 13

5. Ether and Expectation ... 16

6. Quality not Quantity ... 19

7. Late Ambitions ... 23

8. Mental Diversions ... 26

9. Castles in the Air ... 33

10. No Turning Back ... 45

11. The Beginning of the End ... 49

12. So Near But So Far ... 57

13. Dreams and Realities ... 60

14. Revisitation ... 67

15. Facing Up ... 71

16. No More Smoke and Mirrors ... 77

17. Final Arrangements ... 84

18. Better to Give than Receive ... 93

19. The Home Run ... 97

20. Final Touches ... 105

21. Nothing To Do But Wait ... 119

22. The Cost of Living ... 132

23. The Theatre of Life ... 145

24. Start Over   155

25. Life Goes On   169

26. An Old Life – A New Outlook   179

27. The Wind of Change   196

28. Momentum and Emotions   207

29. On and Up   218

30. Love Hurts   228

31. BoyZo to the Last   241

Acknowledgements

My thanks to Bobby Ghainer, a highly experienced Freelance Editor, who skilfully Copy Edited the Final Manuscript.

The 3D front cover illustration was created to my specification by CG Effect, a company specialising in corporate image — www.cgeffect.com

1

Another Year

The lazy drone of jets on the easterly approach to Heathrow sounded ever mournful to David Jenner. Since late afternoon he'd lolled around aimlessly on that old wooden sun lounger, listening to the pretty evensong warble of blackbirds and soft murmur of leafy West London suburban humanity. He'd stared idly into the infinite blue, following the vapour trails of planes too high to be visiting, occasionally letting his gaze drop to the familiar mosaic of garden detail. Easygoing flower beds, undisciplined buddleia, Wisteria tentacles that had long claimed ownership of the conservatory roof and outside loo; close-boarded fencing with the slender upright strips warped and dry – rather like thin fingers of burnt toast ready to snap when buttered.

To the east the deep azure slowly darkened to a rich cobalt blue, David now conscious of the lights of approaching aircraft; illuminated tail fins and neat rows of bright dots along the fuselage. He fondly remembered sitting in this garden as a boy in awe of those silver birds with their propellers and deep-throated engines – Super Constellations, Boeing Stratocruisers, Douglas DC7s – flagships of the sky.

After what had been a warm late summer's day, the sweet smell of dusk hung motionless in the balmy evening atmosphere. But with fading light and clear skies the air quickly cooled to an autumnal freshness, impinging on David's skin like a cold membrane. Idly he ran his outstretched hands across the grass, sensing the incipient dampness of summer's end.

On any other occasion this would have signalled a move indoors, but today he lacked any motivation. It was the 31st of August, the day that each year heralded a deep wave of melancholy. Seasonal Affective

Disorder was not a particularly good fit, though. Within a day or so the mental transition from summer to autumn would be complete – the blues dispelled. But somehow on this occasion the ephemeral twinges of pathos seemed more intense than before and David felt strangely tired.

The night sky advanced until day faded to a pale corona in the west. Colour rendition dulled to a grainy monochrome, and curtains were progressively drawn as the neighbourhood settled down to another evening. With more mental effort than physical David climbed off the lounger, gathered up his 'World's most eligible Bachelor' mug and retired to the kitchen.

Built in 1914, the house was a typical Edwardian semi: busy painted wood detail to the exterior, spacious rooms, and lathe and plaster ceilings that still bore the scars of the Second World War. Still intact were the small bell pushes situated by the fireplace in each room to summon the day-time domestic help of the era. Very little had been done to the house by David since the passing of his parents. Linoleum still featured on the kitchen floor – and the small black solid-fuel Ideal Boiler No. 1 in the kitchen continued its long tradition of churning out hot water. Open fires kept the house warm in winter and open windows cooled it in summer.

They had moved there in 1949 when David was four and all in all he'd spent fifty-six rather unspectacular years in this pleasant domicile just south of the Thames from Hammersmith. The house wasn't so much shabby as dated; but it was familiar and homely to him – a shrine to his parents. And now worth a few bob.

Primary school, eleven-plus failure, Secondary Modern, an aborted apprenticeship in the motor trade, miscellaneous jobs in factories and shops; success and ambition had truly eluded David. And when occasionally ambition had reared its ugly head, it would quietly dissipate without incident within a few days. His innate ambivalence dogged all attempts to proceed usefully in any one direction. Until finally he cracked a more enduring job at Thompson Wigs behind Marylebone Station in their mail order department. And over three and a bit decades he'd managed to climb through their shallow ranks to Sales Manager – Theatrical Wigs and Hair Pieces.

If the daily grind at Thompson Wigs was predictable, so was the journey. Number 73 bus to Hammersmith, then the Underground to

Marylebone via Paddington. David subconsciously knew every crack in the pavement from his house to the bus stop. It was a subliminal thing; his eyes took in the detail, but the swirl of thoughts saturating his mind as he strode along obliterated any recollection of that seven-minute interlude. They were recurring thoughts – always a reflective antithesis of an extremely inconsequential life. Of what could have been.

If only.

Years ago the future hadn't mattered. David's favourite axiom was 'work to live, not live to work' – he detested the idea of being a 'company man'.

And in many respects time had stood still. As living at home with no real responsibilities engendered a lifestyle leading nowhere. It had a 'live for today' ethos with lots of superficial interest seamlessly merging one day with the next – oblivious to the relentless count-down of life's egg timer.

Essentially a loner, David had slowly lost touch with friends from school days and those acquired during his teenage and early twenties years, as one by one they'd dropped out in progressing to marriage and other endeavours. Since then he'd collected a small, motley bunch of friends and acquaintances – mainly quirky individuals who shared his nebulous outlook on life. He was drawn to their offbeat and enter-taining ways, and lack of pretensions, there being little likelihood they would or could upstage him.

In the main, though, David preferred pleasant one-to-one female company. It made no great demands and he selected lady friends who were happy to be scheduled in – as and when. For years the majority of his dates came via the Hammersmith Palais de Dance. And when that became a night club for the younger folk he discovered the Jeanette d'Arcy Dance Studio in Richmond. It was a wonderful source of middle-aged women who were equally in pursuit of male company. The illustrious Ms d'Arcy was polished and charming and everybody's sweetheart; and on or off the dance floor she strutted hither and thither with a majestic pre-eminence. No one had ever seen her in daylight, but in the dim lighting of the dance studio she'd stayed forever young – blond, fixed smile, neck always encased in a wide, black velvet choker.

Although membership was all about dance instruction, the social angle attracted most people, David being no exception. He muddled his way through to Bronze in Ballroom and Latin American dance to keep the peace. Whilst at the same time, in strict tempo, he got to tango.

Ballroom dancing was a licentious excuse for close proximity. 'Your tummies must touch – no light between you!' And David found it possible to run two or three ladies at once – from different nights. Never got rumbled.

It was here he had met Pauline Blakely. She lived on a council estate and didn't have two pennies to rub together. Married once many years ago, she lived alone – parents long gone. Her dad used to drive the Number 9. Mum was a dinner lady at David's primary school – he recognised her from the photo.

But to her credit she was local and ticked most of the boxes. In the idiomatic speak of computer buffs she was plug and play – and within a couple of weeks they'd defaulted to a steady routine.

A sweet lass, Pauline never made any great demands of David. Rather, she got on with making the domestics of his life easier as was her nature. Though she quietly lived in hope – whilst David was mindful to do his own washing.

They'd have nights in and walks down to the river, and occasionally, a trip out to Richmond Park or Kew Gardens. Very occasionally they'd have a day out further afield in David's high-mileage Ford – he'd bought it off Thompson's when they traded up fourteen years earlier.

David's interest in Pauline waxed and waned, and each time it waned the downward inflection came to rest just below the last. Over time the interest factor levelled out to the exclusion of any dynamic variation. In fairness, they both blended well into the grey backdrop of urban life.

The passing of David's parents had triggered thoughts of his own mortality. And by osmosis the realisation slowly filtered into his mind that he had little to show for his adult years. Decades ago he would smugly be an observer on his friends' family lives, knowing there'd be no requirement to cope with dirty nappies and screaming kids. Or financial sacrifices and unsavoury in-laws. But by now his friends had married offspring, and grandchildren, and their lives had substance that his lacked.

His reticence to engage with life more fully had seemed such an easy choice at the time, but he'd not reckoned on the insidious way a shallow lifestyle would come back to haunt him in later years. And that time had arrived.

David locked the kitchen door, and after attending to the usual early evening domestics retired to the lounge with his latest self-improvement book written by the acclaimed Eloise Goodridge, and titled:

'It's never too late'.

2

Some Cracks Appear

The first of September dawned and so did the seasonal blues, intensified by the dismal realities of wasted years. Once out of bed a lighter spirit took over and David stepped through his tried and tested get-ready A to Z and into the placid cool of early autumn. So began another day at Thompson Wigs.

Pulling himself onto the bus David suddenly felt a nauseous sensation in the left-hand side of his body. It lingered for a few seconds and was gone, leaving a feeling of weakness in the pit of his stomach. Though it unsettled him for a while the incident had mellowed away by the time Marylebone tube station drew alongside.

His office was quite small, shoe-horned into what was once a store room, and there was no window. The desk was a tired-looking twin pedestal monstrosity in light oak that had darkened with age; two metal filing cabinets in dreary MOD grey stood to one side, an old-style General Electric office fan atop one of them. In the corner lurked a square table covered with all manner of paperwork and a box of wigs, various. Flooring comprised old-style polished synthetic tiles that might have featured in any 1950s school, factory or supermarket. The wastepaper bin was nausea green, as was the metal light shade which looked straight out of a film noire classic. Rumour had it that the Old Man had bought a job lot of office furniture from the War Office in 1958 when they relocated, much of it still remaining.

Harvey Thompson only believed in spending money on what made money.

The building was originally part of Marylebone Station and had been used as a light engineering workshop for repairing signalling equipment. The lease became available in 1955 and Thompson Wigs moved there from a basement operation in Westbourne Terrace, Paddington. The Old Man subsequently bought the freehold in 1966 when the Great Central Railway company was consigned to history.

It was in March 1972 that David had joined Thompson's – just another job at the time. But a comfortable niche quickly developed and employer and employee seemed to shake down well together. The work was reasonably undemanding and David soon got noticed without trying too hard. Promotion followed – a mixture of horizontal and vertical – though he felt uncomfortable at times in overtaking some of the lifers who considered themselves the heirs apparent.

Harvey Thompson's daughter, Emily, an only child, started work in the Accounts Received office soon after David took over National Newspaper and Journal advertising in 1982. She was a little younger than he and attractive in a homely way; unusual green eyes, long chestnut hair, full hips, delicate bust, small but expressive mouth, pretty hands and a warm, engaging smile. She had a pleasant domestic ring about her that was unchallenging to David's lazy intellect; and an easy rapport sprung up from their frequent close encounters in the narrow corridor.

Out of the blue one day she mentioned wanting to go and see *Tootsie* at the Shepherd's Bush Gaumont, and would he like to join her. A single date lapsed into a relationship. And true to form David suspended time and basked in the casual routine of seeing Emily. He never did get her into the sack, and just as well – Harvey Thompson had started calling him 'Son'.

Alarm bells rang!

Subtly, David applied some distance. Emily sensed the falling mercury but never latched on. Marrying the boss's daughter was surely a fast-track opportunity. But to David the prospect was pure anathema: it invoked the 'R' word – Responsibility. He felt justified in backing out. Emily's knickers had stayed firmly on at all times absolving him of any commitment. Emotional attachment didn't count. He was in the clear.

For a few months the relationship rambled on with David inventing all manner of reasons to justify his lack of enthusiasm. Whilst Emily remained understanding and optimistic. But puzzled.

Then fate took a hand – Harvey Thompson unexpectedly died

whilst at work. They found him face down in a plate of cottage pie in his office. It was his usual practice to have lunch served there.

The mood changed for Emily. Dealing with her father's demise was far reaching, what with the funeral and maintaining stability within the business. Having many long-term employees who knew the ropes well enabled existing impetus to be maintained. But someone at the helm was needed. In the interim Emily became caretaker and advertised for an MD. David might potentially have been Harvey Thompson's choice of successor on the basis of 'keep it in the family', but he paled against those with the right credentials.

Captain Michael Urquart, recently out of the Army, was seen to fit the bill. A dapper man in his early forties, university educated, precise, well versed in business practice and keen to make his mark in civvy street. He'd left the forces with a generous gratuity and was prepared to invest financially in the company.

Old Man Thompson had done well given the supply and demand of his era, but time was right for modernisation and expansion. And Captain Urquart was quick to recognise this. For Emily his appointment was a good choice. She admired his drive and vision and they quickly became close.

David had assumed that when the dust settled he could reel in Emily and maintain her at a comfortable distance. But the moment was gone, her affections now polarised in Michael Urquart's direction. At best, she regarded David with indifference. She married Michael six months later and David slipped back into the uncomplicated realms of employee. He consoled himself in knowing that Emily had been there for the taking, even aspiring to the notion that being MD had been within his grasp. But they were hollow thoughts and failed to dispel his growing sense of inadequacy.

Years passed with David attaining a slow increase in seniority – with a little help from retiring or expiring staff. His personal life followed cycle within cycle; day, month, season, year; start and end synonymous – never progressing. Safe and predictable – pleasantly enjoyable. It was a case of one year's experience over and over. Maintaining this agreeable equilibrium had been easy and life's midspan levelled out into a lazy plateau of self-indulgence. But now some cracks were appearing.

David entered his office, turned on the light, hung up his coat and sat down. Something wasn't quite right – he felt a strange apprehension. It was one of those prophetic moments when one's intuition bears an unspoken message. It left him uneasy, and the unsettling experience at the bus stop flashed across his mind.

3

The Autumn of Life

'Cuppa?' It was Vera – Teas and Lunches.

David quickly surfaced. 'Oh, err, yes please Vera.'

'Two lumps and just a teenie weenie dash of milk?'

Vera knew damn well how David liked his tea, but liked to mock. She winked and flashed that toothy smile. There were lots of teeth and some for later. And when she smiled her top lip was obliged to slide up those prominent incisors. She was a doll – very East Hackney, though Acton born and bred. Vera had been with the outfit a long time, and now, although in her sixties, she still had the sweet touch that endeared her so. Harvey Thompson had been fond of her. Very fond.

The telephone shrilled – first call of the day.

'David Jenner, please.'

It was Rikki from the Theatre Royal ordering for *Pride and Prejudice*. The mid-gender voice had been a puzzle until one day when David had called the theatre the young lass answering had said, 'I'll go and get HIM.' Dispelled for a while, the puzzle returned when he went to see Rikki about an order and was introduced to a rather glamorous 'woman'.

David was never comfortable dealing with people who had no surname. Likewise, he hated being called 'Darling'. But it came with the territory.

Theatrical demand for wigs and hair pieces was reasonably constant except for the manic run-up to Christmas. Pantomimes were a good bread-and-butter line and Thompson's supplied most of the Greater London theatres. It was a balancing act to phase the orders and assure an even workload. And the orders just kept rolling in.

10

Tea arrived.

'Don't let it go cold!'

Vera pinched his right cheek playfully. Then Phil Appleby from Production ambled in.

'Can't get the Synthaform latex for the Apollo order until next week.'

The phone shrilled again, this time Silvia Hewitt from Theatrical Factors – *Brazil Brazil* was closing after only three months; was he interested in fifty exotic headdresses? Pam Brewar stopped by with expenses forms to be signed. And in between David ploughed through his emails before making a start on the monthly sales forecast.

Business as usual.

Most days were same ol' same ol', David easily coping with the daily workload given that many of the orders were repeat business.

Lunchtimes were usually spent strolling round Regent's Park or observing boating life on Regent's Canal. And with Marylebone tube station on the doorstep, Oxford Street was only a few minutes away.

Occasionally Frank Weller from Dispatch would join David for a drink in the Pony and Parrot and they'd put the world to rights. They'd also chew the fat on the shortcomings of their respective lives, resolving nothing; walking away to the same dismal status quo. Frank had joined Thompson's two years before David and they'd served time together in Mail Order. Frank was Bethnal Green, beer, fags and Arsenal FC. He'd caught the tail end of National Service in 1960 – two years of peeling spuds and square bashing at the Army barracks down in Deepcut, Hampshire. A bear of a man, double chin and stubble, yellow teeth, a head of hair thicker than the fur on a Davy Crockett hat; still wore his army belt – spat on his shoes to shine them. Two years of Nasho' weren't wasted on Frank.

They were chalk and cheese, but Frank's raw normality provided a rational peg in the ground for David. When life's perspective blurred he could synch with Frank's uncluttered intellect, discharge the static – set the dials to zero.

Pete Spiller was another of David's buddies. Quiet and unassuming, a slightly built man in his late fifties – hair Brylcreemed back like a 1940s band leader; Joe Loss, maybe. Fourteen years ago his wife had been prescribed a daily tot of whisky to combat premature hardening of the arteries. She'd taken a liking to the medication, now dividing her time between rehab and AA. For all that Pete had an inner calm, his smile warm, fatherly, philosophical. He was happy to bear that cross. In better times Joan, a real cracker, was never short of male attention. With the patience of a saint Pete would wait in hope for those brief but intense flashes of affection that came his way. Now she clung to him for sanity's sake. Occasionally he'd join David on a stroll along the canal, or they'd sip alfresco Costa Coffee on Marylebone Station concourse.

Four o'clock and the day was dragging a bit. David bumped into Nasheima in the corridor. She spoke flirtatiously with those large brown Moroccan eyes. Only nineteen but bright and worldly – curvaceous and confident. According to Nina in Quality Control, Nash worked part time as a belly dancer at the Scheherazade in West Kensington. In conversation she grabbed David's simple mind and fed him unspoken promises. And the afterglow of those provocative communications always left him in no doubt she found him attractive.

A visit to the Gents and a reality check in the mirror popped his bubble of conceit. Greyish receding hair, baggy eyes that didn't recover after a good night's sleep, facial muscles that were losing their fight with gravity. Lips that were beyond Collagen. And adding to this candid image were sinister facial shadows from the harsh white light of a bright but cloudy day that streamed in through rusty, iron-framed windows. David suddenly sensed he was on the cusp of life's downslide. Middle age had been extended by spreading it thinly, but the lining had worn through and metal on metal friction heralded the next phase of nature's wonderful life cycle.

Addressing the tired but stylish urinal, his eyes were drawn to the words 'Shanks & Co Ltd Imperial Nine' that encircled the water flush spout – words he'd read over twenty thousand times. Literally. The gent's loos had once served the GCR blue-collar workers and apart from new soap dispensers and hot-air dryers, little had changed. Finding a dry spot to stand on whilst peeing was a challenge. The cisterns still hissed and gurgled, and no amount of Air-wick could sweeten the air.

Home time loomed.

4

From Bad to Worse

Was it imagination? The waistband of David's suit trousers was beginning to feel uncomfortably tight. He'd noticed it back in August, putting it down to good living. Now he felt an unease about his expanding girth – a gut feeling. The nauseous experience was reoccurring and David's denial slowly deferred to partial acceptance that all might not be well.

Lying in the bath, he pondered his domed abdomen, concluding that geometry and symmetry were within tolerance for his age. But a vertical examination left doubt. Looking down his torso at a shallow angle the soft abdominal flesh just beneath his ribcage was definitely fuller on the left side.

Rising panic now lurked, checked only by hope of a simple explanation. David tried to visualise the inner contents of his torso. Heart, lungs, liver, kidney, large and small intestines, spleen, and possibly a few other bits and pieces. It didn't help, though, as he had only a rudimentary idea of their location. He toyed around with several possibilities: wind, a misplaced organ, a hernia. In background his thoughts lingered on the trouble-free existence he'd enjoyed to date. Maybe the problems of life were backloaded, waiting to wreak their worst as his sixtieth loomed.

Morbid preoccupation set in – a sense of dread never far away. David's social activities and the occasional demands of work gave some respite. But the unknown slowly eroded any remaining tranquillity.

Unable to contain the growing feeling of desperation, David mentioned his symptoms to Frank Weller – as nonchalantly as he could contrive.

'What do you think, Frank?'

'Dunno, Davy. Best go an' see the quack – probly a germ or somefing.'

Opening up to Frank was moderately therapeutic, but overall it did little to relieve the deep sense of foreboding – the knowing that something was amiss within.

Along with the sickening lurches was now a sensation that 'something' was present – something alien. No pain or discomfort – at worst a slightly bloated feeling – but always there. It caused a fissure between the subconscious and conscious minds that allowed anxiety to bleed through – twenty-four hours a day.

In a moment when common sense briefly prevailed over fear David organised to see his GP.

Dr Bharani's warm reassuring manner was halfway to a universal cure. His intelligent hands gently but firmly read David's abdomen, palms and fingers applying a complexity of motion and pressure. Pressing, kneading, stroking, tapping, touching – analysing.

'Are you worried about anything at present?

'No.'

'Work OK?'

'Yes, fine.'

'Motions normal?'

'Yes.'

'How often?'

'Usually once or twice a day.'

'Anything unusual – blood in your stools?'

'No.'

'Any weight loss?'

'No, if anything I've put on weight.'

A sense of relief washed over David. He'd passed the test. Dr Bharani's suspicions amounted to nothing.

'There appears to be a slight swelling in your abdominal cavity – difficult to say what the likely cause is at this stage. First step is to get a few tests done. Are you still covered by BUPA?'

'Yes.'

'OK, I'm going to refer you to Mr Stephens at the Prince Consort Private Hospital, just off Brompton Road. He's a gastroen-terologist – you'll be in good hands.'

If David thought he was off the hook the word 'hospital' cranked his anxiety back up to concert pitch. He'd last been in hospital aged three to have his adenoids and tonsils out. Graphic memories of hallucinations induced by chloroform were quick to emerge. Fifty-six years on and he could still recall the smell and nauseous effect of that primitive anaesthetic.

'You should receive a letter within the next few days.' He sensed David's fear and apprehension and beamed a smile rich in endorphins and Vallium.

Uttering some forced cordialities, David left with a prescription for Siestathol sleeping tablets. Dr Bharani followed him to the front door.

'Don't worry too much and don't look on the Internet to diagnose your symptoms – you'll only frighten yourself!'

The hubbub of early afternoon street life diluted David's morose thoughts. September had maintained a warm, relaxed demeanour and as he strolled home through the sociable residential roads of his childhood, a pleasant sense of well-being drifted through body and soul. Upbeat eased out downbeat. His ailment became trivial – curable.

A letter from Mr Stephens arrived four days later. Please present yourself at the Prince Consort Private Hospital at 11:00 am on 29th September. Eat and drink nothing for twenty-four hours prior. A few sips of water are permissible. Wear loose clothing. Bring along any medication you're currently taking. Fill in the enclosed form and hand in to the receptionist on arrival.

Anxiety was now tempered with a sense of relief. Like most, David assumed the worst. But in addressing the problem he felt in control. Some time ago he had read *How to Stop Worrying and Start Living* by Dale Carnegie. The text centred on a simple philosophy – 'accept the worse and anything less will be a bonus'. He'd pondered this axiom many times. It could be applied to losing one's job or wife. Being made bankrupt, having one's mortgage foreclosed – situations that might be redeemable in the fullness of time. But having one's life foreclosed was maybe stretching things.

David continuously stirred every possible symptom and accompanying rationale into a large mental pot. But the outcome was variable. Sometimes he could extract a happy ending. Other times, he knew for certain.

He was a condemned man.

5

Ether and Expectation

More like a hotel foyer, reception at the Prince Consort Private Hospital oozed commercial efficiency. The lass behind the desk was maybe Rumanian or possibly Polish – Russian at a stretch. Leastways, David concluded that she was definitely a foreigner.

He was logged in and took a seat. Having been raised on vintage copies of *Good Housekeeping*, *Country Life* and *Punch* at his local surgery, David marvelled at the selection of current magazines available. He flicked through *Men's Health*, seeing but not reading, palms moist, heart at the double.

One young man had his leg in plaster. David envied him. A broken leg got better. People wrote silly things on the plaster. Plenty of attention – maybe time off work with pay. A couple to the left told a different story. The man, elderly, was leaning forward, his head cupped in one hand; he wore a dressing gown and slippers. The lady, presumably his wife, looked drawn and pale.

A young Chinese girl sat without emotion – clearly pregnant. Next to her was a woman with an elderly lady. The lady was gesticulating to the woman, maybe her daughter, whilst mouthing words. She had a small flap of material taped to the base of her neck. Now and then the flap rose up to reveal a small hole. David realised that she was breathing through this hole. His mind squirmed.

'Mr Jenner?' There was nothing about Mr Stephens that announced 'gastroenterologist'. He wore a black jacket and grey and black striped trousers – standard kit for a 'Mister' in a private hospital. David took his out-stretched hand and they made acquaintance.

Mr Stephens examined David and then outlined the diagnostics scheduled for the day: a variety of X-Rays and scans along with blood tests.

Throughout, David studied the faces of the nurses and radiologists in the hope of an indicator, but his questions merely drew the same reply: 'Mr Stephens will discuss the results with you.'

Ultrasound scanning was a little unsettling. Something caught the radiologist's interest causing him to thrust the well-lubricated probe deeper and deeper into David's abdomen. The video display unit was out of view – probably for the better.

Then a narrow moving table transported him through the centre of a large white doughnut – CT scanning apparently.

X-raying appeared to have made massive strides since David's last such experience aged three years old. His mother, believing him to have a temperature, had slipped a thermometer into his mouth. For whatever reason he'd bitten the glass bulb, breaking it, and swallowed the mercury. At Putney Hospital they had scratched their heads and sent him on to St Stephens's in Fulham. It was a unique case with little recourse other than to monitor transit of the mercury using an antiquated X-ray machine. David vividly recalled how it had whirred and groaned as the lens assembly descended menacingly towards his stomach.

Then the blood letting. Ten syringes in all, each colour coded. Nearly an armful.

Finally, the obligatory urine sample.

By three twenty-five David was able to clean up. He felt tired and despondent. A snack in the hospital restaurant was recommended – his specialist would see him at four.

Back in front of Mr Stephens David awaited his sentence, but was given a stay. Time was needed to study all of the results. More tests might be necessary – 'all the pieces of the jigsaw puzzle were needed'.

Discussion was minimal, if any, and David soon found himself walking towards Knightsbridge Station clutching an appointment card for a week hence. It seemed a lifetime's wait at the time but some contact sport with tourists and city slickers on the crowded Piccadilly Line distracted his anxiety. Just as rubbing a bruise confuses the nerves and hijacks pain impulses on their way to the brain.

He emerged into the warm hazy sunlight at Hammersmith and

decided to walk home, the day's events replaying on 'repeat'.

On reaching Number 69, his subconscious had crafted an optimistic spin for the future; he felt pleasant and Tuesday week had receded to the horizon.

And after all, why worry today, about what you can worry about tomorrow?

It never failed.

6

Quality not Quantity

A ghastly, cold numbness rose inside David's torso and dissipated through the skin of his arms and neck leaving a clammy residue.

'Malignant tumour?' It was unreal – he wanted to send those words back. The room lurched – his scalp contracted.

'I'm afraid so, Mr Jenner.'

Mr Stephens articulated the devastating news softly, gently – with empathy, sympathy; the hint of a compassionate smile.

In a choked voice that hardly seemed to belong to him David asked, 'Will you remove it?'

Mr Stephens pondered his clasped hands briefly before slowly raising his gaze to meet David's, head on. 'The tumour is too large and complex for surgery, and the blood tests indicate an aggressive spread of malignant cells.'

'What does that mean?'

'It means, Mr Jenner, that there's very little I can do for you. I'm so, so sorry.'

David's heavily traumatised vocal cords jumped an octave. 'How many years do I have left?'

In hushed tones Mr Stephens explained. 'You possibly have about three months. You might want to seek a second opinion – I really am so very sorry.'

Two or three months! Nothing had prepared David for such devastating news. Even on a bad day he'd ascribed only an outside chance to 'terminal'. And even then the most morbid speculation had returned a value of years, not months.

David sat motionless as he struggled to mesh with this brutal moment of truth. So much for the sage advice of Dale Carnegie.

Mr Stephens offered patronising words of comfort that filtered distantly through to David's detached consciousness.

'Think of quality not quantity.'

Support would be provided. An oncologist would prescribe medication and monitor his case.

'Good luck, Mr Jenner.'

Once again David found himself in the street. He heard nothing, felt nothing. His feet took over and propelled him along Brompton Road, past Harrods to Knightsbridge. Then left towards Kensington. He walked and walked; Kensington Gardens slid by, Barkers, Olympia, Hammersmith Broadway. It wasn't until he reached the centre of Hammersmith Bridge that his mind started to defrost.

The day was dull and chilly, offering no consolation. 'A second opinion' – the straw appeared, but David declined to grab it. Such were his symptoms and bodily intuition that he somehow sensed an irrevocable decline had set in, his thoughts transcending any frenetic attempts to buy time. Leaning over the cast-iron balustrade he cast his gaze into the muddy Thames water as it drifted downstream. And he surveyed the tow path he'd cycled so often as a kid. The river vista never changed. Many times he'd stood on the same spot to watch Oxford and Cambridge battle it out on their way to Chiswick Bridge.

Happy days.

Then a strange clarity took over. Someone pulled focus and the world sharpened up as never before. David contemplated the passage of life. Flowers came and went. So did animals. Flies lasted hours or days. Did they know they were living a life? Cradle to grave – his parents had spent their term in this life and moved on. So had most of his relatives. Now the large hour hand of life was casting its shadow over him. He was able to defer to the transitory nature of life, his mind zooming out to the bigger picture. A window of understanding opened briefly and put life's short journey in perspective. Understanding brought calm. Calm brought acceptance.

Acceptance of the worst.

The vibrations and roar of the traffic crossing the bridge sneaked through David's threshold of awareness. Sensation returned – his mind cleared. He wearily turned to complete the last leg, now aware of the pungent smell of nervous sweat as the movement of his arms pumped out the disgusting vapour from within his jacket.

Surroundings became visible. Surroundings that David had never noticed before. Surroundings whose longevity would easily span his coming and going in time.

The main road from Hammersmith Bridge slowly curved to the left with David's turn-off lying on the radius of the bend. Slowly he pressed on, departing the main drag for the tree-lined avenues that led to Number 69. Old Mrs Miller spotted him and waved from her square bay window at Number 63.

He was tired. The house looked tired. Once full of family spirit, three generations, noise, laughter, activity – now just a house. Inside, David slumped in a chair and stared vacuously into the back garden, his mind still trying to unscramble the full ramifications of Mr Stephens's diagnosis.

St Mary's clock struck three-thirty – normally of no significance. But it triggered thoughts of time. Hours, minutes, seconds. David had spent the best years of his life squandering time. Time was the currency given to a new life. Not exchangeable or redeemable. One's allocation unknown 'til the meter ran out.

Mr Stephens's words drifted back – 'quality not quantity'. They made little impact at the time – hackneyed words of a professional mister breaking the bad news for the nth time. But the simple message started to bite. The last few hours seemed to have conferred some belated sensibility on David. Hours became more interesting. They possessed sixty minutes. Optimistically he had nearly 130,000 minutes to play with. He'd expanded time. Take out 37,000 minutes for sleep – rather, make that 30,000. Over 100,000 minutes left.

Three months wasn't looking quite so bleak. In his inimitable way David had massaged perspective to suit. It was an attribute that he'd honed to perfection. As for David, tomorrow rarely came. And now he was putting off the inevitable in earnest.

A hot bath came to mind and David eased his soiled being into the comforting warmth. The abdominal swelling was now developing a personality of its own. He dwelt on the saying 'keep your friends close, but keep your enemies even closer'.

He couldn't get much closer to the enemy.

And then an agitated walk round the neighbourhood whilst daylight persisted. Evening anxiety was difficult to cope with. Too much time to reflect. And ironically TV seemed knee deep in hospital dramas at present. Besides, even his favourite programmes failed to draw his attention for more than a few minutes. Reading was out – his eyes would just glaze over. David had thought about calling Pauline Blakely to break the solitude. But what would he say? She lived in hope that casual sex was the ticket to better things. His conscience stirred moderately and he decided she'd given enough to his cause.

Intense thought dominated the evening. Surprisingly not so much a preoccupation of impending doom – more about a tidy exit.

Given David's secretive nature he had no intention of telling anyone – he'd just GO, leaving no personal audit trail for the inquisitive.

A means to discreetly withdraw from work was needed; resignation required three months' notice. Being already on three months' biological notice made this untenable. Sliding out of view with a doctor's certificate seemed favourite. But coping at work in the interim was a worry. Deep down, though, David knew it would keep the demons in check.

The other closing domestics didn't seem too onerous. There were wills and things – the house definitely wasn't going to find its way to those distant relatives who never wrote. Most likely some deserving charities would get a windfall. The proceeds could have funded a fast and furious lifestyle – out with a bang. But for all David's fickle qualities he couldn't see the value in such self- indulgence.

Tiredness crept up, David happy to conclude the day. The Siestathol had coped well with mild anxiety, inducing sleep with absolutely no side effects. Whatever state of mind David took with him to bed, the Siestathol had guaranteed oblivion for seven hours. Now it would be put fully to the test.

Swallowing the tablet he lay back, hopeful that as before, 420 minutes would flash by.

In no time at all.

7

Late Ambitions

Unlike a bad dream where subconscious experiences feign reality on waking, David surfaced from tranquillity that overran into consciousness. But not for long. Events from the previous day flooded back resurrecting the doom and gloom.

Attempting a calm and nonchalant demeanour at work was challenging. Vera was her chirpy self, managing to make David smile. And smiling helped.

Frank was curious. 'Where y' bin, Davy?'

He surveyed the big man. The epitome of unhealthy living, but with a warm presence that seemed to compensate. David was willing to bet he'd live to a hundred.

Yesterday's tasks added to today's pile. David beavered away, his workload requiring little thought. For the most part he felt well, save for bouts of tiredness. The nauseous spasms weren't so much of a problem. He'd linked them to any straining of his stomach muscles – controllable. But the bulge wasn't to be ignored, its presence increasingly evident; no pain, just an unsettling sensation that was getting louder.

Celia Clarke from Wages stopped by to natter. They went back to the early days. Celia was rounded in body and mind. Voluptuous curves that sat well – a wide mouth and suggestive eyes. Not bad for fifty-six. They'd always been fond of each other, but had become too brother and sister for the sap to rise enough to go critical. She'd sit on the side of his desk and pass on the gossip. David would hear some of what she said whilst admiring her deep, lascivious cleavage. This pleasant visual would often strike a chord in his Hugo Jones boxer shorts.

Today's gossip took in Michael Urquart who was now signing himself 'Captain Urquart' – after twenty years.

Celia giggled: 'Fancy a drink lunch time?'

'Could do – I've just got to pick up a few things at twelve-thirty. How about one o'clock in The Locomotive?'

Drugs prescribed by David's oncologist were the 'few things'. More Siestathol; Euphoridex to combat anxiety; Serenaphyl, an optional night–time anti–depressant; Retrobrax that claimed to put the brakes on bad cell production; taken thrice daily, Vytaboost to make up the shortfall of a poor appetite; and Morpheaze for the pain.

That would come.

Celia had playfully alluded to David's expanding waistline. Mercifully the cool of early autumn justified a jacket, but he wondered for how long his 'condition' could be disguised.

Emily made one of her rare appearances, now matronly and grey after rearing kids for nineteen years. She and David exchanged polite pleasantries on passing. Whatever homely appeal drew David to Emily had long gone. He briefly remembered their first date at the cinema. And how she munched those wretched Maltesers all through the flick.

The Captain barely acknowledged David – perhaps he knew. And at the monthly managers' meetings he'd address him in clipped, impartial and totally indifferent tones.

Back from The Locomotive he got on with the afternoon workload – whilst in background, like a dull ache, his mind churned away endlessly and inconclusively.

Firstly, a session with Jack Waterfield to discuss the best way to get Widow Twanky's wig to rotate and incorporate a flashing blue light. Jack was old school. Shirt and tie and always a brown overall – like the ones auction porters wore; pens and glasses case in the top pocket. His mouth, thin and straight only opened when he spoke. Lips that sealed perfectly. And he spoke as if he had a partial vacuum in his mouth. After a second of strange facial gymnastics his lips would suddenly break open with a pop, and after delivery be snapped shut with the inrush of air.

Later Raymonde, another one-namer, called from the Blue Review. His sibilant words minced down the wires. Could Thompson's make showgirl headdresses using fibre optics, so that changing coloured lights would illuminate each 'hair'.

And pigs may fly.

In the corridor Nash swept past in a cloud of Chanel. She half turned, with a flick of her hips to smile at David, her eyes writing cheques that his sickly body couldn't possibly cash. He knew she was lying.

Time passed with an inevitability. Saturday tomorrow – and one could sense the Friday wind-down. David realised that bodily he felt much the same as he'd done the day before yesterday. Except now he was braced for a different finale. And although resigned to the sand running out, facing the decline of clinical life with all its unknowns was shaping up as a harrowing prospect.

By 4.30 Thompson's had gone quiet and he gladly joined the TGIF brigade.

The ginger tom from Number 57 bounded along the high copings of the front garden walls, level pegging with David as he headed for Number 69. From the tall brick-built gate pillar Victor observed him expectantly as he swung in from the pavement. Momentarily they were eye to eye, and whilst David pondered the capricious instincts of a cat, Victor fixated on his nose, extending an investigative ginger paw. Breaking away he headed up the path to the plaintive note of Victor's disconsolate caterwauling.

Today, on entering the house, he was regaled by the cheerful euphonics of loud pop music emanating from the kitchen – courtesy the radio, timed to switch on at 5.00 pm. It was all about keeping the gremlins at bay when returning to a cold, dark, empty house.

A tin of Big Soup satisfied David's emotionally reduced appetite, supplemented by one of the large Vytaboost capsules – a meal in itself; and out of curiosity, a Euphoridex tablet. For a while he sat pensively at the kitchen table, lulled by the soporific gurgles and mutterings of Ideal Boiler No. 1. Eventually the gentle cadence of domestic plumbing penetrated his thoughts, promoting the idea of a hot bath. And fifteen minutes later he was wallowing in the beneficial heat of steamy water frothed to perfection by Tesco bubble bath. As he lay there idly contemplating his misshapen torso, the Euphoridex finally hit its mark, dispelling anxiety and inspiring the notion of some light relief.

Yes, thought David, I *will* call Pauline.

8

Mental Diversions

'Stayin' the night?'

David hadn't thought that far, but declined. It wasn't that there was any pressure to perform. Rather, pangs of conscience from two days ago resonated and staying the night, even if he laid off the goods, would feed Pauline's hopes. Besides, there was the problem of explaining away the asymmetry down below. Naturally enough he'd not opened up on matters arising. No plans to either.

As usual Pauline passively accepted David's answer. She was very self-contained – happy to fit in with his directionless lifestyle. He often wondered what she did with herself when he wasn't around – not that he really cared; so long he didn't catch anything from her. She seemed to have a conviction that they were going somewhere despite their detached association. A faith maintained for twelve years.

Over the weekend David sensed a growing need to 'make preparations'; a call that sprang from nowhere – an innate sense of duty woken by circumstances. It triggered a domestic stock-taking exercise that quickly spiralled out of control. A serious can of worms.

Paper of every persuasion littered the lounge floor. Bills, policies, deeds, letters, bank statements, guarantees, investments, pension details, tax, pay slips, loan agreements, etc. In addition there were hundreds of black and white family photos that went back to late Victorian times – photos that David never tired of trawling through. In a separate pile an inventory of treasured possessions was accumulating.

Having become a repository for three generations over nearly fifty-five years, every corner in the house yielded its share. Each item told a story, evoked a memory. It was a bittersweet trip down memory lane. And it came with a problem, in that David simply couldn't bring himself to ruthlessly dispose of all this sentimentality in his own lifetime. Nor could he countenance the idea of house clearers job-lotting his life in antique shops and car boot fairs after the event.

A solution came to mind, perhaps a little bizarre. He'd pack up all items of sentimental value and place them in storage – three or four tea chests should suffice. There'd be instructions to hold the cases for a couple of years, whereupon the contents would be auctioned for a good cause. Or burned. It was a pointless exercise, but one that suspended the problem of disposal. At least he could bow out knowing his personal possessions would retain some dignity until he was well down the line.

Each job created two more, and it took the best part of a week to sort and pack. And clear up the debris. Sadly, the very fabric of the house was saturated with nostalgia, but David knew he had to draw a line at some point. With most of the evidence of his life now crated up he was free to craft the final snapshot – enjoy some control over how he'd be remembered.

If he were to be remembered.

It now only remained to have a will prepared. David wasn't too fussed about who got the money providing it would be used effec-tively. He favoured the larger registered charities, but also made a list of needy local organisations and people who'd helped him over time. Plus an allocation to cover the earthworks. The terms of his will got a bit messy, but Mr Paine of Paine, Procter and Pratt managed to distil David's requirements into the sort of legal lingo that wills are made of.

Affairs in order, he felt a sense of relief at having faced the tasks associated in closing down a life. But now with time on his hands the apprehension of things to come started to resurface.

And of late, work had become a little laboured. Trying to maintain interest in a role that was inherently uninteresting, given the altered emphasis on his life, was a losing battle. It signified to David that his withdrawal from Thompson Wigs was reasonably imminent. Dr Bharani was very supportive and had all the answers necessary for long-term sick leave. On David's instruction he would liaise with Edith Rogers in Personnel; no further need for David to be in touch.

The daily grind had been a saviour, but its value was diminishing. Now he just wanted to expend his remaining days savouring the world around him, away from the vapid confines of Thompson Wigs.

November dawned, the increasing dark and cold echoing David's decline. A portable butane gas heater in the hall went part way to keeping off the chill. Whilst the coal-effect gas fire in the sitting room pumped out bucket loads of comforting warmth. Most nights he was resigned to staring into the glowing chunks of artificial coal and letting his mind freewheel amid the changing colours and shapes. And for the most part he managed to keep rising panic in check. But on the rare occasions when desperation, fear and loneliness overwhelmed his fragile psyche he was driven to finding solace in Pauline's company. It was a cruel exploitation and Pauline must have guessed his fickle motives. But she still lived in hope.

So far David had filled four tea chests and they stood in the dining room with a fifth chest accepting the drip feed of final offerings. Now it was left to figure out how to guarantee rediscovery of their contents several years hence. Conventional self-storage was out – rather, a specialist service was needed where instructions could be given for later. Simmonds Brothers Removals had a repository in Putney – he knew about them from regular sightings of their pantechnicons. 'Enjoy a moving experience – Est. 1926'.

However, in the midst of resolving the storage solution, it suddenly dawned on him that he'd not sorted the loft. Not that there was much up there. It was all the usual clutter that wasn't wanted, but which people doggedly hung on to. His only recollection of the loft was that it was dark and dirty. Nevertheless, he didn't want the house clearers finding more nostalgic chapters from his life.

Saturday came round again. Armed with an inspection lamp, David cautiously opened the loft hatch on the upstairs landing. He was dressed for a cold and grimy experience. The naked 100-watt bulb threw strange shadows amidst the beams, rafters and joists of the part-boarded loft. Perched on the rafters of an unboarded area was the old cold-water tank, a masterpiece of zinc-plated steel and rivets. Too big to be removed through the loft hatch it had sat there idly for over forty years. Its successor hissed softly in a far corner.

When they arrived in 1949, David's father had pre-loaded the loft with the contents of their previous one. These treasures had enjoyed peaceful uninterrupted hibernation, waiting for a renewed sense of purpose.

David coiled the inspection lamp lead around a beam to fashion a suspended light and commenced a systematic trawl through the cardboard boxes and old suitcases. The contents were an education. His parents had quietly hoarded just about every official letter and document they'd received since their marriage in 1937. They'd also amassed the birth, marriage and death certificates and wills of their parents, grandparents and relatives. There were more photos. Ones David had never seen – possibly of his father's stepsister. Who was never mentioned.

More interesting was a book of poignant verse and poems penned by his father to his mother during the years of their courtship; it told a story of two people deeply in love – a love that lasted a lifetime.

Boxed sets of 78 records surfaced. Arias, concertos, symphonies; all pristine. His mother's wedding dress along with the silver columns from their wedding cake were packed neatly in a suitcase; in one of the elasticated pockets a lock of his own hair, aged three months.

Then David came across a box of possessions that he thought were long gone. Possessions that he'd outgrown, and which his mother had quietly squirreled away; things that had disappeared so subtly as not to be missed. Why they'd been promoted to the loft was a mystery. A mother's thing, maybe.

Some loose items filled in at the top – mainly bits and pieces from David's train set. Trix–Twin was the bees knees in those days – two locos could run independently on one track. Then there was that record rack fashioned out of green wire with black rubber feet. And still with a motley selection of records intact; scruffy 45s and 78s from the late 1950s.

Excavating further he found comic annuals, letters to his parents from Butlins holiday camp in Bognor Regis, the early transistor radio built from a kit (that never worked); bought in Tottenham Court Road when the place was still knee deep in ex-army surplus shops. And some copies of *Electronics Weekly* from 1959.

At the bottom, neatly bundled, lay the complete collection of

BoyZo Comic, compelling reading at the time. It appeared in 1956 but was the casualty of a Fleet Street merger four years later. Copies still popped up on eBay. On the front page, Zachariah Lightning, in his futuristic uniform – complete with black eye patch, his rugged profile silhouetted against the pink sky of Planet Cerisaephine And a look of retribution that would repel the most dangerous aggressor. As always he was there to protect the Universe; a cautionary tale in every episode. Good always triumphed over evil. Women and children forever safe.

David opened one of the comics. A bouquet of yesteryear newsprint drifted out of the pages, still fresh, triggering vivid recollections. His memory instantly rewound to that magical moment when he opened the inaugural issue with its free cardboard boomerang.

He flicked through several copies; Fists Malone, Hoss Maguire of the Wild West, Jungle Adventures, Professor Inventor, Inspector Hero of the Yard. Things to make, stories, puzzles, games, clubs to join; everything to fire a young mind.

Now seated, David started to work his way down the pile, amazed at how many story lines he recalled. Testament to riveting content and childhood powers of absorption.

And then something caught his eye – something that had fired him forty-six years ago.

On page six, a photograph, in basic colour, of a young girl in her mid to late teens. She was dressed in a pretty uniform – maroon with gold piping – round bell boy's hat inscribed with the letter 'R' in gold, fitted jacket with small epaulettes, and a pleated skirt that ended tastefully an inch or so above her knees. Hands on hips, one foot forward, she cut a classic showgirl pose. Dark ringlets cascaded down creating an attractive vignette around Italianate features. And an engaging smile embodying the sweetness of youth shone from her lovely face.

At the top of the page: 'Competition! Win a trip to New York City!'

Details were given to the right of the photo:

You'll fly to New York on a BOAC de Havilland Comet ♦ Spend a day at the Radio City Music Hall ♦ Enjoy a personal tour of this wonderful theatre with a real live Rockette as your guide ♦ 'Ride the Stage' – descend down a massive 27 feet on one of the four stage sections ♦ View all the machinery that operates this masterpiece of hydraulic engineering ♦ Go backstage during a performance of the Christmas Show ♦ Sit at the console of the largest Wurlitzer theatre organ in the world ♦ Afterwards, go ice skating at the Rockefeller Center ♦ Enjoy another full day's sightseeing before returning home ♦ You'll stay at the Huntingdon Plaza close to Times Square ♦ Your BoyZo tour guide will accompany you to each venue ♦ A whopping ten dollars a day will be yours to spend as you please!

How to enter: In the coupon below, tell us, in exactly twenty words, why you would like to visit New York. Complete the coupon and send it to the address shown. Entrants must be between ten and sixteen years old and hold a current passport. All entries must reach us by 1st of November. A letter to the winner will be sent out by first-class post on 1st of December. The judges' decision is final. No correspondence will be entered into.

David gazed at the young lady dressed so disarmingly in her Rockette's costume, remembering the first time round. Through the eyes of a thirteen year old she'd appeared so adult, so gorgeous; so unreachable. And for a few weeks he'd suffered the pain of unrequited love.

A wave of emotional yearning softly brushed David's heart once more. This time inspired by fond memories of his teen years – happy, carefree days that passed by without warning of impending adulthood. A pleasant mixture of real and surreal engulfed him – the tranquil in-between that ushers in the onset of sleep. For a few seconds he slipped into a comforting reverie – visions of the blissful domestics of those early days. The sweet smell of roasting lamb on Sundays, lazy spirals of classical music permeating the house – the simplicity in which his parents found such profound contentment. The virtual womb he'd never really left.

Sensations of rising cold returned David to the loft. It didn't take too long to mentally catalogue everything; a little longer, though, to hump the contents downstairs. And he was glad to close the loft hatch for the last time.

Tiredness and nausea took a grip. Intrigue had quickened time, but David realised he'd spent over four hours retrieving history. The radio piped up on cue at five o'clock.

Intangible feelings of unwellness were eased away with the habitual hot bath. And Euphoridex pre-empted the evening downer. After a light supper David slid into his favourite chair in readiness to contemplate the glowing coals. Beside him was the collection of *BoyZo Comic*.

Somehow, the trip down *BoyZo* memory lane wasn't quite done – David unsure what fuelled this notion.

Idly browsing the comics triggered nothing. David gave up and stared pensively at flickering images in the fire. Maybe inspiration would come if he gave rein to the peripheral vision of his mind.

His thoughts drifted to the New York competition. It assumed three dimensions in his mind's eye. Things were starting to make a little sense. All manner of disparate thoughts had buzzed around in his head – now slowly they connected.

Issue No. 137, 6 October 1958. David turned to page 6. He read and reread. Holidays had always been to European resorts – he'd never seen America. But the classic skyline of New York fascinated him. So many times it had featured in films – notably black and white ones. Radio City Music Hall – yes, he'd heard of it over time. But its true significance lay in *BoyZo* memories; emotional thoughts from 1958. And a pretty face that was long gone.

Interesting reflections perhaps, but they made no immediate impression on the gathering dark clouds of fate. Mercifully, though, the preoccupation with *BoyZo* started to pay dividends. As such was his intrigue with the competition's itinerary that bubbles finally appeared – the prize was still available! No entry needed – just a trip to the bank. Fantasy and selective thinking chorused; it was a chance to revisit happier times – a means of so fully engaging his mind as to suspend the final countdown. Denial at its very best – fear and anxiety safely quarantined.

Deep down, David knew that a childish element existed to his thinking; that the 1958 New York ambience of his daydreams would be cruelly absent. But he also knew that this crusade would tide him over. And with luck, the Almighty would call time whilst he was still overdosing on nostalgia.

Momentum gathered by the second and the idea became self-perpetuating.

From that moment on, David became a man with a mission.

9

Castles in the Air

Monday morning and the momentum from Sunday's revelations still persisted. David bounced and rattled along the Hammersmith and City Line knowing that Friday would see an inconspicuous withdrawal from Thompson's.

Earlier, he'd dreaded the moment when the clinical threshold for indefinite sick leave cut in. Now he was able to contemplate life after work – ready to proceed with a sense of purpose. The time was right. And besides, he'd grown uncomfortable at the quizzical looks from colleagues sensing unwellness. Even Nash had stopped flirting.

Long inquisitions with his oncologist had readied David for the likely prognosis. Tiredness would increase – vitality decrease; growth of the bulge would accelerate. There would be pain. And although the illness was advancing aggressively, its debilitating effect would be less obvious. More, a silent invasion. Good mobility to the end – his heart would flat-line without warning.

On Tuesday morning he saw Dr Bharani who then initiated the back-office communication with Thompson's. He listened attentively whilst David expounded his plans. A wise and perceptive man, he understood the whys and wherefores of David's escapism.

David managed to appear productive at work, although there was no real substance to his efforts. They'd find the holes eventually, but long after he'd ceased to care. Most of the time his mind was doubling up on the near future – now, all that was left.

The plethora of creative thoughts from Sunday was still no more than a fuzzy cloud of mental energy. It needed to be rationalised into something tangible and achievable, like a synthetic thread being drawn from a pool of molten nylon. David knew for sure that he was going to New York City. His alter ego had trialled the visit several times, but getting body and soul there took some prep.

A stumbling block was money. Plan A had been straightforward – assets willed on. Plan B conflicted. Realising funds would be dependent on selling the house – which would take time. Maybe mortgaging would be the answer. David conferred with several building societies but repayment was an issue at his age. Schemes were available at a higher interest rate, but processing timescales were about thirty days. And that was with his secret kept secret.

Onwards and upwards.

Whilst browsing the money magazines at WH Smiths, David spotted *Autumn's Gold*, one of the journals catering for retirement. On the front, smiling mugshots of a 'retired' couple who didn't look a day over forty-five. But what caught his eye were the words 'The new Heritage Scheme – spend now, don't pay later'.

David scanned the index and found the editorial illustrating this scheme. It was a variation on a theme – owners of mortgage-free properties could raise 95 per cent of the value of their property with no repayment. When the owner passed away, the building society took over ownership. The remaining 5 per cent was kept in hand for emergent admin costs, and any residue was added to the deceased's estate. Home owners over fifty-five were eligible.

On the face of it, a solution was in sight. Put out by the Kettering and Corby Alliance Building Society, the scheme was a bid to cash in on retirement products and services. Terms were good and a fast payout the sweetener that drew David in.

Enquiries with the Kettering and Corby Alliance suggested that an equity release scheme could be completed within two weeks. David made a formal application, quietly in amazement of the self-determination and resolve that came into play. Qualities he'd been short of at Thompson's.

Two days to go until Friday, and a week after that December would kick in. A mental calendar formed up. With a fair wind, he might see in the New Year. The funds should be in place by the end of the first week in December. In a rational moment, David noted that his will had quickly become obsolete. Beneficiaries wouldn't vary, however assets would now be liquid, with a chunk siphoned off to fund the New York City exorcism.

Another trip to Paine, Procter and Pratt. This time, David was persuaded to include them as executors on his will, given his unusual circumstances.

November had been dark and unforgiving. It was another seasonal quirk of David's and the Euphoridex sometimes struggled to break even. For comfort, David slipped on fleece tracksuit bottoms in the evenings. And he'd bought larger waist size trousers as physical comfort suppressed any nagging reminders. He had good and bad days, but the bad days were increasing and he could sense the internal takeover bid.

On Thursday as he headed up the front path after his penultimate day at work, he sensed movement in the front-room net curtains of Number 71. Several minutes after shutting the front door, the bell rang. It was Mrs Pewsey – she'd brought round a cylindrical package left by the postman.

A label reading 'Prince Consort Private Hospital' didn't give anything away. Inside, rolled up, were all the X-ray negatives from David's diagnostic sessions. Out of captivity, the large slippery acetates unfurled and cascaded onto the hall floor. A brief sighting of one of these grisly images was enough for David and he managed to install them back into the document tube with eyes almost closed. For want of a better place, they got parked in the under-stairs cupboard.

Working out his last day at Thompson's with no one aware of his impending departure was an uncomfortable experience. Even Edith Rogers was under the impression he'd be back. And studying the people he'd worked with for so many years became an intrigue. Such a Heinz 57 of shapes, sizes, looks, personalities – and yes, even genders. They'd almost become family.

But they would be here tomorrow, and the next day, and the next month – maybe years. For whatever emotions David read in their faces, he saw no preoccupation with longevity. He wondered what people read from his face. Was he unwittingly allowing people a fleeting glimpse of his soul? Their slight unease in talking to him was unsettling. Perhaps they did know.

In spite of the circumstances of his leaving, David still felt compelled to make a tidy exit. He furtively sifted through his desk drawers for anything secreted away over the years. Several letters surfaced. One from Marjorie Bevan dated 16 July. She'd worked at Thompson's as a trainee wig designer in the late 1980s; another of the homely brigade. David was a great devotee of her bottom but little else. Though he only ever got to sample its texture through layers of material. He'd given her a photo which she treasured. And she would relate how whilst admiring his adorable image, she would try and feed him small pieces of cake. It was at that point he concluded their respective objectives in the relationship were on divergent paths.

And then there was a letter from Christine Lovell. Married, quite a sophisticated woman and desperate to find release from an unhappy union. She'd sought respite with several men at Thompson's and David got his turn. He enjoyed some wonderfully elicit clinches and teased himself with thoughts of things to come. But deep down he felt out of his depth – and that there would be a price somewhere along the line. Christine moved on to the feckless Toby Stevens in Dispatch – only to ditch him when freedom came. Two marriages decimated in the process.

A crumpled form lay under the suspension files in his Pending drawer. David cringed at the contents. Years before one of the evening papers had offered free dating: 'Just complete your profile and return'. 'Name: Jason Strong, Age: 48, Occupation: Managing Director, Looks: very attractive, Income Level: £100,000, Interests: Sport, Investments, Flying, Skiing, Powerboat Racing, International Events, Anthropology.' Fortuitously, a number of female applicants were spared the embarrassment of meeting a date who didn't quite measure up.

For the sake of appearances, David agreed to have a drink with Frank in The Locomotive at lunchtime.

'Everyfing OK, Davy?'

'Sure, Frank.'

David tried to appear nonchalant, but he yearned to bare all to Frank. The big man quietly observed him. He might have been tempted to air any consternation he felt about David, unsubtly, but managed to curb a lifetime's habit. They chatted in a strained atmosphere, both parties nursing inner thoughts that were at variance with their verbalising.

On Monday a simple statement would explain David's temporary absence.

By late afternoon, he'd made preparations for whoever would take over. He'd tried to cover all eventualities, but as his energy faded it became a case of diminishing returns for any further effort.

One last trip to the Gents loo was made for homeward comfort. And for the last time his eyes fell on the words 'Shanks & Co Ltd Imperial Nine'. He passed Jack Fitzgerald on the way out.

'Hiya Dave, got anything planned for the weekend?'

'Not a lot – you?'

The somewhat scripted conversation faded as the loo door closed, and David headed for his office to find the phone warbling. Edith Rogers wanted to see him for a few minutes.

Edith was sweet. Bespectacled, trim, a little schoolmarmish and very efficient. But sweet. No one as yet had peeled away her professional skin. And no one really felt moved to do so. She gave the impression of being the same when viewed from any angle. Edith Rogers all the way through. Like a stick of Brighton rock.

'Hello David, please could you sign this form – it's a declaration needed by our insurers.'

'Fine, Edith.' David signed the form – no need to read it.

'I hope your treatment goes well and we'll look forward to seeing you back here soon.'

'Thanks, Edith.'

Having prepared to slide away unnoticed, David returned to his office and togged up for the final commute. He made his way discreetly to the Goods Inwards entrance – the crew there disappeared at 4.00 pm on a Friday – and met Jack Waterfield coming through the swing doors. Jack stood there momentarily, head and face twitching as some profound words headed from his brain towards the partial vacuum in his mouth. His thin lips parted briefly with a pop. It was the sort of sound made by Granny when she gave you a noisy kiss.

'Have a nice weekend, David.'

'And you, Jack.'

David smiled weakly and slipped into the cold, dark and wet of early December. Throngs of workers heading for two days away from the grind sucked him into their slipstream and he swirled along towards Marylebone Station concourse.

Victor spotted David as he reached the gate and leapt onto the high coping. They were nose to nose as David turned in. Victor engaged David in eye contact and meowed softly without bothering to open his mouth any more than was necessary – as cats do. For a split second, David mused that Victor might be delivering a life-changing message.

A day of mixed emotions started to mellow. David knew he had bigger fish to fry and life at Thompson's had no further relevance. His immediate challenge consumed him more than ever and he powered on with the never-ending list of preparations.

Flying to New York in a de Havilland Comet could now only be accomplished in dreams. The reality was a modern jet – Boeing seven-three-something-or-other; leastways, it probably had two or four engines. David's knowledge of, and interest in aviation languished in boyhood memories.

A one-way ticket was booked with BA, leaving on the 9th of December. With money to burn, David contemplated an upgrade. Years of frugality ruled out first class, and he'd finally settled for Club.

Accommodation was less straight forward. With Christmas a few weeks away, most hotels were booked up for the break. The Huntingdon Plaza was now part of the Fantazia hotel group – and full until mid January. It bothered David that his demise would most likely occur in a hotel room. And that he was seeking accommodation in the full knowledge of this. He reasoned, though, that plenty of people must have croaked in hotels – and would he really care when the time came? And would anyone else? As long as he didn't expire in a plate of cottage pie.

Searching on the Internet gave hope. New York City was steeped in small hotels and David narrowed the field to be within ten minutes of the Rockefeller Center. Sifting the results took time. It was more about finding a hotel that intuitively felt right.

David shortlisted around twelve possibles that drew his attention. Price, area and service levels provided a steer, but photographs conveyed more. Of all the choices, David kept revisiting The Rillington. It nestled between shop fronts on Thirty-fifth Avenue between Eighth and Ninth. 'A bijou art deco masterpiece. Built in 1926 and boasting four hundred rooms. Completely refurbished in 1986.' And there was more. Spats Johnson had occupied the penthouse during prohibition. Better still, F.G. Montague de Ville, the legendary financier, had taken a short cut from the nineteenth floor when Wall Street crashed in 1929.

Thirty-fifth Avenue meant nothing to David. But pictured was the front elevation of The Rillington – an elaborate canopy spanning the entrance and attractive tiered architecture soaring to twenty floors. David was able to read into the inviting look and feel of the hotel. And he increasingly warmed to the prospect of staying there as an emotional avalanche effect wound up his enthusiasm.

Phoning made sense – nearly two-thirty GMT. With a five-hour difference, David assumed he'd get an answer at this time. Someone did answer, a female, he thought, who rattled off some robotic salutation. David started to articulate his requirement, only to be diverted to a further ring tone.

'Holiday Reservation Desk. My name's Caroline – how may I help you?'

The lady had a pleasant accent that belonged nowhere on the planet.

David explained his need for a single room from the 9th of December until the 14th of January. Silence. Then in a laboured way, 'Caroline' reiterated the dates, inserting the years for good measure.

'Yes,' said David emphatically. Another pregnant silence.

'We only have a junior suite left that's available for those dates.'

Mental inhibitors were ready to defend David against shelling out too much. But in the briefest of moments, he converted across to the idea of enjoying a short period of extravagance.

'That'll be fine.'

A junior suite sounded pleasant. Must be like a small flat. Bridging his internal resistance felt good.

David completed the formalities. Now he knew he was going to New York City. He'd finally hauled that large ball bearing up the hill and got it perched at the summit. A small push and no more energy would be needed.

Local curiosity was building up. It was evident that something was happening, though David was evasive but not convincing. Pauline had been sidelined. Telling her the truth would have been unkind and instead she was fed a few white lies that left fleeting hope. David would be in touch when he'd worked out his personal problems. His conscience pricked.

For the most part, he planned to let his current existence lapse by natural defaults. Water always found its own level. Paine, Proctor and Pratt would do the necessary. And after the 9th he had no intention of looking back.

In a self-assessing moment, David realised that the last two months of his life constituted the most profound period in his whole existence. Emotionally, spiritually and intellectually, he'd made up some of the shortfall of a static and wasteful lifestyle. And he was proud of being able to face the last interlude in his life without the need to elicit pity, or bleat 'Why me?' It compounded the inner strength that grew daily in defiance of the onset of frailty.

Four days before his departure, David experienced some back pain. He wondered if this was 'the pain'. It persisted to the point where he took one of the Morpheaze tablets.

'Difficult to say.' Dr Bharani gave David a light examination and asked various questions. 'I should take the Morpheaze if the pain returns – it won't do any harm. But stick to the dose.' He paused, then asked, 'So you're definitely going?'

David nodded.

'I'm going to give you the phone number of a colleague of mine in New York. You'll find him very supportive – Dr Schwartz. Known him a long time – I'll let him know you'll be in touch.'

There was nothing else to say. Dr Bharani walked David to the surgery entrance, where he took David's hands in his own and held them gently. 'Good luck.'

His parting smile to David was full of warmth and understanding. And there was a sadness. Sadness that for all his medical skills and experience, he was powerless to help. This wasn't au revoir, simply goodbye.

Two days before, much to David's relief, the Kettering and Corby Alliance had advanced the money; a sizeable six figure. Timing hadn't really been an issue as it was already a done deal. And he wasn't overly excited by the figure realised. After all, it was still allocated to various beneficiaries. Their cut had dropped a little, although 'little' had yet to be defined. Modern-day banking made life easy for David, as the HSBC had a number of branches in New York City. It seemed he could draw on the money without restriction once stateside.

Mrs Pewsey knocked on the door with some fickle query about the wheelie bins – seemingly close to wetting herself with curiosity. David dispatched her empty handed, but it was a reminder that those gruesome negatives were under the stairs. Using a hacksaw, he cut the mailing tube complete with contents in half and fed them into Ideal Boiler No. 1. He surmised that the smell issuing from the chimney must have been disgusting, but at least he'd get a bowl of hot water out it. After all, the images had no further use – his body had moved on.

Just tomorrow to get through. David performed yet another tour of the house. Nothing of any value or importance was left. Just furniture and everyday tools of living. Simmonds Brothers had picked up the tea chests a week before and in their place were two suitcases containing the life that David would take to New York. Hand luggage was complete with medication, Dr Schwartz's contact details, a letter from his specialist spelling out medical details of the bad news; and carefully folded into an A4 envelope was a *BoyZo* comic. Issue No. 137, 6 October 1958.

Tomorrow came – another day of anticipation; December's dreary cold and wet unrelenting and unrepentant. David eased himself out of bed, mustering some energy for ablutions.

Daylight was only just making itself known, the warm incandescence of the bathroom light overriding any harsh natural rays. He surveyed his willowy frame – slender arms and legs extending from a strangely rotund torso. Face much the same as ever, but with recent events written into the detail. His shrivelled member a forlorn sight.

Physical appearances no longer disturbed him. He now resided in a spiritual sanctuary within and had long since detached from his body – which got him around. Progressive feelings of tiredness and the various accompanying symptoms he could deal with; they ran in background – no conflict with Plan C.

There was little to do but to keep reviewing arrangements and scan the house for overlooked detail. Each iteration revealed another task. Nothing of consequence, though David's mind progressively zoomed in on triviality and micro-thinking took over.

Towards midday the sun came out. A walk down to the river seemed a good idea. Much as he didn't want to wish a second of valuable time away, today was something of a *nul point*. Keeping unproductively occupied was the best he could hope for.

Ambling along the Thames towing path was soothing and memory lane abounded. Visions of paddling along in a home-made boat in the late 1950s with his pal Graham Parker drifted back. They'd found a Second World War hand grenade tucked into a gap in the riverbank stonework. Proudly dropping it onto the counter of the local River Police station got a reaction they'd not expected. A look of terror on the station sergeant's face suggested not all was well. Unlike other lost property, they wouldn't get it back if unclaimed.

A few months earlier, Graham had produced an inflatable dingy – a one-man craft for RAF flyers. They'd paddled out into mid river not knowing a pinprick hole was quietly at work. When the pressure got critically low, the dingy creased in two and shut up like a clam. It was a hot day and the river warm. But did they smell!

Away from the river, David wandered up and down roads he'd frequented with the kids from primary school but had never returned to since. It became a pleasantly sentimental journey. He remembered all their names; even their young faces were fresh in his mind. Some of them had had sad lives – some were no more. Most had just gone their ways. With nearly sixty idyllic years under his belt, David knew he'd no complaints about his lot.

Cool turned to cold as the light faded and David headed up the high street. Years ago it had been well populated with butchers, bakers, grocers, fishmongers and sweet shops. Now it was the domain of gift shops, estate agents and hair salons. But the inviting glow from shop fronts was timeless.

It was nearly five when he reached home. He'd enjoyed making acquaintance with his happily misspent youth, but now he felt quite weary. He decided to have a light supper and go to bed around nine. There was a message on his answering machine.

'It's Frank, Davy – just fort I'd say 'ello. I, err ... I 'ope everyfing's OK. Look after y'self ... you can phone, y'know, err ...'

Frank's voice was subdued. David had always seen him as the easygoing and unsophisticated giant whose thoughts never got too profound. But a new dimension was emerging. A sensitivity that Frank had kept well disguised. The realisation that his unscheduled absence was disturbing the big guy hurt. And it hurt even more knowing that this gentle and kindly soul would learn the real truth in a few weeks' time.

There was no Siestathol that night. David wanted to stay awake and quietly reflect on his life, and re-absorb memories of fifty-five happy years yielded by the house. Propped up in bed he surveyed the room he'd always slept in. When he'd been ill as a child, his mother would leave a small night light on his dressing table. And he'd lie there mesmerised by the small flickering flame and strange shadows it cast. Occasionally he'd woken in the night to witness the moment when the flame dimmed and shrank to nothing, leaving him feeling strangely alone.

He remembered too, how at Christmas time the Salvation Army band would progress slowly up his road playing carols. He'd hear them from afar, and then strain to catch the last audible vestige of sound as they faded into the neighbourhood.

Lying there in the restful dark, David revisited so many happy and fulfilling moments in his life. He felt physically and spiritually at peace and accepted that the greatness of life was profoundly beyond his understanding.

And sleep came.

At 7.00 am the alarm resurrected the real world. Crawling out of bed, David, as always, pumped up the pillow and neatly rearranged the quilt.

At 10.00 am a taxi would take him to Heathrow. And at 12.45 pm, he would take to the skies heading west.

Ablutions this morning excluded any assessment in the mirror, and by 9.00, he was ready. If he had ever wanted time to go slowly, slowly it went whilst waiting for ten o'clock to come around.

At just after ten, the doorbell rang. 'Riverside Taxis, sir, shall I take your luggage?'

David locked up and headed down the path. Victor was on seat. They searched into each other's eyes for a moment and bade silent farewells.

'It is Heathrow, sir?'

'Yes.'

'Which terminal?'

'Four.'

'Anywhere nice, sir?'

'New York City.'

'Holiday, sir?'

'Err, yes.'

It was a simple, mechanical conversation, but with poignant overtones. As they headed for Hammersmith Bridge David asked himself why he was going to New York City? And the answer came back.

He was going there to die.

10

No Turning Back

David surveyed the familiar skyline as his taxi progressed across Chiswick and Brentford on the elevated dual carriageway. Heading to Heathrow on a one-way trip was thought-provoking. As the airport approached, visions of New York City flushed away any doubts. And by the time the taxi pulled up at Terminal 4, every brain cell was pointing stateside.

Lugging the two heavy suitcases to the check-in desk caused David to perspire unnaturally and nausea struck for a few seconds. Relieved of the burden he brightened up and with plenty of time to spare, browsed the array of duty free shops for nearly fifty minutes. After much agonising over the choice of electronic goods, watches, sunglasses and clothes, David spent the princely sum of one pound on a bag of jelly beans.

Gate 92 was all about walking and walkerlatoring. It was with relief that he finally organised himself into the magnificent Club Class seat – a far cry from the compact air travel of his European trips. A day's energy had been dissipated in less than five hours and David reclined limply in his seat until the fatigue subsided. Though he responded well to a complementary glass of champagne; and two meals in seven and a half hours reinstated his hint of pink pallor.

To keep occupied, David had armed himself with a book, crossword puzzles, his Walkman and a small electronic chess set. But for the most part, he switched fitfully between the in-flight music and video choices, cat-napping intermittently. *BoyZo* got several airings – Page 6 held a fascination that went undiminished.

On arriving at JFK airport, the onslaught resumed with the interminable wait at customs in the Aliens queue. David hadn't reckoned on the physical demands of his journey, and waiting by the luggage carousel he felt frail and vulnerable. And alone.

At home, he'd been able to pace his activities, and familiar surroundings gave assurance. There'd been the luxury of setting thresholds of endurance as low as suited him – a warm bed waiting if he transgressed the limits. Rehearsing the trip had been accomplished mentally – no body needed, with a rosy tint adding optimism to his vision. Now, put to the test, David's fragile state of health was struggling to deliver.

His suitcases finally appeared on the carousel and he managed to wrestle them on to his trolley before they embarked on another circuit. By the time he reached the large arrivals hall he was feeling ill with fatigue. Private taxi drivers aggressively accosted him and with little resistance he was marshalled into a car headed for the city.

David gazed at the passing suburban sprawl. It didn't seem to say New York, although different from anything he'd seen at home. And far removed from the classic sights he longed to behold.

Emerging from the Queens Mid-Town Tunnel made all the difference. Noise, traffic, people – it was that he had envisaged. Stimulated and intrigued by his new surroundings, he was able to suppress, for a while, his jaded persona and drink in the cultural delights of each busy street. It was a slow but interesting journey.

The Rillington appeared from nowhere. And yes it was bijou, though looking a little more tired than in the photo. David fumbled around with his wad of dollar bills. They all looked the same – green. For the sake of getting into the hotel he hopelessly over-tipped the driver. The doorman was regaled in a uniform that attempted some level of grandeur, and he had a whistle stuck in his mouth. He gave David a surly nod and summoned help in getting the suitcases into the foyer.

Mercifully, the luggage was taken into care and he proceeded uncluttered to the reception desk.

'NEXT!'

'Deliah' looked at David with total disinterest. A well-upholstered black woman with blonde, finely braded hair, a gold ring on each finger, and the obligatory tattoos on her arm and neck.

'Good afternoon – I'm Mr Jenner.'

'Passport and accommodation voucher!'

David found his passport, though the voucher wasn't so obvious – it was in his hand somewhere with the various travel documents.

But Deliah could spot an accommodation voucher at fifty yards. She leaned forward and whipped the document out of David's hand in the blink of an eye.

'I'll need a credit card imprint.'

David managed to find his Visa card and handed it over. Deliah's fingers played her computer keyboard like a machine gun.

She handed David his passport and two room card-keys.

'Junior Suite 1738. Have a nice day.'

'NEXT!'

Several things came to mind to ask Deliah but David thought better of it and made for the lift.

Junior Suit 1738 wasn't quite what he'd expected. It had a certain incongruous feel with the highly ornate ceiling cornice extending on only three sides of the bedroom and lounge. Almost certainly it would have started life as Room 1738 before being rather inelegantly carved in two. But the bathroom was truly original with a cast-iron bath and dated porcelain furniture. Original too were the radiators – black cast-iron monsters elaborately detailed. The bedroom suite had a classic look about it. And David noted how similar it was to his parent's bedroom furniture which they'd bought back in 1938. Evidence of a 'complete refurbishment' was a little thin on the ground.

He tested the bed. It was firm and looked inviting. Just a 4-foot 6-inch double, but ample for one person. A large window looking eastward was incorporated in the wall adjacent to the left side of the bed; a similar window featured in the small lounge. Furnishings in there were a little more recent and there was a large modern television.

For all its shabbiness, the suite oozed delightful 1920s art deco styling that had matured over time into a pleasant meld of artistic decadence.

A knock at the door. His suitcases had arrived. The porter, a young man in black everything, smiled and walked to the door in slow motion before turning to smile again. David twigged and pulled out his wad of dollars. The porter landed a 10-dollar tip and David resolved to quickly get some small bills. He pondered the porter's nationality; sounded Mexican – maybe Puerto Rican. He was already getting a flavour of the immense cosmopolitan mix. And it fascinated him.

The time locally was 4.18 pm, which meant that he'd been on the go for nearly seventeen hours. Once more fatigue set in and recurrent back pain nagged away. Despite all, hunger still made its point, but he couldn't face the prospect of leaving the room.

A hot soak in the small cast-iron bath never felt so good. As always it was a time for reflection. David replayed the day and enjoyed a modest sense of achievement in making it to New York City. From feeling lonely and detached at the airport, he felt a growing sense of security in his small but homely junior suite. Between bursts of philosophical thought, he idly noted how shabby the bathroom was. Corroded fittings, chipped porcelain, petrified limescale drips around leaking joints – repair on repair on repair.

Having absorbed most of the heat, he crawled out of the bath, pleasantly weakened. A room service menu stood on the bedside table and he phoned through for a Rillington Club Sandwich and a glass of Coke. Another 10-dollar tip. He was too tired to care, though, and only made it half way through the enormous snack.

Tiredness intensified, adding lead weights to David's limbs. And after taking the third Retrobrax and a Morpheaze he slid between the smooth, clean sheets. No Siestathol tonight. The bed felt divinely comfortable. In the last few moments of consciousness he fleetingly wondered whether he would wake up again.

Sleep was instant and it was the deepest and most untroubled that he had enjoyed in well over three months. For sixteen hours, he didn't wake or stir or knowingly dream.

And whilst his body and mind regenerated – the enemy advanced.

11

The Beginning of the End

Daylight slowly permeated David's consciousness. For a while he lay motionless whilst his mind searched for the previous night's bookmark. With memory reloaded, the room started to make sense. Communicating with his body took a little longer.

David realised he must have slept in the same position – start to finish. Propping himself up on one elbow he took stock of the room. Suitcases unopened – first job of the day. A half-eaten Rillington Club Sandwich greeted him from the dressing table.

Another bath, but this time brief. Just a quick dunk in hot water to ease up his aching limbs. In slow time, he got dressed, still feeling delicate but sufficiently refreshed to face the day. After breakfast he'd tackle the suitcases and hopefully that would be the last physically challenging task – ever.

The lift bounced to a halt and a synthetic voice announced 'Hotel Lobby'. Reception faced the row of hotel lifts and Deliah was at her desk looking straight at David as he stepped out. She failed to acknowledge his polite greeting, her gaze unflinching as he moved away. He realised that her eyes and brain were focussed on infinity.

Breakfast was served in Rebecca's Patisserie, a small themed café on the mezzanine floor. It seemed very congenial and David ordered his long-term favourite – scrambled eggs on toast and a cup tea, followed by toast and marmalade. It galled him that for the fixed price he couldn't compete with the big eaters.

Before returning to the room, curiosity demanded a quick look out in the street. As before, it was noise, people and traffic – such a vibrant atmosphere and a must for later.

David stopped by reception on the way back to his room. Deliah

49

was busy, but another lass invited him with a smile.

Chantelle – dusky, slender, pointy, spindly. A mass of frizzy black hair on end, she looked as if she had 230 volts AC plugged into her backside. All eyes and mouth – wisdom teeth visible when she laughed. Nails two inches long – she could dig a ditch. David enquired about Internet facilities.

'Yeah – toon yah TV to d' Hotel menu an' select Internet, then use d' keyboard under d' TV.'

And without prompting – born in Ecuador, lived in Texas and the Bronx, Miss Hoboken 1997. Then, 'Gonna git on d' TV.'

By mid morning the suitcases were empty. Having no further use they got parked under the bed. A knock on the door.

'Can ah clean your room?'

A sweet grey-haired lady from Harlem – Jesse. She'd return later.

David wandered into his personal lounge and half reclined on the settee – such was the extent of his swollen abdomen. Already the euphoria of coming to New York City was cooling slightly. And he'd yet to step outside the hotel. He'd mentally constructed a gold-plated model of this nostalgic visitation; so easy on paper with reality filtered out. Yesterday's travel had been wearisome – lowered his emotional vitality; allowed doubts and anxieties to creep in. Was he simply running away from himself? Or on a hiding to nowhere seeking an elusive Golden Fleece that had evaporated with his youth.

Gazing out of the window he surveyed the city vista. Through a rose-coloured kaleidoscope he'd envisioned joining the throngs of tourists absorbing the wonders of Manhattan. But his sickly body was starting to give out serious messages. It was becoming harder to entirely detach from the depressing reality of his life. Despite meticulous planning David hadn't calculated well for declining health and the impact of unfolding events.

For a while he worked through the amorphous clutter of facts, emotions and feelings until a more rational perspective crystallized out. He acknowledged that keeping his mind engaged with *BoyZo* promises was paramount to coping. And that finding peace of mind lay within.

Finally the whirring wheels, cogs, gears and pinions in David's mind came to rest, and he felt ready for New York City – and the mythological search for 1958.

It was nearly twelve o'clock.

Before venturing out into the street, David called Dr Schwartz to make an appointment. Having medical help at hand would be of comfort.

'Yeah?'

The voice was brash, husky, non-committal.

'Could I speak to Dr Schwartz, please.'

'Speakin'.'

'I'm David Jenner – Dr Bharani gave me your contact details.'

A warmer intonation took over.

'Ah yeah – David. Know all aboutcha. Come an' see me.'

'When would it suit you, Dr Schwartz?'

'Now?'

'Now? Err, yes, I'll leave straight away.'

'I'm at one three six eight West Seventeenth and Seventh – middle bell. Bring your med. See you shortly.'

Click.

Gathering up his pills, David tried to envisage the owner of the voice.

It had been quite cold on arrival the day before so he rugged up well and with a modicum of trepidation headed down to the foyer. Deliah was again staring vacantly at him as he alighted the lift. On moving out of her line of site he gave a fleeting half smile – just in case; and just perceptibly, her little finger moved momentarily in acknowledgement.

David stepped into the hustle and bustle of early afternoon Manhattan having not really considered how he'd get to Dr Schwartz. The doorman was outside, whistle in mouth.

'Taxi?'

The whistle stayed put.

'Please.'

A quick shrill and a yellow cab swept to the curb. David got in, the driver accelerating away without asking for a destination. He leaned forward and read out the address. The driver nodded disinterestedly. They seemed to be heading in the wrong direction. David finally twigged that the one-way system necessitated something of a detour to get on track for West Seventeenth.

Number 1368 shaped up as a door between two shabby

shopfronts. David pushed the middle bell and the intercom crackled into life.

'Yeah?'

'It's David Jenner.'

'First floor.'

The door unlatched with a buzz and David made his way up the first flight of stairs. To the right was an open door and a murky room. A man, sixtyish, bald, swarthy, unshaven, open necked, sleeves rolled to mid forearm, sat slumped behind a large desk. A cigarette dangled from his lips, oblique rays from a desk lamp adding theatrical overtones. The room was styled as a surgery but in a dated way. All manner of medical equipment and supplies littered the floor.

'So you're David?'

He spoke slowly, lazily, the cigarette twitching.

'Yes.'

'Have a seat, David.' Dr Schwartz cocked his head towards a nearby chair.

He sized David up for a few seconds.

'So Bharani sent you?'

'Yes.'

Without removing the cigarette from his mouth, Dr Schwartz leaned forward and tapped the ash into an ashtray.

'Bharani an' me go back some. Yeah. Five years together at the Lincoln Memorial – Queens. Clever man. Good to hear from him'.

David nodded to acknowledge this reminiscence.

'I'm gonna help you, David. Yeah ... I'm gonna help you.'

'Got your med?'

'Yes.'

David laid the bottles and plastic containers on the desk.

'Hmm.' Dr Schwartz read each label. 'Hmm ... how y' feelin'?'

'I get quite tired. The pain's not too bad.'

'Are you worrying?'

'Now and then.'

'I'm gonna give you something, David.'

Dr Schwartz opened a drawer and brought out a small bottle and a disposable hypodermic syringe. He paused to stub out his cigarette and light up another.

'Roll up your sleeve.'

'What are you giving me?'

'You'll feel better – roll up your sleeve.'

David obliged whilst Dr Schwartz charged the syringe and deftly pumped the contents into David's arm.

Within seconds a pleasant warmth radiated throughout his whole body. His limbs felt supple and easy and an immense feeling of well-being suffused his mind.

'How y' feel?'

'Absolutely wonderful, Dr Schwartz. What did you give me?'

He smiled at David. 'You can call me Ferdi – short for Ferdinand.'

'Thanks, err ... Ferdi.'

Ferdi leant back and took a large bottle from a drawer behind. From this he counted twenty yellow capsules into a smaller amber-coloured bottle.

'Take one of these if things get bad.'

'What type of tablets are they?'

'It don't matter – take one when you want to feel better.' He smiled. 'I'm gonna look after you, David.'

Ferdi handed David a card.

'Call me twenty-four hours. Home, surgery, mobile. It don't matter.'

David thanked him.

'David, I want you to take a trip to the Holbrook Institute. It's near the Columbia University – past Harlem. They research abnormal cell behaviour. You could help them.'

How he might help wasn't immediately clear to David, but with the magic fluid coursing round his veins, he would have given the shirt off his back to the first person he met.

'When shall I go?'

'Soon, real soon – tomorrow?'

'OK.'

Ferdi called the institute. He appeared to be well acquainted with the other party.

Could he get there for 11.00 am tomorrow?

David assented. He would be seen by Professor Olufunwa.

'You'll be fine, David. Just do a few tests – helps their research.'

'How much do I owe you, Doctor Sch—, err ... Ferdi?"

Ferdi shook his head and waved his hand.

'I'm doin' it for Bharani — I owe him.'

David got up to go.

'Thanks, Ferdi — I'm so grateful to you.'

'I'm gonna take care of you, David. Remember, call me twenty-four.'

It was more a case of floating down the stairs and back out into the street. The ground seemed further away than usual and David's vision had an odd clarity to it. After conferring with his Eazee-Nav fold-out map, he decided to take a slow walk back along Eighth Avenue.

It was cold and bright, but with a hint of dusk. The street life fascinated David. Such an eclectic mix of shops — everything discounted, a diversity of merchandise. They formed a wonderful linear bazaar stretching northward.

David felt remarkably good as he ambled back to The Rillington — gregarious, uninhibited. He smiled at people — they smiled back. He even said 'hello' — and was rewarded with a 'Hi'.

He'd made a mental note to buy some more trousers. Not that the current ones didn't fit. Standing up was fine, but sitting was getting just a little uncomfortable. And as he walked along David noticed that his swollen abdomen was developing an inertia of its own. At certain speeds a physical resonance took over with the bulge bouncing up and down painfully in opposition to his bodily movement.

Keeping an eye out for a likely clothes shop, he spotted Gerome's Gents' Outfitters. Whereas most shops had a contemporary street market image, Gerome's appeared to belong to another age. In the window, dated clothes on wooden stands. Orange Cellophane on the window to filter the sun, now faded and torn. Garters, cravats, boaters, starched collars. But inside, an Aladdin's cave.

An extremely elderly and wizened man appeared out of the thick foliage of suspended garments. With hands clasped and a disarming smile he approached David.

'Vot vould you like to buy?'

Assumptive selling at its best, mused David.

'I need a pair of trousers.'

'Any particular style or material?'

'Well, I just want something practical that's reasonably smart. Maybe some sort of stretch material. Sometimes I put on weight rather quickly.'

The old man measured David's waist and looked at him a little quizzically. Then he smiled knowingly. 'Good living, eh? Come vith me, I've just the thing.'

From one of the rails, he took down a pair of beige trousers.

'Look.'

David read the label: 'Workaday 3-Size Pants'.

His smiling assistant enthusiastically demonstrated how the trousers could be adjusted for three waist sizes. On each side of the trousers were two pleats or gussets that extended up to the waistband and which could be zipped up. The zips were concealed, rather like the zip fly at the front.

Progressively opening the pairs of zips expanded the waistband from 40 to 44 inches.

David tried them on. It was a struggle in the small changing booth as he could no longer bend forward very far. The 40-inch setting was a little tight, but 42 inches gave an easy fit.

It was a deal. Two pairs. Meticulously, the trousers were folded and tucked into a brown paper bag.

'Are you Mr Gerome?'

The old man smiled broadly. 'Isaac Gerome – yes sir.'

Such a sweet man – David was touched by his gentle charm.

Isaac bid a warm farewell from the doorway and David headed on to The Rillington.

But a mobile phone shop caught his attention and sucked him inside – and shortly blew him out with a snappy top-of-the-range model on a pay-as-you-go tariff.

Turning into Thirty-fifth West, The Rillington's gold canopy was in sight. David smiled at Whistle Man and got a cursory nod back.

Pleasantly tired perhaps but still buoyed along by the fix from Dr Schwartz, David walked confidently through to the lifts. Deliah was off duty, but Chantelle shot him a patronising mouthful of teeth.

A hot soak was as beneficial as ever. Reclined back amid the steam he observed the patchy bathroom repairs and shabby details that were fast becoming old friends. Garbled voices and music from the lounge television held his attention until the threat of overheating ended the therapy. Donning the white Rillington bath robe he repaired to the settee with a Coke to watch television idly.

It was a little after six and the brigade of slick power dressers were delivering the day's news in their assertive mid-town media voices.

Then the NBC Manhattan Round-up; delivered by a woman clearly in a class of her own – Maria Arabella. Smiling dark eyes, Latin looks, full, hour-glass curves, confidence and poise. She was a delicious amalgam of age, maturity and natural beauty. Maria spoke one to one with every viewer, her voice soft and inviting. She captivated David in her personal radiance. The warm, seductive timbre of her voice pleasured his eardrums. But he heard no words.

Wearied by the trip out and the overrun of fatigue from the previous day, he opted for a Rillington Club Sandwich in front of the TV. And as the magic jab from Dr Schwartz faded, so the pain and physical and emotional discomfort returned.

He managed to put away most of the sandwich before sinking gratefully into bed, and debated whether to take a Morpheaze, but settled for a Siestathol. Throughout, he'd taken the thrice-daily Retrobrax. It had no side effects and he could only hope it was working on his behalf. A bottle of twenty faceless tablets on the dressing table awaited deployment.

Whilst Siestathol prepared to turn out the lights there was time for reflection. Day One had been absorbed with some necessary domestics and Day Two was already partially accounted for. The shear overhead of living was creating an unforeseen burden. Whilst the limitations of a sickly body were becoming bleakly apparent.

But the dream persisted.

In the last few moments of consciousness it occurred to David that he must soon make the final preparations.

12

So Near But So Far

'Please come in Mr Jenner – I hope you didn't have too much difficulty finding us.'

Professor Olufunwa turned out to be a charming middle-aged woman. Slender, fair, gold-rimmed spectacles – a pleasantly lived-in face. In a crowd she'd blend with humanity, but here at the Holbrook Institute her professional aura reigned supreme.

David was taken to a small ante-room and settled in a chair. Professor Olufunwa sat to one side of him, but facing and close.

'Let me tell you about the work we do here.'

She explained that the Institute was funded from donations and researched malignant cell behaviour. And that they depended on monitoring the progressive cell behaviour of people with advanced disease.

Whilst talking, she took David's blood pressure. He felt comforted by her touch – gentle, knowing, seeing hands. The hands of a doctor. The tools of her trade.

'We'd like to conduct some blood tests and then take a few small biopsy specimens. There might be just a little discomfort.'

She smiled and gently squeezed David's arm. It made everything right.

Dr Rozanski was summoned. Pale, shaven head, a tattoo on his neck depicting two entwined cobras and something tattooed on each finger and thumb. And David counted six gold earrings in each of his ear lobes. He had one eye at home and the other away, and they took turns at looking in David's direction. Unsure as to which eye was sighted, and not wishing to offend, David concentrated on the bridge of Dr Rozanski's nose. Later, whilst following him to the procedure room, he noticed a large eye tattooed on the back of his head.

'Dr Rozanski will look after you.'

First a DNA swab.

Then another armful of blood. David tried to peer discreetly at the tattoos on Dr Rozanski's hands. Sensing his interest the doctor smiled and, putting his hands side by side, the word C A S A B L A N C A formed up.

'I watch it every day. It guides my Karma. "Play it again, Sam!"' He tilted his head back and shrieked with maniac laughter.

Taking biopsy samples involved more than a little discomfort. Large needles were eased through David's abdomen for the purpose of accessing the diseased entrails within.

To conclude, David sipped a cup of tea whilst Dr Olufunwa in-filled a little more about their operation. He would be known only by a number. They would need to see him every three days for a similar set of tests. As recompense for submitting to the tests, the Institute would provide his ongoing medication via Dr Schwartz. And please would he sign a declaration absolving the Institute of any responsibility for his medical condition.

'How did you get on with our Dr Rozanski – Katz?'

She smiled with veiled amusement.

'Fine, err ... thanks.'

'Oh, good – he's a brilliant haematologist.'

Dr Olufunwa walked David to the entrance and softly touched his arm.

'Thank you, Mr Jenner. We'll see you on Wednesday at eleven o'clock.'

A taxi was waiting.

Although it went unsaid, David accepted that his reduced life expectancy made him an ideal research subject for the Holbrook. And he wondered how Dr Schwartz was rewarded for steering terminal cases their way. If, though, he had doubts about the institute's authenticity, ten minutes on The Rillington Internet facility revealed a high regard by the medical fraternity.

Whilst addressing issues of mortality, David bit the bullet and consulted the Yellow Pages for funeral services. 'Eternal Slumbers' on West Twenty-first seemed as good as any — 'Michael' would receive him tomorrow at 11.30 am.

The morning's exertion caught up – pain, now more extensive than before started its nag, and a dreadful melancholy set in compounded by an overbearing sense of unwellness. A Morpheaze partially eased the pain. But David needed to escape his body. Throwing caution to the wind he swallowed a deep slug of Rillington Springs bottled water. Now there were only nineteen Doc Schwartz specials left.

Nearly fifteen minutes and no reaction. Then the active ingredients fired up. First, light-headedness, then nausea; followed by a warm glow that started within, working its way out until his skin tingled with pleasure. Now he was motoring.

Lunch at Rebecca's Patisserie seemed apt – and then a taxi to Macy's. Given the circumstances, it was a pointless exercise. But David happily floated around the store absorbing the festive atmosphere and buying unneeded trinkets. And he revelled in being accosted by the legions of vibrant young sales staff who appeared to be so taken with him.

Sixth Avenue and another army of shoppers – his head on a swivel, he drank in the world and its wives, and engaged with New York City.

After about two and a half hours of heaving around the streets, his body sensors said 'OK', but lack of energy told another story. He slumped into a taxi and managed, just, to walk unaided into the hotel and make his way to his suite. Jesse was finishing up as David ungraciously collapsed on the bed. It was a lesson.

Six o'clock – Maria Arabella and evening room service had become a ritual.

At nine, David selected his night-time cocktail and slid between the freshly laundered sheets. By the bed was his new phone – that was ever silent.

13

Dreams and Realities

Eternal Slumbers sat rather conspicuously amid the everyday Manhattan shops – a large smoked-glass facade with little to suggest the line of business; save the name in beautifully embossed gold letters.

Twin glass doors silently opened as David approached, leading to a circular lobby. In the centre, a marble pedestal with 'The Flame of Eternal Slumber' burning serenely. Delicate aromatic vapours pervaded – an ever-changing fragrance. Distant echoes of a heavenly choir completed the spiritual setting.

Two glass panels silently parted and 'Michael' appeared. He glided smoothly and silently towards David as if on wheels, hands lightly clasped, a half smile that catered for any occasion.

'I am Michael – welcome to the home of Eternal Slumbers.'

His voice was soft, measured, emotional tones delicately balanced to harmonise with his unbearably immaculate persona.

Yet two more smoked glass doors opened.

"Please, Mr. Jenner, come through into our Tranquillity Suite.'

Dim lighting complimented the soft strains of 'Ave Maria', the air fragrant with a hint of wisteria and honeysuckle. To one side, a full-size sculpture of a woman, arms gently outstretched, her smiling countenance elevated and bathed in soft golden rays of the 'Sun'.

Beautiful murals graced the wall – scenes of peaceful meadows, placid waters, Elysian cloud formations; sacred edifices and symbols that belonged to no known faith or culture.

Michael directed David to a large Chesterfield settee and gracefully slid into a chair to the side.

'May I offer you some refreshment, Mr Jenner?'

'I'd like a nice cup of tea, please.'

Without appearing to action this request, Michael continued. 'We are honoured, Mr Jenner, that you have chosen Eternal Slumbers to take your loved one on their final journey of peace and love.'

At this juncture, David was becoming a little uncomfortable – he was used to the simplicity of Fred Marshall and Son in the high street on the respective occasions of his parents' passing. The thought occurred that it might have been better to have paid Dr Schwartz to do the necessary.

From nowhere a shadowy figure discretely brought in David's tea.

'Well, actually, I wanted pay for my own funeral. Err ... that is, in advance.'

He expected a break in Michael's smooth delivery, but it didn't come. Michael switched seamlessly to Eternal Slumbers Pre-paid Packages mode. And his smile morphed into one of sincerity, warmth, trust and joy.

'Eternal Slumbers will be proud to personally take you on that final journey of peace and love – when the time comes. Let me share with you our services to those we've lost and the bereaved.'

Long velvet curtains opened to reveal a wide screen. For the next fifteen minutes a soft, deep, male voice-over, oozing sincerity and compassion, accompanied a tasteful exposition of Eternal Slumbers' caring services.

The curtains closed.

Now on the defensive David explained, 'I really didn't want anything too expensive.'

'Of course you don't, Mr Jenner. I so admire you for your humble wishes – a rare thing. BUT, we must think of those who'll mourn your sad passing. I beg you not to deprive them of cherished memories that will forever sustain them. It will be their day as well as yours. We truly care for those left behind – Mr Jenner.'

David realised he was snookered. A recycled cardboard coffin would have done the trick. And he could hardly explain that the 'bereaved' would comprise Doc Schwartz with a half-smoked Lucky Strike stuck to his lips.

He finally signed up to a Serenity-Plus package, managing to talk his way out of a lead-lined casket with gold-plated fittings, the gospel choir and professional mourners.

With his 10 per cent off for on-the-day signing the bill came to a frightening 9000 bucks, although he also got a week's holiday for two in Las Vegas thrown in. It contrasted starkly with the Co-op funeral package he'd bought many years ago for £200. And most of that was paid off with Green Shield stamps.

Not once, David observed, did Michael let slip his polished image, demeanour or stylised verbal delivery.

Stepping out to the din of traffic on West Twenty-first was surprisingly refreshing.

'The Rillington, please.'

David had stopped looking for signs that the taxi driver had heard, or better still, understood his destination.

Sorting his final journey of 'Peace and Love' had taken nearly two hours.

Deliah's eyes tracked David as he made for the lift. He elected to ignore her today, though in his peripheral vision as the lift doors raced towards each other, he could sense her stare.

Having arranged the final details of his material life, David felt able to progress the nostalgic journey. But then it occurred to him that on his passing, who would tell Eternal Slumbers, or for that matter, Mr Paine? Another solicitor was needed. It was never ending. He realised that with the epicentre of his existence now in New York City, a parallel life had sprung up.

The Yellow Pages came up trumps – again. Wrightman Goodfellow of LawServices4U could see him at 3.30 pm.

Jomayra arrived with David's lunchtime snack. A sweet lass of eighteen – pretty, petite, a faultless coffee complexion. They'd chatted before – parents still in Puerto Rica, five brothers, vegetarian – and she had ambitions. He knew the key words that would loosen her tongue for a while and break the solitude. Today's stimulus was mention of her wannabe modelling career. He was rewarded with Jomayra's smiling, animated face and youthful enthusiasm as she gushed about her future prospects. Worth every cent of the five bucks tip.

Post food, and in preparation for 3.30, David relaxed on the settee whilst watching some pithy daytime TV drama.

LawServices4U were only three blocks away. With documents and pills at the ready David took a slow walk. He wasn't sure what to expect, but was learning to expect the unexpected. It was neither a seedy office nor a palatial suite of chambers. More, a newly fitted shop-front, staffed by immaculate suits and skirts. It had the ring of a franchised business – very logo orientated.

Wrightman Goodfellow was as good as his name – a big, genial American, early thirties, and straight out of the movies.

'How y' doin'?'

After a knuckle crackin' handshake, David was led to one of the consultation rooms.

'How can I help you, Mr Jenner – David, isn't it?'

David spun a rather flaky story about the need for various people to be informed should 'anything happen to him'.

'Hope y' ain't plannin' on dying just yet, David,' quipped the big man, throwing himself back in his chair and grinning broadly.

In a trice, David realised the need for honesty.

'Well, actually—'

Wrightman's jocular expression faded.

'I don't have very long.'

'I'm, err ... so very sorry, sir.' His voice now subdued and awkward he asked, 'What sort of timescale are you hopeful of, sir?'

'Possibly about two weeks.'

Wrightman struggled to find words that might seem appropriate. Like David, he'd assumed years, not weeks.

David tried to put Wrightman at ease. Smiling, he said, 'It's something I have to deal with, Mr Goodfellow – don't let it bother you.'

They quietly worked through David's requirements.

On completion, Wrightman accompanied David to the door and gently shook his hand.

'We'll be sure to carry out all of your requests, sir.'

Around thirty seconds later, as David hailed down a taxi, a voice called out, 'Mr Jenner, sir!'

It was Wrightman, breathless, holding out a business card. 'I've written my personal mobile number on the back. Please call me any time, Mr Jenner. I'm here for you, sir.'

David knew there'd be no need to call, but he was touched his plight had so easily penetrated Wrightman's professional veneer.

Back at The Rillington, David called Dr Schwartz. On this occasion he used his new mobile – it came with 20 dollars credit.

'YEAH?'

'Oh, err ... it's David Jenner.'

Ferdi's voice softened. 'Ah, David – how y' feelin'?'

'Not too bad.'

'Did they treat you OK at the Holbrook?'

'Yes.'

David passed on the LawServices4U details.

'Thanks, David. I'm here for you, David – twenty-four.'

A nagging question surfaced.

'Dr Schwartz, err ...'

'Ferdi!

'Err... Ferdi, how will the hotel staff know what to do when, err...?'

'I'm gonna look after you David, don't worry. I'm here for you, David – twenty-four.'

Click!

David bathed and caught the back end of Manhattan Roundup. He didn't feel too bad, considering. Early nights and ten hours had dispelled the fatigue of journeying to New York City. But in equal measures, advancing sickness was quietly filling the void.

Tomorrow he could start indulging the happy memories of 1958. Whilst planning the trip, there'd been a crock of gold at the rainbow's end. What lay there now was less certain. Radio City Music Hall would hold the answers.

David made for O'Banion's restaurant just off the lobby. If nothing else, his appetite was still in good shape. Don Rodriguez, the hotel manager, was bustling about. Forever sewn into a green blazer and grey flannels, you could spot him a mile off. He had a staccato sixty a day twang that carried like a foghorn over still waters; and a moustache that could upstage the largest yard broom.

Don smiled on passing and rattled off some slick cordiality. Quick, slick repartee wasn't David's forte, and his 'slick' retort came out as a garbled spoonerism.

The maître d' lisped a welcome; would he like to sit with someone? Social conversations being thin on the ground, David accepted. His date was a fat lady up from North Carolina to take in Saks Fifth Avenue winter collection. She – Roberta – oozed a charismatic vulgarity, and held sway with her potted bio of four weddings and a funeral – and three divorces. Tummy tucked down to 10 per cent capacity she could still ingest a 16-ounce rump steak. 'Bobbie', as she preferred, had 'gotten from forty-one to twenty-five stone' and was 'mighty proud of ma new body'. Whatever the transformation, she still had a magnificent cleavage – deep enough to transport a pet Chihuahua or incubate an ostrich egg.

'And you, Mr Jenner?'

She eyed him coyly.

David managed to crank out a phoney story that loosely parodied his life. But it lacked the juke box glitz he ascribed to his companion's life and times.

It made no odds, though.

With the spectre of Mrs Jenner laid, Bobbie confessed her fondness for Englishmen. Under different circumstances David might have enjoyed some cat and mouse with an amorous divorcee, but that moment had gone. Nevertheless, an hour and a bit of light relief over dinner had put a pleasant spin on the evening. Tiredness kicked in and the crisp Rillington bed linen beckoned. It was getting close to nine o'clock and he excused himself on the basis of an early start.

'Sweet dreams, honey.' The big lady flashed him a winning smile. 'Got somethin' good lined up?'

'Oh, just some sightseeing – I'll probably make a day of it.'

Bobbie winked.

'Might bump into ya in town.'

In getting up from the table David was careful to play around with his unbuttoned jacked in a way that disguised his portly feature.

Suite 1738 was as he left it, save for the down-turned quilt and Rillington Deluxe Chocolate Éclair left on the pillow by Jesse. Solitude waited in the wings. And wait it did whilst Roberta's exuberance pleasantly percolated David's thoughts. Her warm slipstream had been uplifting, transcending any considerations of size and weight. He reflected how, in his halcyon, pre-bad news days, he would probably have dismissed her out of hand. Like so many, his sociological outlook was based on shallow values.

Now, he loved all humanity, albeit in the same vein that a condemned man finds religion. He'd finally come of age and could see life from the other end.

In the few minutes before lights out David pondered what

tomorrow would bring. For the nth time he read *BoyZo*, page 6. That darling young girl's smile hadn't changed in forty-six years. In daydreams, the power of nostalgic thought played tricks with David's mind, only to spill over into reality with false promises. He so hoped tomorrow, to connect with *BoyZo* days; but the how, when and wherefore were way beyond his understanding.

Slowing time no longer served a purpose. Nine am could come as quickly as it wished. And it did – with a little help from Siestathol.

Morning light surfaced without a hitch. For a while David idly gazed at the easterly skyline until it registered that snow was falling. Easing himself out of bed he viewed the scene below – white pavements and slushy streets.

Morning times were never good. And they only got worse. The process of kick-starting his body became more and more laboured, and today he struggled against overwhelming lethargy and discomfort.

After ablutions at quarter pace David got dressed. It was with a deep sense of despair that he found the need to open the second pair of zipped gussets on his Workaday 3-Size Pants.

From a trim 34-inch waist, he'd now bloated to 44 inches.

14

Revisitation

Feeling sickly and mentally defeated David knew that the day couldn't progress, at least not for a while. He reasoned that a light breakfast might help. Rebecca's Patisserie was a café too far but room service was good for coffee and Danish.

Having found a receptive ear, Jomayra arrived well primed to regale David – chapter and verse.

But her sweet voice grated on his jaded senses and he searched clumsily for a means of dismissing her – she left with a 10-dollar bill, confused and subdued.

Eating brought a modicum of comfort, but no more so than on a good day. Moreover, David knew that Morpheaze and Euphoridex would struggle to meet the demands of *BoyZo* expectations.

There seemed no contest – a large mouthful of Rillington Springs water reduced the count to eighteen Doc Schwartz bombs in the small amber bottle. Reliably, after about fifteen minutes, the room performed a couple of revolutions and nausea cut in. He felt the coffee and Danish head north, hovering in his gullet for a second before dropping back with a gurgle.

Within ten seconds David felt able to tackle the day – and more. The transition from bad to great lay at each end of the spectrum. A contrast ratio of at least five thousand. Had he really felt unwell?

Although now able to conquer the world, common sense still prevailed and he knew he'd no more than two and a half hours before reverting to a pumpkin.

Dressed for the weather he hit the lift. In the lobby he spotted a large but curvaceous lady heading for O'Banion's. It was Roberta. With more front than Atlantic City she'd looked good across a table, and David found her equally easy on the eye as she perambulated her 350 pounds with regal grace. She'd every ounce of flesh under control – truly mind over matter. Four-inch stilettos were invented for her – especially red ones.

But David's Dutch courage fell a little short of being accosted by Roberta and he fiddled with his watch behind a pillar until the coast was clear.

A shrill warble from Whistle Man and he was on his way to Radio City Music Hall. Today's expedition had deliberately been mentally partitioned away. It was to be the climax of his nostalgic journey and savoured afresh rather than diluted with reheated daydreams.

In the weeks prior he'd boned up on the hallowed venue to ensure good mileage when he finally got touch and feel.

Turning into West Fiftieth Street the blue and red neon illuminations of Radio City Music Hall suddenly appeared. Whatever magical expectation David had of this moment, it was truly fulfilled.

People milled every which way as the morning show emptied onto the pavement. The Stage Door Tour, he was told, was to the side of the building in Fifty-first.

Standing by the entrance was a large black doorman. This magnificent human monolith was a sight to behold. Machined from a single block of finest Macassar ebony he stood 6 foot 6 high and spanned 4 foot 31/2 inches – tie, suit, shirt, socks and shoes colour coded to match his perfect Afro-American complexion. Every strand of facial stubble fully retracted. Large black pupils that obliterated the whites.

Egged on by the Ferdi effect David pulled out *BoyZo*, page 6, lovingly stowed in an A4 Perspex wallet.

Holding up the wallet he announced boldly, 'I've come to Ride the Stage.'

No doubt this catchphrase had bubbled up in the fertile imagination of some long-gone *BoyZo* employee. And David didn't really expect his declaration to make any impact, especially to someone who wasn't even a twinkle when Armstrong stepped onto the moon.

But the chemical high promoted the need to tell *someone* he'd arrived. Even if he *was* forty-six years late.

The doorman stared at David impassively for a few seconds.

Then his large black pupils rotated down momentarily to interrogate the strange offering, returning back to re-examine this pasty faced limey.

'D' next Stage Door Tour starts at twelve o'clock. Ya'll need t' git in laan tru' d' door an' to yo left.'

Having dispatched this edict the doorman's face went back on standby.

Inside, David bought a ticket and hovered around with the other curious tourists. Twelve o'clock proved a little flexible, but by and by a young man in a smart maroon blazer, and suitably badged, rounded up his charges and delivered a scene setter for the tour.

They wended their way through the magnificent art deco lobbies, chambers, passages and staircases that show goers never got to see. Samuel Lionel 'Roxy' Rothafel's office was one of the highlights with its high ceiling, striking design and original furnishings.

David sponged up every detail, stopping to smell and feel some of the fittings. Occasionally he'd discreetly re-acquaint with page 6 – such was his need to reference the occasion back to 1958. And now and then as he engaged with the yesteryear ambiance he became convinced his sweet love's spiritual essence was close as hand.

Seeing and experiencing the stage would be the grand finale – he burned with anticipation.

Next, they assembled in a small room in readiness to meet a real live Rockette. Through a private door stepped the most exquisite young lady David had ever seen. She had pretty blond hair and wore a short-skirted costume with white heels, and her lovely face could only be likened to fine porcelain. Beautifully posed and with striking confidence, she described life in America's most famous dancing troupe. Throughout, maintaining a natural, attentive smile.

At the end, everyone had the opportunity of a photo with their arm slipped around the waist of this sweet lady. David declined. Such perfection made him feel shabby and self-conscious of the bulge.

They would now, their tour guide announced, wend their way to a small cinema where they'd view a short video. The news unsettled David – a video suggested conclusion.

'But we haven't seen the stage or the Wurlitzer yet.'

'Yes, I know – whilst there are shows running we can't visit the stage area.'

It was crushing news. For whatever impossible and unlikely fantasy he was enacting, the prospect of experiencing the *BoyZo* prize itinerary was the one thing that successfully contrived to shut out morbid desperation.

He endured the video and shortly found himself in the street being jostled around by the next house.

There was one more port of call in this disappointing pilgrimage. Around the back of the theatre was the famed seasonal ice rink, nestling in a hollow adjacent to the shops and attractions of the Rockefeller Center. In his dreams David might have zoomed around the ice. But he was happy just to see the skating masses stumbling and slithering their way around, and loving every second. He lingered for about ten minutes enjoying the festive atmosphere; observing the young families out together, their lives still to be lived.

With around twenty minutes of 'safe' time left David was happy to hail a cab. Whatever his disappointment, mingling with the happy throngs had jollied him up a little. He forged a path through the busy lobby round to the lift. Checking the reception desk for signs of life no longer interested him. It was a mutually patronising exercise. Express lift 4 disgorged half a dozen bodies and waited for instructions. As David stepped in a voice called out.

'Good afternoon, Mr Jenner.'

He glanced in the mirror to the rear of the lift compartment.

It was Deliah. And through the bronze-tinted glass there appeared to be…

The hint of a smile.

15

Facing Up

The morning had been one of loaded anticipation. Of hope that life's full circle would create a reunion with teenage emotions and memories. That in walking the theatre's inner sanctum he'd absorb the spiritual ether of long ago, somehow encountering the darling lass from page 6, if only to feel her brush his heart once again.

He felt hollow and wretched.

Fanning out the various items of literature on the bed, David slowly perused each one. Information, pictures, colours, shapes – each one offering a fascinating slant on this wonderful venue. Today's visit should have been all embracing – no need to attend a show. He knew the *BoyZo* prize itinerary by heart: 'Go backstage during a live performance – "Ride the stage" – descend a massive twenty-seven feet on one of the four stage sections.'

It hadn't happened.

He contemplated approaching the box office for a show cancellation. But emotional judgment said no. A second trip might devalue the first one and damage the delicate fabric of misty dreams.

Glumly David gathered up the brochures and binned them. And he propped up the Perspex wallet on the dressing table.

He'd not eaten since morning and a Rillington Club Sandwich started to come on strong. By association, his shabby treatment of Jomayra nagged.

'Oh, hello, this is Mr Jenner in suite 1738. Would it be possible to have a Rillington Club Sandwich and a coke?'

'Yes sir – around twenty minutes.'

'Is it possible that Jomayra could bring it up?'

'I'll see, sir – I think she's getting ready to leave ... yes sir, she'll be up with your order.'

A warm welcome greeted Jomayra.

'I'm so sorry about this morning – I was feeling ill, but so looking forward to hearing all about your plans. Would you have time to tell me now?'

Would she have time? Her darling little face glowed.

David took to the settee and motioned Jomayra to sit down.

'Now, about your plans to follow a modelling career ...'

He tucked into his club sandwich – no need to talk. Just nod approvingly now and then.

Jomayra let rip. He'd heard the first three chapters before, but she still needed to talk. Far from dismissing her as a wannabe this, that and the other, he now respected her determination to succeed. From a poor background in Puerto Rica, she'd saved enough to reach America, and was working two jobs in the hope of funding modelling school.

David listened with growing interest, drawn by Jomayra's ebullience as she expounded her hopes and dreams at full chat. For a while she became the daughter David might have wished for in another existence. No longer was she fodder for those solitary moments.

'What do you think, Mr Jenner?'

'Follow your dream, Jomayra, and you'll get there.'

'Do you think I would make a good model?'

'The very best.'

And David meant it.

This time Jomayra left on a high. And with another 10-dollar bill. As she made off down the hallway David's fatherly instincts faltered a tad, as he couldn't help but notice that ...

She had a lovely butt.

From bitter disappointment, David's spirits had risen. Jomayra had dispelled his self-indulgent thoughts – buoyed him with her youthful resolve.

Tomorrow, the Holbrook Institute, and a further donation of body fluids and biopsy specimens.

David decided to veg out on the settee until after the Manhattan Roundup, and then, energy permitting, have a light snack in Rebecca's Patisserie.

A knock on the door.

'Can ah make your room up, Mr Jenner – sir?'

Jesse – David let her in.

'How is you today Mr Jenner, sir?'

David beheld this gentle, grey-haired lady with fondness.

'Oh, I'm fine, Jesse – and how are you?'

'Ah'm good, sir – thank you.'

Jesse turned to start her chores.

'Have you worked here long, Jesse?'

'Well, let me see now ...' She eased herself onto the side of the bed. 'Ah started here at fifteen, and in three weeks time ah'll be seventy-five. So, Mr Jenner, sir, I guess ah'm comin' up for sixty years.'

'Sixty years?' David was astounded.

'Yes sir, Mr Jenner – this hotel has been ma life. Mind you, Mr Jenner, sir, ah only works part time now. Ma husband, you know, he worked all his life for the bus company. Now he stays home and watches the ball game on the Tee Vee.'

'Are you having a holiday this year?'

Jesse laughed and stood up. 'Ah ain't had a holiday in forty years, Mr Jenner, sir. You see, The Rillington Hotel is ma holiday.' Turning to start making the bed, she hesitated. 'You know, Mr Jenner, sir, sometimes ma husband and I goes over to Pier Ninety-Three and looks at them big cruise ships. We just wonders the faraway places all them rich folks go to.'

She gazed distantly out of the window for a few seconds and then turned to David with a broad smile.

'Would you believe, Mr Jenner, sir, I ain't never been out of the state of New York! Best get on, sir.'

David made for the lounge and turned on the television. He flicked through the channels and finally watched a re-run of the Benny Hill Show.

'Have a nice day, Mr Jenner, sir.'

Looking up, David bid Jesse the same.

And from the dressing table the pretty teenager in her bell boy's uniform smiled hauntingly at him.

After several more episodes of UK classic TV David switched over for the Manhattan Roundup.

Ed Razaadi was just finishing off the sports results. David liked

Ed. He had such a pleasant, well-balanced manner about him. A full head of well-groomed salt-and-pepper hair, grey sports jacket, brown shirt – tanned. An image David coveted.

Over to Maria Arabella, who as always looked devastatingly beautiful. And more so tonight, in a red dress that would have gotten any other woman arrested.

She focussed on the plight of the Kwi-Megei refugees – so named after the boat they'd arrived on. Numbering forty-nine men, women and children, they'd fled a vicious military coup in the coastal province of Chumimbah, South East Asia, and made a perilous trip aboard a rusty, overloaded fishing boat in the hope of being taken in by Uncle Sam.

Intercepted by the US Coastguard in the Hudson River, permission to berth had been refused. With nowhere to go they had hung around in the estuary, until exhausted, hungry and bedraggled, but otherwise intact, they were subsequently taken ashore whilst officials figured if they were aliens.

America, it seemed, was on the threshold of opening its big heart to them. For the time being, and whilst the usual bureaucracy clanked away, they were encamped in a small draughty warehouse on the west side river front just south of the Holland Tunnel.

News clips depicted the refugees huddled over fires with their sparse possessions. In the interim the Red Cross had kitted them out with the basics – sleeping bags, food, cooking utensils and hand-me-downs.

It touched David and further distanced him from his own malaise.

In conclusion, Maria flashed David her special smile.

From popping a Ferdi special earlier, his bloodstream had normalised to having just the regular contents. He didn't feel too bad, although a spasm of pain was gaining momentum. Some Morpheaze and he was back in business heading for the lobby.

Rebecca's bustled with tourists and business visitors alike and David was happy to sit in a corner by himself. He nodded to a couple of nodding acquaintances, knowing they'd never advance beyond nodding, but it smacked of a pleasant camaraderie.

After a Rillington Special Burger and curly fries, David bought a bar of chocolate and yesterday's copy of the *Daily Mail*.

Of all films, *Tootsie* was showing on TCM. He recalled Emily and her Maltesers. Fact was, he didn't see much of the film in his attempt to be amorous. With his chocolate and a low alcohol lager David successfully took in the whole flick this time round.

Each day, he could feel the useful span of time closing in. And each day he felt the need to retire a little earlier. Bed time that night was 9.15. It was like growing up in reverse.

Morning brought a better prospect than twenty-four hours before. True to David's oncologist, days would be good and bad, with bad getting worse. For the sake of the Holbrook, he avoided any med.

By 10.30, he'd fired up and managed coffee and toast in Rebecca's. And on the dot, he was welcomed by Professor Olufunwa.

As before, she led him to the small ante-room. And as before, she pulled up a chair to be facing and alongside. But this time, allowing her thigh to connect quite firmly with his own.

Whilst gently stroking David's arm as she deployed the blood pressure monitor, she spoke in soft tones.

'How much longer do you have, David?'

'I'm not really sure. Maybe a week or so.'

It was a bizarre conversation, but David quickly fell prey to the professor's charm.

'Would you consider donating your diseased organs to our institute for research?'

He'd not thought further than Eternal Slumbers, but there seemed no good reason to refuse.

'Yes – OK.'

'Thank you, Mr Jenner.'

'And as you know, we are funded entirely through donations – perhaps you might remember us.'

David was perhaps a little taken back, but he was big enough and old enough to understand the sentiment.

'Of course.'

Such questions were unlikely to promote a meaningful blood pressure reading and David doubted the equipment was even switched on.

Katz attended him in the procedure room along with a pleasant Asian nurse. Taking blood was OK. But the biopsy was akin to taking a sample of the earth's core prior to drilling for oil. On this occasion, he was injected with a substance that would ostensibly attach itself to malignant cells and provide diagnostic information for next time.

Katz returned David to the ante-room. With a slightly unbalanced smile he declared, 'We'll see you again – "As time goes by".'

Professor Olufunwa chatted to David whilst he sipped his fluid-replacement tea.

He shyly noted how unusual the professor's surname was.

'My late husband was Holbrook Olufunwa – he was Nigerian. I lost him to Hodgkinson's Disease twelve years ago, and started the institute in his honour.'

'I hope you didn't mind my asking.'

'Not at all.'

Tea finished and donor consent signed, the Professor wheeled David to the entrance.

'We're here for you, Mr Jenner. Please call us any time you feel the need to.'

She handed him a card.

'These are the out-of-hours numbers.'

'Please could we see you again in two days' time?'

David's expression must have belied his mental questioning of two days rather than three.

Professor Olufunwa explained. 'You've entered a critical phase of cell transformation.' She smiled.

'Remember, Mr Jenner, we're here for you.'

'Goodbye, Professor Olufunwa.'

'If you prefer, you can call me Alice.'

David detected a certain sadness in her face.

'Goodbye … Alice.'

Instead of heading back to the hotel David directed the driver to Gerome's on Eighth Avenue, as he knew the Workaday 3-Size Pants 40-44 would only be good for another day or so.

16

No More Smoke and Mirrors

Isaac Gerome appeared out of the fabric jungle smiling broadly. 'Why, Mr Jenner, vot a pleasure to see you.'

'Hello Mr Gerome, I wanted two pairs of the Workaday 3-Size Pants, forty-six to fifty-inch, please.'

'Are these for you?'

'Oh, no. A friend of mine was so impressed he asked me to get him some.'

'Ah – ve'll have to put you on a commission!'

Isaac laughed mischievously.

David took the brown parcel and strolled back towards the hotel. Although rugged up, the cold penetrated deeply and a sickly weakness set in that drained him physically and mentally. The Rillington gold canopy never looked so good. As he laboured his way across the lobby to the lifts a ritzy voice rang out.

'HEL-LO Mr Jenner!'

Roberta was advancing on him, face a picture of sensual anticipation – her curvaceous chassis swaying with each slow, deliberate step.

Getting closer to David her expression changed to one of concern. She looked deep into David's troubled eyes, raising her arms and gently cupping his face in her hands.

'Honey, you're not well, are you?'

David slowly shook his head. For the first time, he felt emotionally demoralised, and tears welled up.

Roberta gently relieved him of the brown paper bag.

'Honey, I'm gonna look after you.'

Slipping her arm around his waist, she steered him to the lift.

'What floor, honey?'

'Err, seventeenth.'

Head bowed, David succumbed to the firm support of this kindly lady. Once in the suite, she helped remove his coat and scarf.

Her voice was soft and comforting.

'Tell me about it, honey.' David tried to talk, but emotion choked him, and tears flowed. Roberta wrapped her large fleshy arms about him and held him like a child.

'Let it out, honey.'

Within a few minutes, he was able to summon up some composure. He'd not wept since his teen years.

'I'm so sorry.' David could only look at the floor.

Roberta took his hands.

'It's OK, honey, there's a time for everything. Why don'tcha get comfy on the settee whilst I order some coffee.'

Roberta rattled off some no-nonsense instructions to room service and then elegantly slid her curves into an armchair.

In soft, empathetic tones she asked him, 'Why not start at the beginning, honey?'

He explained that he'd not been too well of recent and had decided to come and see New York City whilst still reasonably mobile. That treatment was waiting on his return. That all would be well – the outlook was optimistic.

Coffee arrived. They sipped in silence for a minute or so.

Then Roberta tenderly took David's hand in hers.

She was no fool.

'May I call you David?'

'Of course.'

'Now, David, honey, tell me the truth.'

Part of the truth sat on the dressing table. David silently handed the A4 folder to Roberta.

Armed with the facts of the *BoyZo* competition, she turned to him.

'And how does this fit in, sweetie?'

David described his illness and the prognosis, and how he'd found the old comics.

He lightly touched the photograph.

'At thirteen I was so in love with her. Most of the readers must have felt the same. I tried to escape into the competition. It was my way of dealing with terminal illness. I kidded myself if I came here and followed the prize itinerary I'd somehow connect with 1958. That through some wonderful metamorphosis I'd see the young lady in the photograph again. She holds a romantic fascination for me that just won't go away. I built up such a ridiculous fantasy, and now it's all gone flat. I feel such a fool.'

'You poor baby. Do you have family in the UK?'

'None at all. I have a few friends, but I think I've rather burned all my bridges.'

'And you're here all by yourself?'

David nodded.

'You poor, poor baby.'

'I do have a local doctor who's taking care of me.'

'David, I go back home on Christmas Eve, but until then I'll be here for you. I'm in suite 2016. Call me any time, day or night.'

'Thank you Roberta, err ... Bobbie.'

David knew that she meant it. She had a heart of gold and he loved her for it.

'Why don't you join me for dinner tonight – we can talk some more.'

'I'd like that – thank you.'

At the door, Roberta kissed David softly on the cheek.

'I'll see you at seven.'

For a while, David gazed reflectively at the world outside. Keeping his conscious mind drugged with nostalgia hadn't worked out. In his heart there were dimensions that defied the bounds of the physical world. But it seemed that memories could only ever be memories.

Nevertheless, events of the last few days had somehow left him stronger. Re-engineered his values. It had been a strange ride – now he was able to face the reality of his situation.

Installing page 6 back in the wallet, David returned it to the dressing table. He couldn't resist a quick glance at that familiar smile. In spite of all that had gone before – she still had his heart in tow.

Dinner with Roberta was easy on the soul. Gone was the flamboyance. Gone was the need for any pretence on his side.

'Tell me about yourself, David, honey.'

She listened quietly whilst David laid bare his simple, aimless, unproductive life – opening up recesses of his mind hitherto untapped.

'It's taken me nearly sixty years to grow up, Bobbie, and now it's too late.'

She held his hands.

'Don't punish yourself, honey. Most of us just punch the clock each day to keep this big ol' world turning, and we don't necessarily have anything to show for it.'

David understood the sentiment but his personal sense of failure was well dug in. He'd daydreamed of doing something prolific to redress the balance. Something gallant, creative, romantic, memorable – whatever. But always 'tomorrow'. Now he was running out of tomorrows.

At around ten to nine he excused himself. Turning to leave, Roberta lightly caught his hand.

'Remember David, honey – I'm here for you – room 2016. Anytime.'

A comforting gesture and David counted his blessings. He'd envisaged very little social contact whilst chasing down the dream and assumed his passing would go virtually unnoticed. But in the space of a few days a supportive network of humanity was in the making.

Talking had cleared his mind – left him able to make some frank admissions to himself. The Walter Mitty escapism in the *BoyZo* flight of fancy was clearly doomed from the start. But something to replace it was beginning to shape up. Something to reliably see him through. It embodied a degree of self-indulgence, perhaps. But the effect would be the same.

He recalled the main war cry of Eloise Goodridge in her book: 'It's never too late'.

'Don't bemoan the failings of yesterday's yesterday, enjoy the rewards of tomorrow's tomorrow – today.'

He'd yet to fully digest the logic, but knew there was a motivational message in there somewhere. And motivate him it did.

On reaching his suite, David put Wrightman Goodfellow's invitation to the test.

'Hi, this is Wrightman.'

Jovial bonhomie abounded.

'Hello Mr Goodfellow, this is Mr Jenner – I hope you don't mind my calling at this time.'

Wrightman's voice softened.

'Mr Jenner, sir, I invited you to call me anytime, and I meant it. How can I help you, sir?'

'May I see you tomorrow?'

'Yes Mr Jenner, sir – name the time.'

'Would eleven am be OK – err … I realise you might be busy?'

'There's nothing I can't reschedule. I'll look forward to seeing you at that time, sir.'

Once again, David was focussed – able to put doom on a back burner. This time round it was real world stuff.

In the morning, he rose at 8.30. Switching to the new Workaday 3-Size Pants set for 46 inches no longer triggered a downer. Their predecessors took a walk with the trash.

As a matter of course he downed a Doc Schwartz pick-me-up, with one held for later. And also popped a Morpheaze to pre-empt pain. Today, there were things to be accomplished – a willing body was paramount.

First stop – the HSBC Bank on Eighth and West Fifty- third. Chantelle flashed her tonsils, Whistle Man warbled something – and the taxi driver grunted.

The bank cashier swiftly took on board David's requirements.

'Yes sir, we can do that for you today – there'll be a small charge for the same day electronic transfer.'

Manipulating large sums of money was alien to David, though quite a novelty, and he marvelled at the slick execution of his request.

But then, this was America.

Time for a Dunkin' Doughnut and coffee in lieu of breakfast. And then a slow walk five blocks south to LawServices4U. With his bloated midriff walking had to be slow. To dampen the painful counter motions he'd adopted the practice of supporting the bulge with hands clasped underneath. A white dog collar would have completed the ministerial stance.

Wrightman's quiet, understanding demeanour carried over from their last meeting. Sympathetic smiles rippled down the line as David passed through – they'd surely been primed up. Tabling a copy of his will, he explained a wish to re-assign some of his bequests. That he wanted to donate anonymously to causes he'd first-hand experience of.

And in his lifetime.

Leaving most of his estate to large international charities made sense at the time. But this way he could get a buzz from being an observer on the happiness and goodwill he was to confer.

'I'd like to make a substantial donation to the Holbrook Institute.'

Wrightman struggled to suppress his surprise at the vast sum.

Jomayra would be going through modelling school, and Jesse and her husband would take a special journey to Pier 93.

'Please notify the recipients straight away, Mr Goodfellow – I'll have the funds transferred to you tomorrow".

Wrightman understood the urgency, and more. He'd 'Fax the revised Will to Paine, Proctor and Pratt this afternoon, Mr Jenner, sir. And I'll be sure to courier a copy to you at The Rillington.'

'And there's something else, Mr Goodfellow.'

David explained his requirement and in the process gave a sheet of paper to Wrightman.

'I hope you can do this in the time allowed.'

Wrightman surveyed his frail client. Most people wanted to engage in vitriolic combat with their spouse, or sue the pants off some unfortunate organisation or individual.

And Wrightman was their man. If they didn't feel hateful or acrimonious, or the need for vengeance or retribution, Wrightman would incite these emotions. For he was never happier than when enjoying the adrenalin rush of demolishing his clients' adversaries in court.

But here was a man who wanted, without pretension, to anonymously give most of his material wealth to people in need.

In humble tones he assured David, 'I will have everything ready for you in forty-eight hours – I give you my word, sir, whatever it takes.'

David's will now only served to divvy up whatever small residue remained on his passing.

Business arrangements had driven the conversation and with no latitude for concluding on a high note, they walked in silence to the front door. Wrightman gently shook hands with David.

'I shall see you in two days' time, sir.'

David thanked him.

'Call me, Mr Jenner, sir, anytime – I'm here for you. I mean it, sir.'

Nodding in acknowledgement, David headed towards Eighth Avenue.

Walking back was OK to begin, sufficient of ingredient X still present. Three blocks on though, withdrawal set in, and with it, worse than ever, those ghastly sensations of mortality. Junior Suite 1738 never felt so welcome. Clearly the uppers were losing their grip and David accepted, philosophically, a growing drug dependence. Plan C had foundered. But rising from the ashes was its successor – a program of unbridled benevolence.

Plan D.

17

Final Arrangements

Having got the new bequests sorted, David felt a spiritual uplift equivalent to at least two Euphoridex. Feeling somewhat physically wretched though, and with nothing further scheduled for the day, he elected to bypass the pills and instead take to the settee and let his mind freewheel amidst the potpourri of cable TV trivia.

Midway through an episode of *Bonanza*, there was a knock at the door – Don Rodriguez the manager in his trademark snappy green blazer and grey flannels. And that wonderfully crisp gravel voice straight from a TV ad.

'Hope I haven't disturbed you, Mr Jenner. Just a courtesy call to check that everything's OK for you, sir.'

David, with his undemanding needs, assured Mr Rodriguez, 'There's nothing I can think of – but thanks anyway.'

Don smiled and nodded pensively whilst lightly tapping the door post.

'That's good, Mr Jenner, sir.'

He nodded, smiled and tapped some more.

With a final nod and tap he turned to leave, but swung back again.

'You know, Mr Jenner, sir, we're here for you – I mean, err ... HEY buddy, Mr Jenner, SIR, you want anything, just call. HEY! I mean anytime, sir. Yeah! – we're here for you!'

With a sharp smack to the doorpost the green blazer was gone.

Was Don Rodriguez just being a good ambassador, or had he got wind of sickness and frailty? David drew a blank and returned to *Bonanza* to catch Hoss and Little Joe tying up the baddie.

Thirty-nine channels of mediocre early afternoon cable television became the casualty of a wave of apprehension. David could feel all of the terminal threads in his life reaching a point of convergence. At times, his immediate existence seemed detached from reality. As if he was an observer on himself. But it all distilled down to a waiting game. One in which time was tight – and yet interminably slow.

Amazingly his stomach appeared to stay outside of the equation. And Edwin arrived shortly with a chicken salad and an ice-cold Bud.

A good-looking young black kid from Greenville, Mississippi, Edwin had no particular aspirations for the future, but nevertheless exuded the sparkling energy of youth. Permed and oiled hair, diamond ear stud, faultless complexion and a smile that could energise a street-load of lights. Some day he'd go back home to work in his dad's lumber yard. But for now soaking up the city culture and courting his Venezuelan chick was more compelling.

David often wondered what these lively youngsters saw when engaging with him. A sickly old geezer of fifty-nine? It seemed unlikely. They were too young to disguise their inner feelings with a convincing degree of sophistication. Their smiles and exuberance indicated a lack of deceit and whatever they perceived was wholly acceptable to them. It bore the hallmark of that caring relationship a child has with their grandfather. He might be bald, toothless, ugly and unsanitary, but nature bonded the generations with an unconditional love.

The chicken salad found a sweet spot in his stomach, and along with a Morpheaze David felt sufficiently inspired to take a stroll along Eighth Avenue, this time heading north.

Wintry cold from the morning had reformed to a mild light drizzle – pleasant and refreshing as it tickled his face. He ambled along, observing the shapes, sizes, colours, cultures and ages. Three months ago his interest in people was set to the urban average. Now he was a confirmed people watcher, reading their faces to gauge happiness or adversity – observing them move around like an army of industrious ants in slow motion whilst they got on with the business. This was life in the raw – everyone busy earning a crust or foraging for the necessities of life.

For so many of these people, life would be a struggle from beginning to end.

But for David, the challenges and problems of a progressive

existence had been removed, his life reduced to little more than expending each of his remaining days. It left him free to savour his environment, to enjoy his senses at a much more subtle level. To notice things that would normally have slipped beneath the radar. As his life moved to its conclusion, David's perception of everything became sweeter and more tolerable. Smells became more interesting – the smell of people, roasted peanuts and chestnuts, damp pavements; traffic exhaust fumes intrigued his nostrils. Even the rancid stink of garbage in greasy side alleys had its own fascination.

People bumped and jostled, umbrella canopies caught his head, traffic roared and horns blared. Devices of irritation that might once have offended his senses now found a receptive subject in David. And he welcomed them as glorious manifestations of life itself.

Having just crossed Forty-sixth West, David noticed a shabbily dressed individual slowly moving into his path. His instinctive deflection to the right was mirrored by the oncomer. Within seconds he was face on with an amazing, reddish, greyish beard. It radiated out in an inverted semi-circle and joined seamlessly with a thick head of reddish, greyish hair.

Attached to the beard was a weathered face and two very intense eyes. And all this was attached to a raincoat that had picked up enough grease and oil to qualify as a waxed trench coat. From the smell alone a blind man could have described this creature.

It was evidently no chance meeting.

'How y' doin', buddy?'

Equipped with his philanthropic affection for anything that moved, David, far from feeling repulsed by this visual and odorous confrontation, sensed a value-added experience in the making; a chance to savour humanity in its native state.

'I'm fine, thanks.'

'Can you spare a man a buck or two?'

Cocking his head to one side, lips pursed and eyes wide and expectant, Beard Man waited for his victim to capitulate.

David was now in the business of sparing quite a few bucks. But rather than hand over a wad of notes, he decided to offer the healthy option.

'Would you like a hot cup of tea and maybe something to eat?'

It wasn't quite the response Beard Man was expecting. Most

people either ignored him or hastily shelled out some cash to get him out of their face and rid the pong.

'Hmm – TEA? – don't touch the stuff. Now if you said "whisky" we could be in business.'

'OK, whisky, then – are you hungry?'

'Err ... yeah, buddy – if whisky goes with hungry, them I'm hungry.'

He laughed. 'Y' gonna take me to the Waldorf?'

A cup of tea and a sandwich would have been easy to rustle up in the street. Whisky and a sandwich was something else.

Given his condition, and his current state of mind, David didn't really care how this unlikely interlude panned out. He revelled in his new-found ability to strip away inhibitions and convention, and step boldly out of his comfort zone. To be brave and wise and tolerant. And with death waiting in the wings, to ensure quality towered over quantity.

'Well, maybe not the Waldorf.'

David quickly scanned the shopfronts for a licensed café that would take a stinking street dweller.

'There's a place round the corner in Forty-sixth – Scotty's. They'll take anyone with money – even me!' He laughed again. 'Sure you want to do this, brother?'

'Yes. Incidentally, I'm David.'

'RED!'

He gave David a sidelong look of bemusement.

'Let's go buddy – whisky's callin'.'

They found a quiet, dark corner in Scotty's. It was a dive – around thirty years overdue for a facelift. But booze and food were on. And he and thee blended with the other clientele.

David invited Red to 'Have what ever you want' – which he did.

Whilst Red shovelled all the trimmings down his throat along with a tumbler of double malt, David quietly studied him. Here was a man living rough, who'd probably ingested most known germs and viruses, eaten poorly and indulged all the bad lifestyle taboos. And yet he appeared to be disgustingly healthy. There seemed to be a lesson embedded somewhere.

Glancing up from the trough, Red caught David's eye and perhaps felt obliged to show a superficial interest in his sponsor.

'So what brings you here, brother?'

'Just wanted to see New York.'

'You sound like a Limey.'

David smiled. 'That's right – West London.'

Red engaged with his plate again and then ordered double bread and butter pudding with custard, ice cream and chocolate sauce.

David got bold. 'How would you describe yourself, Red?'

'Describe myself? I'm a TRAMP! Folks try to give me fancy names. But I'm a TRAMP!'

'Where do you come from originally?'

'Springfield Missouri – born and bred.'

Red's dessert arrived and his spoon became a blur. After scraping the pattern clean, he finally slumped back in his seat.

'Well, brother, err ... David you said? Don't get a whole load a' tucker like that every day.' He belched appreciatively. 'Yeah – Springfield, Missouri. Wife left me in 1967 for another woman, lost my job, lost my home. Bummed it for a few years on the railroad. Came to New York nigh on thirty years ago – never looked back. You just on holiday?'

David pondered the route to go on this one. And whilst he did so, he could hear himself saying rather mechanically, 'Well, actually, I've come here to die.'

Red hit 'Pause' for a couple of seconds.

'Hmm ... I take it you mean by your own hand?'

"Oh, no – I'm terminally ill. Got an inoperable tumour.'

'That's bad. Err ... when do you think you might be dyin'?'

'One week – two at the very most.'

'A WEEK? Hmm ... that's *real* bad.' Red drained his glass and gave David the eye. 'Mighty fine drop of malt.'

David recognised the look of expectation

'Have another. Have as many as you want.'

'Well thanks, brother – my lucky day.'

He grunted and belched a few more times, and studied David pensively for a while.

'Hmm. So you're spending your last week doin' good around the neighbourhood?'

David nodded. 'Something like that.'

His guest leaned forward.

'You look OK to me, brother. Sure the Doc's got it right?'

'Yes – there's no mistake.'

'Hmm. My buddy Smoky-T makes a brew – cures everything. Grinds up leaves an' bark an' bones an' stuff. Not sure what else goes in there – don't wanna know. I takes it for everything. Tastes like python piss. Had a large wart on my chin. A swig of the brew an' it just fell off.'

'That's amazing.'

'Can get you some, brother – have you right in no time.'

Politely declining, he made his excuses to leave, anxious to get back before energy levels went into crisis.

'Change your mind – I'm doin' Seventh tomorrow and Sixth the day after.'

David bade his lunch date farewell.

'Where y' stayin', brother?'

'The Rilling...' He tried to suck the words back in.

Red laughed raucously. 'Don't worry, brother, I ain't gonna come an' show you up.'

David pressed a 20-dollar bill into Red's palm.

'Take care.'

'And you, good buddy.'

Once back on Eighth, he hailed a cab.

Entering the foyer he detoured to the hotel shop. A latent craving for Cadbury's Bournville chocolate surfaced – he'd spotted it on the counter a couple of days ago: 'Special import from Britain'. It wasn't just the taste. The Rillington had quickly become 'home', but David still sought that tenuous link with a lifetime's happy memories across the pond. Five dollars bought two bars of memory lane.

Deliah, as usual, appeared to be on Planet X. She had a wonderful gift for being able to transport everything but her body to another place and time. But as David intercepted the exclusion zone, her face snapped to attention.

'Good afternoon Mr Jenner.'

A radiant, pre-programmed smile spilled out. It was quite a transformation using just seventeen muscles, as the aphorism claims. On target for Deliah who was economical with movement,

It caught David unawares.

'Oh, err ... good afternoon.'

Insincere bonhomie flew around like the proverbial at The Rillington, and as he walked into a waiting lift, David waited for the meaningless follow-up.

'Have a nice evening Mr Jenner.'

It amused him and seventeen muscles pulled his face into a stupid grin as he went up in the world.

It was a few minutes short of 5.00 pm, and Jesse was finishing up. Her sweet smile never changed.

'Had a good day, Mr Jenner, sir?'

Jesse's sincerity was refreshing.

'Yes thanks, Jesse.'

It would be Jesse's turn tomorrow to have an extremely good day.

'How about you?'

A dreamy quality crept into her smile.

'Well Mr Jenner, sir, thank you for askin'. Ah can honestly say that today has been good. But you know, sir, all ma days is good days – Lord's been kind to me.' Making to gather up her cleaning equipment she looked up. 'Did you like them Rillington Fudge Delights ah left you last night?'

'Oh yes, Jesse – they were delicious.'

She winked at David.

'See what ah can do tonight sir.' On closing the door behind her Jesse chuckled softly. 'That's if you's a GOOD boy.'

Easing himself onto the settee, David sipped a cup of Junior Suite 1738 tea made with his own fair hand. Not quite what 'mother makes', but nevertheless, a good companion to Bournville chocolate. His fondness for this brand went back a long way. Once a week his paternal grandfather would visit from Shepherds Bush and give him a half crown and two bars of Cadbury's Bournville chocolate.

Aged seven, it was a treat and his mother would siphon off a shilling for saving stamps. Sweets, comics and Saturday morning pictures absorbed the rest. At seventeen, there having been no adjustment for inflation, the weekly half crown just about made a packet of fags and a box of matches. But Bournville chocolate was inflation proof – every bar as good as the last. Even at the end, semi-comatose with morphine, his grandfather had slipped the usual into David's hand from his hospital bed.

Swilling a final mouthful of tea to collect the sticky residue of dark chocolate from around his teeth, David laid back and contemplated the ceiling. His brain pressed 'Play' on the cerebral poker machine to establish mood. Most times the reels returned a row of cherries. But as chance would have it they synchronised on 'Moribund', switching his thoughts to darker issues.

Rising panic had been contained by keeping his mind soggy with the self-satisfaction of benevolence. But it seemed that periodically his psyche needed to re-acquaint with the stark and gruesome facts. David dwelt on the pain and physical discomfort that was worsening significantly day by day, knowing that slowly it was getting the upper hand. And he wondered how long it would be until bed became his only salvation. At the onset, he'd agonised about the means of coping as play drew to a close. But as the physical evidence of his malaise piled up, his question was answered.

He'd feel too ill to give a damn.

His mind, having bled off some morbid thoughts, flicked the reels again and came up with a row of cherries. And David, without knowing why, felt the barometer needle move round to 'Sunny'.

From over yonder, the remaining bar of chocolate begged to be eaten. He made another cup of tea and obliged, slipping back into memory lane.

Eventually rejoining the real world, David noted the Manhattan Roundup to be some twenty minutes away. Sufficient time to soak up a little heat. Rillington water was always hot and plentiful, and it gave relief where chemical means failed.

Whilst undressing, David caught site of himself in the mirror. His appearance was becoming even more bizarre. Eight months pregnant might have been apt, but for the lopsided bulge. Out in the street, a complete cover-up was achieved with winter clothing. But around the hotel, he assumed people would recognise a large beer gut and leave it at that. Workaday 3-Size Pants helped, their full cut disguising his skinny legs and giving a more uniform impression of portliness.

A little overcooked, David slid out of the bath and flopped back on the settee in his Rillington superior soft white towelling bath robe.

Ed Razaadi, as always, met expectations with his smooth, understated delivery. A man with nothing to prove, who never wore the same sports jacket and shirt twice. The more he observed Ed's easy, confident manner and appealing charisma, the more he wished he'd cultivated his own appearance and personality when it mattered. It brought home that he'd ambled through life in grey primer, never bothering to acquire the final paint job.

Then it was over to Maria Arabella. Today she was casually perched against the front of her desk, displaying her magnificent Venusian curves, and clad in a tantalising little blue and gold number. If Maria's upper torso had enthralled David, her lower torso tripled the thrill. The initial news items flew over his head as he watched her sensuous lips mouthing words that registered only as sexual overtones.

Realising that his tackle was in full view, David hastily adjusted his bath robe. Such was the realism of Maria's presence.

The awaited update on the Kwi-Megei refugees got his attention. He now had a vested interest in these poor displaced souls. Today, there were more images of despairing men, women and children huddled round their fires, albeit perhaps a little less disorientated, but still in limbo as to the future. Unofficial reports suggested that they would almost certainly be allowed to stay under the asylum laws. Most such situations went that way. But the wheels of officialdom would keep this one going for a while longer until announcing a decision that the people had already taken as fact.

David felt good in the knowledge that the refugees' lives were about to change in a way they would never have imagined.

Plan D would see to that.

Camera 3 closed in on Maria whilst she told David she'd look forward to seeing him the same time tomorrow.

His next date was at seven with Roberta.

18

Better to Give than Receive

A repetitive electronic sound struck up from the bedroom. It persisted and prompted David to clamber off the settee and find the origin. It came from beside the bed – his mobile phone was ringing!

He fumbled blindly with the phone and succeeded in losing the call. But it warbled into life a few seconds later.

'Hello?'

For all he knew it could be someone from Mars calling.

'Hi David – it's Ferdi.'

'Err … oh, hello Ferdi, how did you know my number?'

'Easy! It showed up on my call indicator when you last phoned me. Anyway, David, just checkin' to see if you're OK and needing more med.'

David was 'OK' as he could be under the circumstances.

'I'm coping, thanks. I could do with some more Siestathol and Morpheaze.'

'OK, I'll have it sent over.'

'Thanks.'

'What about the other med – the one I prescribed?'

'I've got eleven left – just taking them as and when.'

'Good'.'

After several seconds, Ferdi continued, but in a quieter, slightly patronising tone.

'I, err … gather you signed up with the Holbrook.'

That was a puzzle.

'Signed up?'

David sensed a modicum of awkwardness from the other end.

'Yes, err … that is, the Institute will be able to examine you – afterwards.'

Afterwards?

The penny dropped with David.

'Yes, I've signed up.'

'Well yeah, that's err ... good.'

His voice sharpened up again.

'Get the stuff to you tomorrow.'

'Here for you, David, twenty-four seven – don't forget – gonna look after you.'

'Thanks Ferdi, I really—'

Click.

There was something more than a little dodgy about Doc Schwartz. By no stretch of the imagination was he the respected family GP. And definitely getting a backhander from the Holbrook Institute. Something of a 'Mister Fixit' – probably kept a string of wealthy showbiz clients well primed with the magic shot. No questions asked.

It made no odds – David knew that when things really went pear-shaped, he'd be glad to call on Ferdi's talents.

Preparations for dinner followed. Workaday 3-Size Pants really lacked any social graces. Designed with an army combats theme, they clashed with his jacket – of which the button and buttonhole would never meet again. But it was the best image he could present.

Roberta spotted David from across O'Banion's. She sashayed through the tables to meet him, all bust and bangles, arms outstretched and smiling affectionately.

Once again those full, firm, fleshy arms held him in a gentle motherly embrace.

'It's good to see you, David, honey – been thinkin' 'bout you all day.'

'And it's good to see you, Bobbie.'

She smelt good – Coty Nuance. Tantalising memories of the Jeanette d'Arcy Dance Studio drifted back – Phyllis Gray. She all but drank the stuff.

There were no more revelations from David tonight. His mental sluice gates had been fully raised prior. Roberta now knew as much about him as he did, and as a woman, probably more. He felt safe in her worldly aura, and the thought did occur that to expire whilst swathed in her generous arms would not be an unpleasant way to go.

They kept away from David's situation. Roberta did, however, stroke his fingers coyly and ask if he was 'Still pining for your little girl?'

To which David sheepishly gave a 'Yes'.

Instead, the conversation, of its own accord, turned to the more poignant events in Roberta's life. Her first husband was cruelly taken away in a failed parachute jump.

'The love of my life.' Her eyes brimmed. 'We met at college. I was so slim in those days.'

A slim Roberta! David tried to visualise a skinny version – like a distorted image in a fairground hall of mirrors. He had a theory that over time people assumed a natural weight – a preordained mass that looked right. Definitely the case with Roberta, whose curves had a very pleasing inertia.

'I went on to marry three more times, but things just went wrong.' She smiled. 'But I have plenty to be grateful for. I was pregnant with Chris when I lost my husband – he lives with his wife in Mexico. Don't see him as often as I'd like.'

Time with Roberta was well spent. It buffered David's mind from the constant awareness of his downward trajectory.

As the dinner date progressed, incipient back and abdominal pain took a hold, making further socialising untenable.

'I'll have to go, Bobbie.'

'I understand, honey.'

She fondly squeezed his hand.

'I'll be here tomorrow night, honey, if you feel like some company.'

He turned to navigate through the tables.

'David!'

Roberta caught up with him. Her smile was caring and warm, but interlaced with sadness and a sense of despair.

'Call me any time, David – don't be alone. 2017.'

For a second, they logged on to each other's hearts.

'Thank you, Bobbie – I will.'

He would gladly have extended his lifespan, if only to ease the hurt of this sweet lady. For the two days before she departed, he resolved not to add to her emotional burden and instead give every impression of personal well-being.

Passing through the lobby he nodded cursorily to a couple of his co-nodders, anxious not to be waylaid. Don hesitated as he passed, but maybe sensed timing was bad. And a strident 'Have a good evening, Mr Jenner' from Chantelle missed its target, ending life as a fading echo in the lift shaft.

Evenings were drawing in for David. By 8.40 he was safely installed in bed, pilled up and ready for Siestathol lights out. Both tomorrow and Christmas Eve would have their demands. And then Plan D would be fully implemented. He knew at that point he'd be happy to move over and succumb to the inevitable.

City lights of different colours and intensities softly illuminated Junior Suite 1738, giving a restful quiet. From the dressing table his illusive sweetheart from 1958 smiled. Happy, sunny *BoyZo* days and tender love at thirteen were David's last conscious thoughts before Siestathol pulled the plug.

19

The Home Run

For a change, David awoke to bright sun streaming into the room. His mind came out of suspended animation and let the *BoyZo* daydream from twelve hours earlier run its brief course.

The Holbrook Institute were expecting him at 11.00 am, and before that he had to call in at the HSBC Bank to organise a same-day transfer to LawServices4U.

As before, no med before the fluids and flesh session. Besides, he'd dismissed the Retrobrax and Vytaboost as little more than placebos and given them a free ride around the sewers of Manhattan.

Getting ready was gently paced. Twelve hours sleep had given some respite. Though getting from horizontal to vertical was the test. He felt dizzy and nauseous as the bulge came under the influence of gravity. It necessitated sinking back onto the side of the bed until everything biological had started to harmonise.

A cup of tea and a packet of Rillington shortbread biscuits gave his stomach something to do whilst finishing the getting-ready etceteras. It helped, and as his organs fired up one by one, so he reached the critical momentum to tackle the outside world.

Today would be a taxi job throughout. All the usual physical nasties were lurking in background, waiting for a chance get the upper hand. For some reason the driver took a route past the Radio City Music Hall. It made David's heart lurch, stirring those festering emotions. Emotions fuelled by a lingering conviction that *BoyZo* love from 1958 was captivated in those timeless art deco chambers and corridors. That time was no more than human invention. Logic and common sense had broken that spell. But in his heart nothing had changed.

He'd consciously avoided passing the theatre and yet its gravitational pull was unrelenting.

Whilst revisiting those insoluble yearnings the taxi had stopped, driver and car waiting impassively for David to make the first move.

Organising the funds transfer was straightforward. Jackson McClelland – an unlikely name for a coffee-coloured kid from Panama City – smilingly did the business, as before. Festooned in studs, earrings and tattoos, and wearing a red bandanna he deftly set up the transaction. David quite envied the younger generations for their freedom in self-expression. In his day it was Old Spice aftershave, Weaver to Wearer or Burton suits. If you were brave, a pink shirt. And after going for a pee at a Saturday night dance, be sure to brush the talcum powder off your fly afterwards.

'What message shall I add Mr Jenner?'

'Oh, just say "To Wrightman Goodfellow from David Jenner".'

A vast pile of bucks was heading Wrightman's way. Even in sterling, the Kettering and Corby loan had seemed enormous – enough to buy a couple of streets up North somewhere.

There was sufficient left in the account to tide David over for a few weeks. The residue would get cabled back to the Hammersmith branch, courtesy of LawServices4U.

Afterwards.

On to the Holbrook. It was somewhere on the East side – uptown. David had no great interest in the location. A taxi got him there and back – wherever. Professor Olufunwa was there to meet and greet. But at least the blood pressure formalities were skipped. Business was business today and she led him directly to the procedure room.

Katz prepared his kit and David peed in a bottle. Then blood was drawn by a pretty Filipino nurse. Ten syringes on this occasion. No wonder the cup of tea and biscuit afterwards.

One at a time, Katz sank the biopsy tubes. David felt no pain – he was assured as before that they'd been coated with local anaesthetic. In any event, he'd written off what lay below – and was surprised that such intrusive diagnostics were being performed whilst he was still warm.

With all the boreholes patched up, Katz turned to David and slowly closed his left eye. Tattooed on his eyelid was 'YES'. A similar exercise revealed 'NO' on his right eyelid.

'Decisions Decisions!' he giggled childishly.

Professor Olufunwa came by and touched David's arm reassuringly.

'We need to drip a compound into your arm – it'll help with our analysis.'

In another room, he was directed to a couch and hooked up for around thirty minutes whilst substances unknown were piped aboard.

Afterwards, Alice spent a few moments with David in the anteroom for the obligatory tea break.

'How are you feeling?'

'Not too bad, thanks.'

'You might feel a little queasy later.'

She smiled and took her glasses off. David had dismissed her as nondescript. But she looked sweet today. Quite a babe.

'We'd like you to come in Boxing Day – could you manage it?'

Crossing her legs elegantly and letting her skirt ride up two tads, she increased her smile by 10 kilowatts. David assented. He was a sucker for shapely calves. And Alice knew how to get the right sound out of an empty vessel.

Having his body pillaged made him feel, at times, like a living corpse. However he endorsed her determination to find cures. After all, in a big way, he'd put his money where his mouth was.

On the way back, a stop at Walgreen's to pick up some small brown envelopes, the remaining two blocks taken at a gentle stroll. By now he was running on empty and fading.

Mohamed on the concierge desk intercepted David as he beelined for the lift.

'Some guy left this for you.'

He held out an item wrapped in a brown paper bag.

'He said you've gotta drink all of it.'

Shades of Red filtered back.

'What did the guy look like?'

'Dunno, boss – CARL!'

Two hundred decibels summoned Whistle Man from the street.

'Hey, Carl, describe the dude who left this.'

Carl spat out his whistle. With a voice like crushed razor blades he elucidated. 'Some stinkin' tramp – beard an' a greasy coat. Sez "Is there a David here – Englishman?" – describes you. I sez "Yeah".'

'Gives me the bag – sez y' gotta drink it all.'

He hurriedly thanked Mohamed.

'No sweat, boss.'

David continued to the lift, spurred by a feeling of unnatural tiredness, which from experience would quickly mature into exhaustion.

Finally home, he hit the bed and lay spreadeagled whilst molecule by molecule his blood re-acquired lost sugar.

It took an hour or so to regenerate. Along with the returning energy levels came the beginnings of an abdominal pain spasm. But it got cut short with a couple of Morpheaze. And for the sake of some quality time David gulped a Ferdi special. The tablets catalyzed an immense amount of energy from seemingly nowhere. Though he was convinced there was a price to pay somewhere along the line – but hopefully, not in his lifetime.

The required uplift quickly materialised – so much so that he felt able to recline on the settee and watch the city in motion. Whatever was ported in from the drip didn't cause any queasiness. But he felt strange – strangely strange; albeit not in an unpleasant way.

A Rillington burger and curly fries suddenly seemed a good idea. Not being sure whether Jomayra had got the good news yet, he asked for Edwin.

While he munched, Edwin lingered and expounded life through the eyes of a twenty-year-old male with too much testosterone and very little ambition. His Venezuelan beauty had been summarily dismissed in favour of a white girl from the Upper East Side – with a rich daddy.

'Is Jomayra in today, Edwin?'

'She came in earlier, Mr Jenner, but went home, sayin' she had somethin' important to do. Said she'd come back later today. Seemed excited an' all.'

It sounded as though one of the letters organised by Wrightman had made it. David pondered on Jesse's likely demeanour when she appeared later.

Edwin chattered some more in his juvenile street jive until David finally gave him 10 bucks severance pay.

He'd not forgotten the brown paper bag – still on the bed where he'd dumped it unceremoniously earlier. An hour earlier he might have flushed the contents. But hyper on the Ferdi effect, his Mr Hyde alter ego goaded him to swig it down.

Out of the bag came a bottle, clear glass, which might have originally contained cough mixture, or plant food, or a tonic. Or meths. Whatever the substance, there would have been 250 ml of it. Now it contained a fluid that appeared black and viscous. Like used engine oil.

He gingerly removed the screw top and had a sniff. A plethora of bouquets teased his nostrils, each one stimulating recognition, but nothing nameable. It certainly didn't smell as unpleasant as it looked. Maybe python piss wasn't such bad stuff. Red's anecdotal recommendation came to mind. He envisioned his tumour 'dropping off' with no place to go.

Getting the goo into his stomach was the problem. David considered two options. Favourite was to gulp the contents down quickly followed by a mouthful of Rillington Springs. Fear of long-term effects had no relevance. Option one foundered, though, with the prospect of writhing in agony as his stomach lining dissolved.

Option two got the vote. David pressed the opening to his lips and flicked the bottle upwards so to thinly coat the tip of his tongue. Smacking his lips wine tasting style revealed the primary flavour as sulphurous with a bitter afterglow – and a definite hint of some faceless liquor.

He got a little braver and sucked in a small slug, suspending it on his tongue for a second before coating it with saliva and tossing it to his epiglottis for dispatch down the hatch. Slug two got savoured and swallowed gently. With his mouth and gullet now lubricated with the black stuff, the sulphurous experience had become masked by a more focussed taste of bitter liquorish – still with an alcoholic resonance in background.

Confidence growing, David imbibed larger slurps, each one modified in flavour by the previous one. And each one with its complementary aftertaste. He stopped halfway through the contents to allow for any delayed reaction. But apart from a warm sensation in his throat and stomach little else surfaced. With conviction he guzzled the remainder and instinctively reached for the Rillington Springs – but hesitated. Emanating from the peat-like essence imparted by the last gulp was a sweet and somewhat intriguing taste – a taste that David felt the need to hang on to. It seemed to say so much.

Yet so little.

Sitting back he lightly humoured the situation. For all its strange tastes and aromas he didn't believe the concoction would get to the parts that conventional medicine failed to reach. But he did wonder if some mental cooperation might reinforce its biological endeavours.

Closing his eyes David tried to visualise Red's panacea waging war on the bad things. His mind's eye view evoked colours and shapes that mimicked the anatomical bits and pieces to be annihilated.

But mind over matter was rudely interrupted by some vigorous activity in his stomach. It seemed likely that rejection had set in. However, after some rumbling and gurgling, the contents of his stomach decided to head due south – out of mind and out of sight.

For a few hours.

With a dull thud Red's recycled bottle landed in the waste bin. It was the usual story. A small, gossamer thin plastic bin liner that detached and sank to the bottom when anything heavier than a paper clip was trashed.

But David didn't care.

His idle gaze settled on page 6. She smiled at him. And it *was* at him. He smiled back. For a moment he yearned to be back at Number 69, opening that issue of *BoyZo* for the first time, with the prospect of entering the competition and fulfilling dreams of a young heart. But on this occasion armed with all the hindsight of his fifty-nine years.

A slow return to the jaded norm came about as the final dregs of his latest Ferdi fix ended up as salty waste and hit the porcelain. From an original three hours or so, the feel-good now sustained for less than ninety minutes. Mindful of Roberta's sweet offer of company tonight, David realised it would involve another Ferdi special. But equally, it was apparent that his body could only deliver energy on demand so many more times. And he debated the worth of losing another life for an hour's company with Roberta.

A knock at the door dispelled David's pharmaceutical dilemma. It was coming up to 4.00 pm – probably Jesse.

She floated into the room in a state of blissful joy, seemingly unaware of David. And for several minutes tiddled aimlessly around with a feather duster whilst humming a tuneless tune. Good news was at work.

Stopping midstream, Jesse flopped into a small armchair by the dressing table, her legs spreadeagled, head thrown back.

'Well, LORDY, LORDY!' She laughed, raising her head to give David a somewhat asymmetric smile. 'Mr Jenner, SIR, ah'm gonna tell you – ma ship's come in, an' me an' ma Joshua is getting on that ship at Pier 93, and we is gonna see the WORLD.'

David beamed back – a genuine smile; and he enjoyed a heady flush of delight. Because here was the payback – witnessing the immeasurable happiness of this sweet old lady from Harlem.

He invited her to 'Tell me about it', which she did. At length.

'Well it's like this, Mr Jenner, sir – the West Side Travel Company is doin' a cruise promotion and they picked me an' Joshua out of the white pages. Now sir, this is what they called random selection.'

David enjoyed a mental chortle. There was random and there was RANDOM.

'And you know, sir, we is goin' FIRST CLASS! Yes sir, Mr Jenner, and Joshua an' me has been given extra money so we can dress right to hobnob with them first-class folks.'

By now, David had positioned himself on the side of the bed in order to give Jesse his undivided attention.

As she leaned forward to deliver the next proclamation a familiar essence tweaked his nose – one which bore a striking resemblance to gin. Jesse caught him sniffing and her face creased with mirth.

'Yes Mr Jenner, ah've been on the gin – Mr Rodriguez, he gave me a shot to calm me down an' he says to have one later. But you know, sir, ah had the one for later straight after the first one.'

She dissolved into peels of laughter again.

And continued.

'We is going for a MONTH! – yes sir. And a limousine is to collect Joshua and me and bring us home after.' Lowering her voice a little, she went on, 'We is goin' to have one thousand dollars each to spend! But there's one thing we have to do, Mr Jenner, and that is to write a letter to the West Side Travel Company and tell them about the trip. It's called "User feedback" – so they tell us. An' they use this information to improve their service – yes sir.'

As if David didn't know. He'd quite enjoyed crafting the means by which the recipients of his donations would receive their share. It was all about creating a simple smokescreen to isolate LawServices4U from the equation – but with it, an element of fun.

Jesse went quiet for a few seconds and gazed at some cerebral point on the ceiling. Then her eyes slowly reconnected with David's.

She leaned forward and gently laid her hand on David's wrist.

'You know, son, everything comes to those who wait. Me an' Joshua has been waitin' a long time, and now it's our time.' She squeezed his wrist gently. 'You're still a young man, but your time will come.' She patted his hand and eased herself out of the chair. 'Best be getting' on Mr Jenner, sir.'

Jesse took up with the dusting, quietly reaffirming to herself that, 'Yes sir, ma ship's come in.'

Back in her joyful reverie, she proceeded to croak out 'How Great Thou Art' – though not quite to the standard of the immortal Mahalia Jackson.

David retired to the settee. His mind picked up the threads from earlier and tossed the dinnertime options around, finally ending in stalemate. But he needn't have agonised on this.

The decision had already been made.

20

Final Touches

The room telephone shrilled with that dulcet tone recognisable from so many American movies.

It was Roberta – her voice soft and comforting.

'Hi David, honey – I've been thinking about tonight. You know, sweetie, we don't have to meet at O'Banion's.'

David might have toyed with not seeing Roberta, but confronted with the real prospect of this keened his need to sample her charismatic warmth for the last time.

He needn't have worried, though.

'It's just an idea, honey, but maybe we could dine at your suite. It would be so much more comfortable for you, and I'd promise to leave if you get tired.'

He allowed a wry smile to escape. In better times it would have been an offer well received for different reasons. But here and now an offer to be gratefully accepted for its integrity.

'That would be lovely, Roberta. Thanks.'

'I'll see you at seven, honey.'

David settled back on the settee.

Darkness may have fallen, but the Manhattan son et lumière was in full swing. It would have kept his attention but for the even stranger sensations gathering in what seemed every nerve ending in his body. An increased sensitivity – a heightened awareness. To what, he wasn't sure.

And aided and abetted by the discomfort factor as the dark fluid navigated his intestines.

Having vowed to present nothing less than a nonchalant, 'I'm having a good day' front to Roberta, bodily sensations got moved to

105

the back burner whilst David contemplated the means of buoying tonight's mood.

Two Euphoridex would do the trick, and hopefully Red's med would keep a low profile during the seven 'til nine slot. He pressed the second pair of Workaday 3-Size Pants using a small travel iron and set them to 46 inches. And out came a dark-blue XXL fleece designed to hide the bulge.

At 6.30 he would bath quickly and be ready to receive Roberta just before 7.00. Enjoying Roberta's company from the comfort and security of the settee would be a luxury.

For half an hour David relaxed with a cup of home-made tea and a Snickers Bar. *The Liberace Show* kept him entertained whilst waiting for Maria. It smacked of lazy Sunday afternoons and a small black and white telly.

His concentration was variable though, as apart from the regular abdominal discomfort, there were some more pronounced goings on. David estimated the alimentary journey would need his involvement sooner than later.

Tonight he was in for a treat. Ed handed over to Maria, who was standing amid the Manhattan Roundup set wearing a tight, brief and somewhat diaphanous white satin dress – that was just about legal. And surrounded by a montage of electronic images she probably couldn't see. For Maria, no clipboard, or wafer-thin laptop computer, or other stereotyped newscaster accessories to occupy her hands.

She simply stood there, hands lightly clasped, looking devastatingly beautiful. And if that wasn't enough, she walked slowly, deliberately, provocatively to a large screen that added graphic detail to her news delivery. David was mesmerised by the sight of the smooth fabric of Maria's dress struggling to contain those wonderfully dynamic curves.

Two days before, in the *Manhattan Mercury*, Ms Arabella had featured in a TV editorial. Her career was as impressive as her Latin looks. But what had caught David's attention was her recent divorce from Roland Krugenstein, owner of Planet Bee-Bop, a specialist music publishing outfit in Queens. It gave him a degree of meaningless satisfaction knowing that she was ...

Still available.

Fleeting mention was made of the Kwi-Megei refugees, their

future still in the balance. But other stories were now dominating. In particular the headless body found in a Harlem pork pie factory.

As the 6.30 ads hit the screen David made for the bathroom. Getting up re-awakened his large intestine, though he reckoned on fifteen minutes grace. For a minute or so the soothing heat of the bath calmed his bowel. But unsavoury tell-tale bubbles started to break the surface and he went violently into labour.

Exiting the water so quickly as to leave a jelly mould outline of his body he made the pedestal with a second to spare. Even as he strove to cope with this explosive movement, David managed to visualise everything malignant being successfully ejected at the speed of sound.

Within seven or eight minutes, the angry muscles had relaxed. David curbed his curiosity and with eyes straight ahead completed the paperwork.

Now pleasantly relaxed he slipped back into the bath. Whatever Red's medication hadn't done, it would have left the inside of his colon with a healthy baby pink glow.

Lighter in body and soul, uplifted even further with the Euphoridex, David was ready to boogie – if only from the settee.

Roberta arrived a few minutes after seven, her smile and jovial demeanour not wholly convincing. Whilst David greeted her with the easy conviviality he'd rehearsed earlier.

They circled each other emotionally whilst trying to gauge true states of mind. With David sitting as upright as circumstances would allow, and Roberta poured into a club armchair, they engaged in some light repartee.

To his 'How has your day had been?' Roberta replied that she'd spent the morning shopping and the afternoon visiting friends.

Nodding with fake interest David continued, 'And have you bought all the things you'd hoped for on this trip?'

Shallow though the question was, it pushed the right buttons and triggered her underlying passion for retail therapy.

Beaming broadly, she announced, 'Sure have, honey – nine cases in all shipped to ma home address.'

But the lights went out as quickly as they'd come on.

Shoehorning herself out of the chair Roberta slid alongside David. And with his hand gently sandwiched between hers, she surveyed him fondly for a few moments before asking, 'How are you feeling today, honey?'

A question attempting to elicit how good David was feeling rather than how bad. For as much as David wished to maintain a high note, so too it was clear Roberta had no desire to revisit his sad plight.

Smiling breezily he nodded with affirmation. 'Pretty good today, Bobbie – managed to get quite a few things done.'

It had the optimism of futile hope – no more or less than Roberta might have expected.

Room service took the dinner order and they managed some more inconsequential chit-chat – punctuated by reflective quiet and unspoken communication.

Two knocks signalled food. In answering David realised he'd not reckoned on Jomayra being on the other side – which she was. And her sweet face was afire with excitement. He tried to appear nonchalant but knew he'd have to listen while she waxed ecstatic and Roberta looked on.

She managed to de-trolley the food without feeding the carpet. And David pretended to examine his food, whilst wondering when Jomayra would reach critical mass. Roberta clearly had no inkling of this loaded moment.

'Mr Jenner, sir!'

It was 'Show Time' and David prepared to be entertained.

'Yes, Jomayra?'

'I'm going to be a MODEL!'

She almost shouted the last word, totally oblivious to Roberta's bemused looks.

David responded with a slightly quizzical intonation. 'Oh, I thought you'd already decided that.'

He brought Roberta into the picture. 'Jomayra was telling me she plans to be a model.'

'That's right, Mr Jenner,' she gasped, 'but before, I couldn't afford modelling school. Then this morning I got a letter from the Models and Manikins agency – their talent scout spotted me last week and they're going to sponsor me at college and then give me a job!'

David dropped his knife and fork and slumped back in his seat, his face a picture of surprised delight.

'Jomayra! That's fantastic!' And playfully feigning concern he added, 'I hope you won't be leaving too soon.'

He allowed Jomayra a few more minutes to offload and then gently moved her on with an invitation to tell him in detail about this opportunity when she had more time; along with the mandatory 10 bucks.

Jomayra's elation warmed David's heart. He would have preferred the experience one to one. But somehow it dispelled the uncertain atmosphere between himself and Roberta. And they munched away amid companionable silence.

Despite the pleasant diversion, tonight's rendezvous was limited by sombre undertones. Conversation stayed within the past and present tense. And David knew his comely friend was fighting back the words and feelings that had no place at this gentle meeting of the hearts.

They reminisced about happy times in their lives. Of their child-hood days when the earth was still flat. Of people and places they'd treasured. And time passed unnoticed – 8.00, 9.00, 10.00. At 10.30 they both knew it was time to conclude the bittersweet experience.

Reaching into her handbag, Roberta withdrew a card, and gently pressed it into David's hand.

'David, honey, you can get me on these numbers any time.'

'I'm leaving at ten tomorrow, but I'll come and say goodbye.'

She hugged him affectionately and took off; whilst he gratefully hit the hay, unable to stave off deferred tiredness any longer.

There was no sun to greet David as the 24th dawned, and he slowly surfaced to the murky silhouettes of bedroom detail. Today's challenges would provide a sense of purpose for the next twelve or so hours and conclude Plan D. But in background dismal thoughts hovered; for from tomorrow there'd be little more to do other than tread water.

Roberta's goodbye at 10.00 motivated David to extract himself from the cosy bedding. His body felt even more leaden than yesterday. But he skipped the Euphoridex lest it argue with the heavy stuff needed to get through the midday appointment with Wrightman.

At 46 inches, the Workaday 3-Size Pants were slightly less than a snug fit. For the sake of an extra degree of comfort the second pair of zip gussets were loosed. It gave an easy feel analogous to wearing tracksuit bottoms. By 9.30 he was as sartorial as ever he was likely to be again – and sipping a cup of Rillington passion fruit tea whilst waiting.

Roberta's arrival was timely and without ceremony. Eyes obscured with large dark sunglasses she held David momentarily in a tight embrace, and in choked tones whispered, 'Love y' honey.'

Turning swiftly to leave, her reddened eyes and wet cheeks were briefly visible.

Then she was gone.

He felt horribly empty – a wave of sorrow painfully traversing his throat. Powerless to ease Roberta's hurt, he knew there'd be more heartache when Don phoned her in a few days' time.

Edwin arrived with the continental breakfast, keen to gas some more – this time about his woes. David was far from receptive to more empty chatter but the kid needed to offload. Uptown girl had dumped him for a penniless street artist. Who would, no doubt, amuse her for a while. Such was the fickleness of an idle rich girl. It took some understanding for Edwin – worldliness he'd yet to acquire. His former Venezuelan chick didn't want to know either. It all sounded vaguely familiar to David as he slowly tackled the large carbohydrate spread – good value for $3.50.

Lethargy from earlier persisted. Just attending to the simple domestics of everyday life was becoming increasingly laboured. And he could no longer contemplate hitting the street for trivial reasons. Strange sensations persisted from the day before. David read nothing of significance, but accepted they were all part and parcel of the journey. He'd earlier taken some Morpheaze. Not for pain – but simply to deaden the growing sense of physical wretchedness.

With around forty minutes to kill he browsed *BoyZo* page 6. As always, hoping to glean hidden significance previously missed. And forever searching the eyes of the sweet lass for a romantic message.

Allowing fifteen minutes reaction time, the large yellow bomb went down. And by 11.45 David was ready to rock and roll. His sense of well-being urged him to walk. Common sense prevailed, though, and Carl blew him a taxi.

Wrightman quietly led the way to a consulting room.

'I managed to find an interpreter through The Association of

Language Colleges. I've also had the letter independently verified to check it replicates the content you requested.'

He produced a document that had some semblance to a letter – but written in the symbolic language of the Far East. David studied the meaningless content, happy in the knowledge it would expedite the last phase of Plan D.

'Thank you, Mr Goodfellow.'

'How many copies would you like, sir?'

'Would it be possible to have fifty?'

'Of course Mr Jenner.'

Whilst the letter was being copied Wrightman confirmed that, 'The funds reached us yesterday and we have arranged for the inter-mediaries to receive the amounts today; they will translate the money into whatever benefits you specified for each recipient.'

'Laura' slipped in with an envelope containing the copies.

There was little else to say, and in conclusion David proffered to Wrightman that he should deduct his fees from the balance that would be temporarily in his safekeeping.

With eyes downcast Wrightman shook his head slowly. And looking up at David with a sad smile, replied softly, 'No charge, Mr Jenner, sir.'

'But Mr Wrightman, I must—'

Objection overruled.

'Mr Jenner, I have felt privileged to act for you in these matters. And sir, may it be one day that I can be as noble as you.'

Further objections fell on deaf ears. Wrightman slowly stood up and held his large hand out to David.

'I'm proud to know you, sir.'

At the door they quietly shook hands again.

'I'm here for you, Mr Jenner, sir, anytime.'

It was another sad goodbye.

Within ten minutes he was stepping under the familiar gold awning. Carl appeared to smile at him. And Don Rodriguez spun round en route and bid him cheerily, 'Have a good one, Mr Jenner, SIR!' From a further 20 yards he honked out, 'Anything we can get you, buddy, err ... sir?'

David declined. On passing reception Chantelle exposed the back of her throat and loudly invited David to:

'Have a great afternoon, Mr Jenner.'

As well as pulling energy out of a hat, the uppers also bolstered David's appetite – maybe that was the trade. And he would choose the dishes that pandered to his taste buds rather than the scales. There seemed no future in healthy eating.

Lunch arrived courtesy of Chalina – a new lass. Somewhat shy, but happy to loosen up with a few verbal prods from David – and then difficult to shut up. She'd arrived from Santa Lucia, Ecuador, aged nineteen – another escapee from poverty. With no money, she'd managed the journey by working the cruise lines. It was a roundabout route taking three months, but brought her to Pier 93 with a small residue of earnings.

Her Latin skin was of the lighter tones, maybe Honduras mahogany, and she had the beauty of youth, but nothing that might endure when spring faded, save her solid, athletic curves.

Jomayra's good fortune had gotten around beneath stairs, and Chalina lamented that she too would 'like a career in modelling', claiming to have 'the perfect figure for it'.

She would, David noted, do better as a lifeguard, but cheered her on regardless.

Anxious to get stuck in he finally told Chalina, 'It's been lovely talking to you.'

She took the hint without offence and hovered with an expectant smile. It seemed his 10-buck tips had become legendary.

A Rillington mixed grill with side salad and curly fries was followed by sticky toffee pudding with vanilla, strawberry and chocolate ice cream. And a Bud. Reclining back on the settee he browsed the cable channels and settled for *Wagon Train*. But as blood migrated to his stomach for a sugar fix, so his eyelids grew heavy. And for two hours he enjoyed a light sleep, with *Wagon Train* dialogue filtering strangely into dreams that could never be recalled.

He surfaced to the inimitable humour of *I Love Lucy*.

One O' something had become a few minutes to four and there were things to do for later. A sense of urgency cleared the mental fog; which dispersed leaving David hungover from the feel-good of earlier. A painkiller helped.

Out came the photocopied letters and the brown envelopes from the day before. Though the symbolic Far Eastern wordage made little sense, he knew with confidence that it conveyed the same simple message he'd crafted and passed on to Wrightman.

It read:

Dear Kwi–Megei Refugee,

You have a friend. A lawyer has been appointed to help
you stay in America. You will receive $10,000 through a
trust to help you make a new life. You will become
an American.
Take this letter to the address shown.
Good luck.

Your friend.

David was able to rest easy knowing Wrightman would deliver the promises. And each copy was carefully folded into a brown envelope, the flap licked and sealed. Occasional sips from a Bud diluted the bitter aftertaste of cheap glue.

Tonight at around 11.00 he planned to deliver the envelopes personally. Wrightman had established the exact whereabouts and provided a map. It seemed straightforward enough. All he needed was a willing body. Given his poor track record for staying conscious beyond 9.00 pm David had reservations. Yet he so wanted to witness first hand these displaced people and to have the ultimate fulfilment of personally handing them a future.

Lying down, he attempted sleep, but food and rest from earlier made drowsiness hard to come by. When eventually his conscious and unconscious thoughts became pleasantly confused – someone knocked; Jesse as it turned out.

She was still on cloud nine and content to potter around whilst continuing to murder the best of Mahalia Jackson. With the bedroom temporally requisitioned there was little recourse other than to slump into the deep impression in the settee – moulded to perfection over time. After the Manhattan Roundup he aimlessly channel hopped, looking but not seeing, now resigned to unproductively wiling the evening away.

However, in background nascent pain and feelings of unwellness quietly conspired to sabotage David's plans, intensifying until they were sufficiently real as to catch his mind's eye. Though it worried him not, given his assumption that a bomb from the amber bottle would reliably pull energy and feel-good out of a hat.

But by 7.30, David's state of malaise was turning ugly – and his faith in getting to the party by pharmaceutical means was fast on the wane.

By 8.30, wracked with nauseous pain and overpowering physical wretchedness, he finally accepted that embarking on the evening's sortie was a hopeless enterprise.

There were no alternatives to hand. And tomorrow would be too late as deep down David knew that nothing short of a stretcher would transport him there and back. Bitterly disappointed he accepted he'd have to task Wrightman with anonymous delivery of the envelopes.

However, in the penultimate moment to admitting defeat, two words spontaneously formed in his mind – like a moving neon marquee.

DOCTOR SCHWARTZ!

That intravenous pick-me-up from his first visit had eclipsed anything since. But it was a long shot.

'YEAH!'

'It's David Jenner.'

Ferdi's voice softened; husky, wheezy – patronising. 'Ah, David – just thinkin' 'bout you. Is there something I can do for you?'

'Well, err … Ferdi, I need to go out tonight for a while, but I feel so bad. I don't think the pills—'

'What time are y' goin' out?'

'Eleven o'clock.'

'Be over at ten-thirty – I'm here for you, David.'

'Thanks F—'

Click!

It was difficult to believe, feeling as he did, that anything could sufficiently energise his sickly being.

In the meantime, with just over two hours to kill, there was little to do other than painfully shuffle around getting his kit ready; and then flop back in front of the TV in the hope of some mental distraction.

Ferdi arrived on cue – saliva-soaked cigarette poked into the side of his mouth.

'Mind if I smoke?'

He was telling rather than asking.

'No.'

David quietly observed Doc Fixit. In the bright light of Junior Suite 1738 he looked shorter, balder, fatter and seedier. And he stunk of whisky.

Whilst unloading the necessary from his shabby leather Gladstone bag, Ferdi gave assurances. 'Gonna make you feel better, David.'

David smiled, apprehensive of the cocktail in prep.

'How long do y' need to be out?'

'Err, about an hour, Ferdi'.

Ferdi stroked his stubbly chin.

'Hmm – don't wanna overdo it.'

He sucked up the magic stuff into a hypodermic large enough to ice a cake with.

'Make sure you're back by twelve.'

This time, with a rubber tourniquet strapped around his upper arm, David received a shot that would have revived an elephant. Within ten seconds of removing the tourniquet a hideous wave of nausea and giddiness hit – displaced within seconds by a blindingly powerful sense of well-being that coursed his body with a rhapsodic vibrance.

'Oh, Ferdi, I feel marvellous.'

Face flushed, eyes as large as saucers, he leapt to his feet. Now he felt like the keep-fit junky who craves exercise.

'Best take it easy, David. Gotta make it last.'

'Whatever did you give me, Ferdi?'

Ferdi laughed raucously.

'Y' don't wanna know, David, y' don't wanna know.'

Whilst packing up Ferdi asked, 'Do y' want me to wait?'

Predictably, David's alter ego declined. As at that point he couldn't envisage feeling anything but devastatingly good.

Ferdi departed and David dressed up for the cold. Dividing the pile of brown envelopes in two, he stowed them in separate side pockets. And with a street map, torch and plenty of bucks, he floated off to the lift.

Maybelline, the evening receptionist, got a loud 'YO!' on the way through. And anxious to retain anonymity, with hood raised, he walked to Eighth before hailing a cab.

To avoid confusion, the driver was just given the numeric street references, there being no recognisable destination. Traffic made for slow progress until the docklands of Lower Town loomed. Out of familiar territory, the cabbie nosed his way slowly to the given junction.

A request to wait received a sullen nod. David had done his geography homework meticulously beforehand. Bright lighting from overhead crane gantries helped – but they also cast dark, confusing shadows.

He found Shed 27A without too much trouble. It was a large, single-pitch-roof building, probably clad in corrugated-iron sheet. And old. Small windows ran along the side and the entrance comprised nothing more than a door-shaped aperture. A small all-weather bulkhead light burned above the entrance.

David cautiously entered the shed. It was dark save for shadowy detail rendered by the warm glow from open fires on the concrete floor. And as his eyes normalised to the dim incandescence, he perceived a sea of faces silently tracking him like a cluster of synchronised radar dishes. The faces of forty-nine refugees huddled in sleeping bags, quilts and blankets. He tried to read their faces, but blank expressions told they were beyond emotion. These gentle people now waited impassively to discover their fate. Glad, perhaps, just to be alive.

Anxious to show a friendly demeanour – dispel fears – David followed simple instincts. Sinking to his haunches, he pulled back his hood, smiled and held his palm up to indicate 'peace'. And uttered a soft 'Hello'.

It elicited not one iota of reaction.

With all eyes on him David drew the first envelope and slowly offered it to the nearest soul. Two delicate hands appeared from within the bedding and gently took delivery. One by one the process was repeated to completion.

Mission accomplished, and mindful of time, he walked to the entrance, turning for one last look. Forty-nine silent faces were angled at him, each one clutching an envelope in both hands. It was a poignant photograph he took away in his heart.

Swiftly he retraced his steps. Around one hundred yards on he heard a loud scream. And then another one. And another and another. Until the excited din of forty-nine oriental voices shattered the cold silence of winter. David smiled, hooded up and hurried on to the taxi.

But it wasn't there.

A small flutter of panic sprang up. Time was tight and he felt marooned in unknown territory. Walking briskly in what he believed was an easterly direction eventually led to Hudson Street, a busy main road. But it was nearly ten minutes before an available cab came by. Now nearly 11.40 the feel-good energy level was on reserve, wasted by anxiety and unnecessary exertion. Heading up Ninth David felt the pendulum swing through zero and onto the scale marked 'Feel-bad'.

Getting out on the corner of Ninth and Thirty-fifth, he stuffed a twenty in the cabbie's hand. Tonight was a serious Cinderella job. He staggered along Thirty-fifth as the big hand headed for the vertical. And into The Rillington Foyer, collapsing onto one of the red leather settees.

Jason the night porter anxiously came over.

'Are you OK, sir?'

David was far from OK.

'Just came over a little weak.'

'Are you staying here?'

'Err ... yes – Mr Jenner, Junior Suite 1738.'

'OK, sir, I'm gonna get you up to your room.'

A few minutes rest drummed up enough energy to stand. Jason gently led David to the lift and delivered him to the suite.

'Will you be alright sir?'

He was feeling worse by the minute and simply wanted to make it to bed.

'Yes thanks.'

Jason left, not completely convinced.

Managing to pull off most garments, he took a wavering pee and fell into bed. Now paying the price of the intense high David plumbed the depths of withdrawal most ghastly. In desperation he grabbed the Euphoridex, Morpheaze and Siestathol bottles on the bedside table and swilled down a careless combination of what seemed appropriate. And sweating profusely, his heart pounding like an errant kettle drum, he waited for relief to come.

Maybe even for his heart to be stilled.

As chemicals galore hit the red stuff his eyes lost coordination, one image becoming two – slowly diverging; with everything visual reduced to strange colours and shapes.

And his eyes rolled upwards out of view as unnatural sleep took over.

21

Nothing to do but Wait

David raised his arms sideways until they were horizontal. Then, with no more than a thought, he rose up to a height of perhaps fifteen feet and tilted forward – like a plane.

Now he was flying.

It was warm and sunny and the air smelled sweet – of trees, grass, flowers, shrubs, earth, of happiness. Of life.

His mother waved as she hung out the washing. And his dad saluted him with a trowel from the veggie patch. Next door Charlie Duggan winked as he mowed the lawn. Whilst Mrs Wallace at Number 65 waved from the scullery window.

And Rex barked.

David leaned gently to the left and turned towards the river. Over the trees and lush green foliage – red terra cotta Edwardian roofs, quiet roads and the occasional car. Effortlessly he swept right through 90 degrees and drifted along the towing path. Rounding the bend, Hammersmith Bridge came into view. And there was the gang from primary school – up to no good. Little Kenny Barratt, shock of curly black hair, toothy grin, large mischievous eyes. Maureen Kelly, straight fair hair, pink bow, butter wouldn't melt in her mouth. Eric Miller, tubby, dirty knees, torn trousers, no front teeth, catapult. Jane Adams, long dark hair, petite, pretty, freckles – a right little monkey. And Bruce Thomas, pale, thin, quiet, clumsy leg iron. Polio. They waved and smiled as David passed – smiles untouched by the future burdens of their lives.

Now he was approaching Thompson Wigs. A row of beaming faces greeted him. Vera blew a kiss, Frank was laughing – 'Ullo Davy'. Pete looked happy – Joan was with him, short skirt, seductive smile, glossy lipstick; she'd yet to hit the bottle. Nasheima flashed him messages as never before. Celia was slouched up against the wall, top button undone – she looked inviting. Jack Waterfield was struggling to say something – thin lips Superglued. Captain Urquart was in uniform – he waved his cap. 'Good show, David!' And there was Emily. She looked so young and appealing – and was holding something up to David. It was a bag of Maltesers. And Old Man Thompson was perched on the wing of his beloved vintage Mk1 Bentley Continental – he gave the thumbs-up. RAF style.

Now he was lying in bed in Junior Suite 1738. Victor was on the ledge outside the window. He was smiling – face larger than normal. David smiled back.

A sweet young girl stood at the foot of his bed illuminated by a shaft of light. It was his *BoyZo* love – no longer a coarse half-tone image. She was here for real – three dimensional; sparkling eyes, radiant face, thick beautiful hair and that pretty uniform. And she was smiling so endearingly at him. David smiled back and tears of happiness coursed his cheeks.

Greyness descended. And distant pain – confused hallucinations. For seemingly a long time David's mind clung desperately to the utopian happiness of dreams. Then restful sleep – broken only by the physical stimuli of a gradual return to consciousness.

Slowly he reconnected to his sickly body – soaked in perspiration and weak. Every detail of his dreams had been captured for vivid recall. And over and over the virtual encounter with *BoyZo* love replayed.

With no incentive to rise, he stayed put, for an age lost in idle thoughts; of wonderment at how much more clinical deterioration was needed to carry him off. He finally managed to strain round to see the time – nearly one o'clock. It dawned on him suddenly that this was Christmas Day. But the festive spirit eluded him.

He fancied there was a soft tap at the door. It came again. David managed a rather weak 'Come in', forgetting the need for a key. But his visitor was equipped – Don Rodriguez.

Quietly Don bid David 'A happy Christmas, Mr Jenner' and asked, 'Can we get you anything, sir?'

David sensed a kindly note of concern.

'Could I have some tea and toast please?'

'Sure thing, Mr Jenner, SIR! Comin' right up.'

De-bedding was accomplished as usual, though laboured on this occasion. Thus he swivelled himself around to be parallel with the headboard, legs hanging out. And then pushed down with his hands on the mattress to get into a sitting position.

David surveyed the bedside table debris from the day before. Uncapped white plastic containers amid scattered tablets. But on the corner of the table nearest the bed was a small dark object he failed to recognise – that definitely wasn't there last night. It was a disk the size of a nickel covered in maroon velvet, with a gold band around the circumference and the letter 'R' in gold, in the centre. At the back, a tiny brass ring.

Clearly it was a button and David immediately made the connection. His scalp prickled – pulse quickened. Taking the button and *BoyZo* page 6 to the window for closer inspection revealed a perfect match with the buttons on his sweetheart's Rockette uniform. It was unreal. He'd almost expected a button to be missing from the uniform – as in a strange Edgar Allen Poe story.

Stale and grimy from a strange night, and mind racing, he managed a quick shower. And slipping into the Rillington bath robe, took up residence in the usual hollow. He played and toyed with the button. It exuded a barely discernable fragrance. But one that evoked a powerful sense of the past. He derived a strange comfort from this small object. Bizarre and strange, but it pandered to David's imagination and he became convinced that the button was connected to his sweetheart as she drifted around, captive between the past and present.

Don himself arrived with the tea and toast. David thanked him and explained that, 'I'm afraid the bed has got in a bit of a mess.'

But Don was ahead of him. 'Juanita's on her way to fix it up – we're gonna look after you buddy, err ... Mr Jenner.'

He got to the door.

'Whatever you need, buddy, just call.'

And with a smart tap to the doorpost he was off.

With Plan D now accomplished, David was happy to give in to the limitations of his body. Though he wondered if he'd make it out of Junior Suite 1738 again – save in a box. And there didn't seem much hope of a trip to the Holbrook Institute the next day.

On the breakfast tray was an envelope – a deluxe Rillington

Christmas card personally signed by most of the staff. The tea and toast tasted divine, prompting a repeat order.

Juanita stopped by and made good the ravages of last night.

For most of the afternoon David just lay watching Christmas TV. He'd placed the button on a sheet of hotel letterhead; every now and then handling it, smelling it, still pondering what strange warp of time or matter could have engineered its appearance.

Manhattan Roundup had been shunted to a later slot due to festive specials. Not that it mattered. For the time being Maria Arabella was on an emotional back burner. And he didn't expect breaking news to cover the refugees. Their good luck couldn't be exercised until Immigration opened up shop two days hence.

By 5.00 pm David was feeling decidedly better. Purged now of most 'substances' he felt weak and jaded, but able to cope. As usual, his stomach managed to soldier on regardless and Jomayra arrived with a decent spread. Still on hold from last time, she delivered the 5-dollar tour of her burgeoning career. Which cost David 10 bucks.

Maria strutted her stuff at 8.00 pm. A heart-warming story of kindness and generosity on Christmas Day – the Kwi-Megei folk had been saved by a mystery benefactor. All's well that ends well. David had underestimated the eyes and ears of the news machine. It seemed the refugees in their excitement had run amok in the street until police and a government interpreter calmed the situation. Other stations were broadcasting variants of the story.

By nine, David was back between the sheets, enjoying the tactile experience of freshly laundered cotton. Eighteen inches away, where he had first found it, was the button. As he drifted off, David wondered if *BoyZo* love would visit him again – maybe this time for real.

Alas, the only visitation was from deep restful sleep.

Eleven hours later gentle rays of wintry early morning sun brightened the room. David reached out and took the button to savour once again the faint enigmatic fragrance.

Yesterday the Holbrook was an institute too far. But today it was achievable. The usual morning ritual got him away in a taxi. No bore holes today. Just the usual fluid samples and some more diagnostic fluids decanted into his arm.

Alice seemed in good spirits.

'We'll be able to run the tests so much quicker when our new blood analysis suite is installed.'

David assumed this to be funded by a very substantial grant from the Louise Metièr Medical Trust.

And 'Please could you attend again on the twenty eighth.'

Back at The Rillington foyer Mohamed nodded. 'Have a good one, boss.'

He bought some magazines and more Bournville chocolate.

Don bustled by. 'HEY buddy, err ... sir, err ... Mr Jenner, SIR – how y' doin'?'

'Not too bad thanks.'

'Just call, Mr Jenner – SIR.'

With no door post to tap, Don gave David a social tap on the arm with clenched fist and spun off towards O'Banion's.

For the rest of the day David was content to read, eat and sleep, relying on his room service entourage for paid company as and when.

And in background, he never stopped pondering the metaphysics of a maroon velvet button.

The 26th seamlessly ran into the 27th. With nothing doing and no desire to do anything, David got through the day as before, propped up by Morpheaze when wretchedness or pain struck. Several times he ventured to the lobby simply to escape the confinement of his suite. He longed once more to hear Roberta's soothing voice, knowing it could never be.

At one point, the monotony was sufficiently overbearing that the next day's Holbrook visit became an attractive prospect.

Back to normal, Manhattan Roundup ran its course, and with a rejigged spin to the refugee story. There'd been sightings. The taxi driver enjoyed a brief moment of glory with some highly embellished account. And the usual crew claiming to be 'The Friend' came out of the woodwork. Maria had a low-cut dress – was she trying to win him back?

Halfway through *Brief Encounter*, David's mobile struck up.

'David – Ferdi. How's things?'

It seemed a rather patronising call. Maybe Ferdi was awaiting his commission.

'Fine, Ferdi.'

'Did y' make out all right the other night?'

'Yes thanks.'

'Gave y' some strong stuff, David – was a little worried about y'.'

There didn't seem much substance to the conversation.

'Holbrook OK an' that?'

Yes, thought David, and in a few days time my organs will arrive in plastic Tupperware boxes.

'Yes.'

'Here for you, David – twenty-four. Can come to you any time.'

David sensed there was more.

'Err, y' know David, I'm conducting some research. It's sorta related to your problem.'

'Really?'

'Yeah – err … costs quite a bit y' know. Ten thousand should cover it. Yeah, well, just thought I'd mention it in passing. Don't forget, David – here twenty-four.'

Click.

Not for one moment did David imagine Ferdi knew of his Holbrook donation. More likely he had suspicions about the twenty-fifth. In any event, the greedy gnome was wasting his time.

Missing ten minutes of the flick was of no consequence. David knew the plot inside out. A familiar theme at present – unrequited love. It ended at 9.35 by which time he was ready for bed, but by no means exhausted. A gentle routine made the difference.

Less tired than usual, David's mind churned away over something and nothing. So much so that he downed a Siestathol – and slept before the first sheep had sailed past.

In the morning, refreshed and having puzzled once more over the maroon button, David set off for the Holbrook; where he received a cordial greeting from Alice, though she seemed a little agitated and preoccupied.

'David, we need to take some marrowbone jelly from you. It will be painful, but it's critical to our research – do we have your consent?'

Couldn't they wait until he was on the slab!

'I suppose so.'

This wasn't the social trip he'd envisaged yesterday when solitude was getting the upper hand.

Urine and blood were taken as usual. And Katz drilled for oil in a couple of places.

Extracting the marrowbone jelly was exceedingly painful. And after a thirty-minute recovery break, he was hooked up to yet another diagnostic drip.

Alice sat with David in the ante-room. She appeared genuinely concerned at subjecting him to such harsh clinical rigours.

'How are you feeling now?'

A bit wobbly.'

She squeezed his hand.

'The anaesthetic should last you for another hour, and then take one of these if you're in pain. I can't tell you haw grateful we are, David.' Then, squeezing David's hand more firmly she asked if he would allow them to take more samples in two days time.

'Does that mean more marrowbone jelly?'

'It's quite possible, David.'

He pondered this one, but knew deep down that the answer had to be. 'Yes.'

Back at The Rillington, he stayed on track with the easy routine. And pigged out on the room service menu. By late afternoon he was bored and took a ride down to the lobby shop for more magazines and crossword puzzles.

Most nodding acquaintances had moved on, replaced though by the growing numbers of staff he'd befriended. And he nodded much as before.

On returning Jesse was sorting the room. She gave him a cheeky smile.

'And how is you, Mr Jenner, sir?'

'Not bad at all, Jesse.'

She tiddled with the pillowcases.

'Hear you wasn't so good the other night.'

'Oh, I probably drank too much.'

It amused Jesse.

'You youngsters is ALL the same. And remember what ah said, Mr Jenner, sir – your time will come. Ya jus' gotta be patient.'

Ma time, David lamented to himself, sure is gonna come – and soon!

Whilst Jesse finished the bathroom, David made tea and watched *Miami Vice*.

Again Maria showcased the refugees' plight – which had taken a dramatic turn. Kindly officials had granted them a stay and they'd been moved to a hostel. Now a sub-plot was taking hold – the 'Friend'. Evidence was sparse; the 'Friend' took a ride from the corner of Ninth and Thirty- fifth to Shed 27A. Sketchy descriptions from the refugees narrowed the field. All in all not much for the local gum-shoes to go on.

Later, TCM was showing *IF* – another movie half seen from the back row. This time with Beryl Higginbottom in 1969. And he spent two hours filling in the sizeable gaps.

The 29th came and went uneventfully. Having conserved his energy, David was becoming restless, though loath to venture out fearing a bad turn.

Dawned the 30th and David found the need to tighten his Workaday 3-Size Pants from 50 back to 48 inches. In the final throws of a malignant takeover he was losing weight. Gloom struck.

He pushed on to the Holbrook and was marshalled somewhat brusquely by Alice to the procedure room. After the usual donations he eyed Alice hopefully.

'Sorry David, but we need to extract the marrowbone jelly just once more.'

Today Alice was no nonsense – on a roll with whatever nasties they were sucking out of his body.

Last time Katz had jumped him from behind with that enormous needle. Now he knew the score.

Later, the usual intravenous bit. This time, though, conducted in a small store room.

Alice connected the drip.

'Sorry about the noise, David, but we're having the other room refurbished in readiness for the new diagnostic equipment. And we're also getting a small Scanning Electron Microscope for body tissue research.'

And a bacon slicer, no doubt, he reflected, to section my entrails for examination.

'Please David, may we see you on New Year's Day – it's important. I promise, no more needles.'

Her tone had a compelling ring.

As always, he agreed.

Groggy and sore he headed back. Relieved at being on the far side of marrowbone jelly extraction, his appetite surged. And breaking with tradition, lunch was taken in Rebecca's Patisserie.

Mid-afternoon there was a knock — an attractive brunette power-suited in navy.

'Would you be Mr David Jenner?"

Confident and a little brash, her voice had an assertive edge. David felt slightly intimidated.

'Err ... yes.'

With a steely smile and poised to cross the threshold she asked, 'May I come in for a minute?'

'Err ... what's this about?'

She moved forward and David instinctively moved back.

'I can explain — shall we sit down?' Like a hawk she scanned in every detail of the bedroom and proceeded into the lounge. 'May I?'

She took one of the club chairs and David filled his usual impression.

'Jennifer York — Manhattan Roundup news team.'

David shook her extended hand.

So they were on to him. He felt a little unnerved. 'THE' Manhattan Roundup!

In assumptive tones she announced that:

'Mr Jenner, from information we've received we believe you might be the "Friend" of the Kwi-Megei refugees. And we'd like you to provide an anonymous account of how you accomplished every-thing. I promise you, your identity would be kept secret.'

If David excelled at anything, it was looking completely blank.

'I'm sorry I rarely read the papers — what did you say they were called?'

Some of the gloss fell away.

'But you did go out late on the twenty-fifth, did you not?'

'I had to go to Walgreen's for some medication — I've not been too well, you know.'

The stuff of Oscars. Jennifer's face fell.

'What time did you return?'

'Umm ... let me see — must have been just before twelve.'

'A whole hour?'

David knew he'd shaken the scent.

'Well, I stopped for a coffee and doughnut on the way back.' Wide eyed, he explained, 'I've got a real thing about doughnuts with coffee icing.'

Ms York left as briskly as she'd arrived. Confused and disappointed.

Katz's needle had been more painful than last time. Residual aching and soreness appeared immune to the tablets Alice had provided. Though if nothing else the pain diffused any restlessness and David was happy to weather things out sprawled on the settee.

Maria gave a low-key update on the 'Friend'; who, it appeared, was still at large. Elvis hadn't quite left the building. A few more sightings were mentioned along with a suggestion of some leads. But David ascribed all that as fodder to maintain the storyline. An emotional thank you was delivered by the refugees in their native tongue – to their 'Friend'. David waved back and smiled; and wondered how Wrightman had so slickly covered his tracks.

By 9.30 tiredness took over. David waddled into the bathroom supporting the bulge for the closing rituals before taking once more to his bed. Lying on his stomach was a luxury long gone. Facing the ceiling wasn't too bad, although it came with an uncertain centre of gravity. Curled up on his left side was favourite as the bulge connected well with the mattress. A right-hand foetal position necessitated having a pillow for the asymmetric bulge to rest on.

But no need for pills tonight. Benefits from relaxing more and not getting overstretched were becoming evident. David slipped his hand under the pillow and held the button. He felt complete – and *BoyZo* sleep came easily.

The dawning of New Year's Eve left David untouched. As a teenager he'd once gone to Trafalgar Square to watch revellers frolic in the cold fountains – happy ever since to observe the same event on TV. If anything occupied his mind it was the prospect of still being around on the 1st of January.

Breakfast was ordered. Today, though, his taste buds begged for savoury – a full English. It arrived courtesy of Edwin – who was happy again. A wealthy widow of fifty-two was pandering to his every need.

Stoked up with food he was content to relax and observe life on the streets, planning to venture out briefly later on to break the inevitable monotony. At minus 5 degrees it would be a challenge for his Thermo-Snug quilted coat.

A reflective moment was shattered by the phone.

Mohamed from Concierge.

'Hi Mr Jenner – you have a visitor. Shall I send them up?'

'Oh, err … yes please.'

'OK boss.'

Visitor? David had visions of Ferdi fronting up to promote his dodgy research. A polite tap heralded the caller – who turned out to be a young man. A very attractive young man. Attractive almost to the point of being err … beautiful. And wearing the most magnificent full-length fur coat.

Mr Jenner?'

Defensiveness sprung up.

'Who are you, please?'

'Oh, I'm Dominic – a colleague of Jennifer. I believe you met her yesterday.'

He spoke with a theatrical flourish that complimented his easy and unthreatening mien. It seemed the Manhattan Roundup crew were attempting to cover all bases.

'Oh, err … YES.'

There seemed no harm in asking him in. A few word games might help the day along.

Although more discrete than Ms York, Dominic's eyes left nothing untouched.

'I was unable to be of any help to Jennifer in finding this person.'

'Oh, yes, I know Mr Jenner. A shame though. We are able to pay quite a large sum to the real "Friend" for their story.'

Being wooed with a wad of bucks came as no surprise to David. But unfortunately for Dominic he was in the business of giving, not taking, money.

'Gosh.'

Dominic engaged him in some light exploratory. And David fielded his questions to perfection. Despite snappy replies, he sensed Dominic was assembling the jigsaw.

His guest stood up.

'Thank you so much for your time, Mr Jenner.'

Heading out he admired David's coat in some detail.

'I bet that's warm, Mr Jenner.'

'It's OK – got it in Shepherds Bush market.'

'Haven't heard of that one – is it far?'

'Oh, about three thousand miles.'

The penny dropped and they both chortled like schoolboys.

'So will you be going anywhere today, Mr Jenner?'

'I'll have a stroll around this afternoon.'

'Anywhere nice?'

'Oh, probably just around the local streets.'

Dominic bid him a pleasant day and left.

Back in the lounge, David made a cup of Rillington banana and cherry tea and wondered how many more of Maria's acolytes would have a crack at him. Inspired by his flying visit to Thompson Wigs, he tried to imagine what his friends and colleagues would all be doing now. And then for the umpteenth time he examined the button, and wondered if the paranormal was simply a gap in human understanding.

By around 2.00 he'd exhausted all avenues in staving off boredom. Rugged up courtesy of Thermo-Snug he boarded lift 3, and strolled along Thirty-fifth towards Eighth, anxious to keep the gold canopy in sight. It was something of an aimless exercise as he didn't feel ill enough to be bedridden, nor well enough to leave the hotel for any length of time. And walking with the bulge was uncomfortable. Nevertheless, he indulged his enjoyment of people watching.

Progressively he became aware of a vehicle that was idling along a few yards behind. He paid little attention at first but became curious on realising its speed was synched to his. It was a large black 4 X 4 with darkly tinted windows. Discretely he observed its reflection in shop windows and then panned his gaze round slowly from bonnet to boot as if looking nonchalantly to the other side of the street.

Momentarily, as his line of sight swept the windows, he saw the faintest outline of faces within. His subconscious quickly returned a match with images filed under 'Shed 27A'. Now openly staring at the vehicle it noisily sped off with the rhythmic bolero of a beefy V8 motor. But in the penultimate moment before it swept off David caught a dim outline of the driver.

It was Dominic!

No alarm bells rang. He understood the love-hate relationship between media and public. Whatever connections were made would amount to little more than speculation. Though it would sell copy. And he knew if the truth later surfaced he wouldn't be around to account for it. It was all a game.

With around 400 calories pleasantly burned off David felt happy to head back. Carl nodded and winked. Mohamed offered a 'Hi boss'. Jomayra passed with a food tray and nearly scorched his face with her radiance. He was one of the family now, but alas too late.

Then up to the seventeenth armed with magazines and chocolate. Once in, street togs were shed for the comfy options. But as he prepared to veg out, the word 'food' popped up from nowhere. It was becoming apparent that even without a Ferdi upper, his appetite was on the increase. It made sense though, as now he was eating for two!

22

The Cost of Living

David waded through a room service order that even Red would have struggled with. And for an hour or so drifted in and out of consciousness whilst his overloaded stomach beavered away. Head a little clearer he browsed the magazines prior to the 6.00 pm slot. Maria added little to the 'Friend' story but mentioned some possible new developments.

In the middle of *Peyton Place* David's mobile struck up with the new funky ring tone he'd selected in place of the dreary default.

Soft and professional, an easily recognised voice.

'Good evening, Mr Jenner, it's Wrightman Goodfellow – I apologise if this is not a good time to call you.'

Hearing from Wrightman was no imposition. And besides, some friendly contact with the outside world never went amiss.

'It's nice to hear from you, Mr Goodfellow.'

With his usual quiet sincerity Wrightman went on to advise David, 'I just wish to report, sir, that all of you requests have now been implemented. The money held in trust for the refugees is now with Immigration, and they have kindly undertaken to administer the terms.'

'Mr Goodfellow, I am so very grateful to you.'

'It has been my pleasure, sir, and I remain at your service.'

'Thank you.'

'Good night, Mr Jenner, sir.'

At 9.30 David turned in, having watched some of the televised preamble to New Year festivities. It was back to Alice and the Holbrook tomorrow. To get there without a chemical prop demanded a good night's sleep.

Whatever celebrations had raged into the wee hours were of no consequence to David as the first light brought him round. Getting body and mind sorted for a 10.30 departure was foremost. Set at 48 inches, David had to dismally accept his Workaday 3-Size Pants were getting looser. Braced for a crisp minus 6 degrees he made off.

A nurse ushered him into the ante-room, where after five minutes, Alice joined him. Facing and alongside she cupped his face and scrutinised.

'How are you feeling, David?'

'Not too bad – eating OK but losing a bit of weight.'

She examined his skin, looked in his eyes, and Ah Hmm'd quite a few times. As doctors do.

'Right! We'll take the usual samples.'

Ten slugs of blood were drawn.

'David, we'd like to get a CT scan of your abdomen performed. Do you feel well enough for a ride to the Harlem Hospital Centre? Katz will drive you.'

It seemed preordained. The Holbrook certainly wanted their pound of flesh before the Tupperware containers arrived.

Edict delivered, Alice picked up the kidney dish full of blood phials and was gone to analyse the samples herself.

Katz gave David one of his less sinister smiles.

'I'll see you at the front.'

Expecting a small Japanese car or a Ford, he was taken by surprise when a colossal 1966 Oldsmobile Toronado screeched to a halt. A massive gas guzzler from way back, it had a two-tone finish – blue and rust. The passenger door flew open and David entered the classic monster.

With a defective heater and worn-out shock absorbers, he shivered whilst they heaved and bounced their way to the Harlem Hospital.

Katz proudly announced:

'It's my baby. Gonna be worth something one day.'

'Something', David calculated, might even go negative when Katz paid to get it towed to the breakers.

Feeling decidedly queasy he followed Katz to the X-ray department. It seemed Alice had influence here and he was quickly prepped up for scanning – which took twenty-five minutes.

'We just need to wait for the negs.'

He and Katz had a cup of hospital tea in the meantime. And just before 12.30 David was back in the ante-room.

'David.'

Alice assumed softer tones.

'We would dearly like you to see us tomorrow.'

There was urgency. David felt like the hospital patient moved to a bed reserved for those who won't survive the night.

His dejection was clear – Alice spoke more tenderly.

'Katz could pick you up.'

'Will I have to have more X-rays?'

'No, and we won't keep you long.'

David agreed, but declined a roller-coaster lift from Katz. Tomorrow's visit would have to be the last. He'd been glad to help the Holbrook but now wanted peace and dignity as the end of the line loomed.

Outside The Rillington was a black Cadillac Escalade super stretch-limo. No doubt, David mused, the chariot of some visiting A-list member. Heading for the lift he was apprehended by Don.

'Hi Mr Jenner, sir.'

He appeared unnaturally keen to engage David.

'Hello Mr Rodriguez.'

Don smiled and feigned interest.

'Doin' anything special?'

'Not really. I'll have lunch in my room and probably do a few bits and pieces.'

'HEY! Sounds good, buddy, err ... Mr Jenner.' Don smiled, nodded and continued the light repartee. 'So, err ... you'll maybe stick around for a while and let your lunch go down?'

It was all said with a relaxed nonchalance.

'I expect so.'

'Well, HEY! Have a good one, Mr Jenner, SIR!'

A little miffed, he took lift 1, now rather indifferent to Deliah's mechanical greetings. Lunch arrived in no time. And the usually garrulous Edwin quickly slid away. Food never tasted so good, all washed down with a complementary glass of house Chardonnay. Edwin must have hovered outside. For as the last crumb was downed, so he knocked to take away the dirties.

Back on the settee David got pensive. Waiting around for his body to pack up and with no more challenges was a little unnerving. Staying occupied was key. Taking a sheet of hotel paper he brain-stormed things to do or make. Perhaps a quick autobiography – as it would be a complete one, bar a day or so. Something to leave for posterity; 'The David Jenner Story'. Or maybe a fund-raising initiative with Junior Suite 1738 as the operations centre. His flight of fancy was interrupted by the house phone.

This time Don Rodriguez.

'Hi Mr Jenner, sir, you have a visitor – OK to send them up?'

Why 'them' and not 'he' or 'she'? And what gender variant should he expect this time.

There was a knock – distinctive from all others.

David shuffled over in his easy togs and opened the door – and stood there, totally agog at the sight that greeted him.

It was Maria Arabella!

She was more beautiful than he could ever have imagined. No longer a pixelated image composed of red, blue and green dots on his room television. Wearing a full-length camel-hair coat sash-tied to emphasise her curves, and hair elegantly styled, she was straight off the cover of *Vogue*. And her perfume swirled around David drawing him seductively into her personal space.

For several seconds Maria smiled 'THAT' smile at David – the one saying 'I've known you for ever and I'm so pleased to see you'.

And then she spoke with that warm confidence – her smile never faltering. 'Hello Mr Jenner, I'm Maria Arabella from the Manhattan Roundup – you might have seen the program.'

Maria Arabella was speaking to HIM – David Jenner!

She continued, 'I apologies for disturbing you, but I wonder if we could talk for a few minutes.'

Whatever strange, gormless apparition Maria Arabella saw standing before her, she maintained the composure of royalty.

For a moment David descended into gibberish, finally getting out a strangled 'yes'.

'Err … would you like to sit down, Miss Arabella?"

Maria was already heading for the lounge and lowered her heavenly being onto the settee. Making for a club armchair himself, Maria patted the space next to her. 'Come and join me, David.'

Nervously he obliged, knowing he was almost certainly a gonner.

'Err ... alright, Miss Arabella.'

She smiled at him, quietly observing.

'Please call me Maria.'

'Oh, err ... alright, err ... Maria.'

'And may I call you David?'

'Yes, err ... please do.'

'So, David, you've come all the way from England?'

'Yes.'

Fears of an inquisition proved groundless. Maria chatted to David about his life and what he'd been up to in New York City. In the sway of her charm he felt completely at ease.

'You know, David, we were so convinced that you were the "Friend".' And with a somewhat quizzical look, she asked, 'Are you sure it's not you, David?'

'Oh no, definitely not me.'

'Well, our team will just have to keep looking.'

From her bag she pulled out a half bottle of champagne and two flutes.

'David, I brought this along in the hope we could have celebrated you being the Friend. But it's been lovely talking to you and so perhaps we could toast the New Year.'

Something about this arrangement sat badly with David. A few days before in the *Manhattan Mercury*, an article had advised on avoidance of being slipped a date-rape drug. Having his body played like a theme park by Maria Arabella was probably unlikely. And if it did happen, the worst part would be not to remember the experience. More realistically, David pondered the likelihood of a truth drug.

Eagle eyed he watched the champers being decanted. Neither glass seemed to be saying 'take me', and neither was closer than the other. In the end he selected at random and they toasted 'wealth, health and happiness'.

Gathering up the empties she stood to go. And turning to David she observed his wan features, her parting smile filled with genuine compassion.

'Thank you for talking to me, David. I've enjoyed it.'

Alone in the room David wondered if it had just been a dream.

It so unsettled him that any further attempts at continuing the creative thinking from earlier went by the way. At six he tuned in to see Maria for the second time in one day. And for the rest of the evening wallowed in Walter Mitty escapism.

The 2nd of January brought no cheer. Another pair of gussets required zipping to keep his pants up – now down to 46 inches. His body was ebbing away.

Alice marched him into the ante-room – the mood wasn't good. Holding some sheets of paper she strutted back and forth, messing with her hair in agitation.

'Now, you reported losing weight – right?'

'Yes.'

'Hmm – so you've been weighing yourself?'

'No.'

'So HOW do you know you're losing weight?' Alice was becoming quite hostile.

'Well, my trousers are getting loose'.

'Hmm – we'd better weigh you.'

David's heart sank. ANOTHER trip would have to follow.

'KATZ! Bring me those blood analysis reports.'

Casablanca Man scuttled in with the necessary.

Flicking through the sheaf of papers she continued, 'You see, David, there are changes we can't account for.' Waving several documents under his nose, she went on, 'Your results from the twenty-eighth of December indicated a slight drop in malignant cell count. Those of the thirtieth showed a dramatic drop. And yesterday's analysis failed to detect ANY!'

She was angry.

'We've been so meticulous in tracking the progression of cell behaviour. Your CT scan clearly showed the tumour and some scare tissue on the affected organs.'

Confused at what Alice was saying, and perplexed by her demeanour David asked, 'So, what does all this mean?'

Swinging round to face David head on she barked, 'Frankly, I just DON'T KNOW!'

With that she marched off. And the swirl of air generated by her departure gently surrounded David. It was laden with the fragrance of sweet fresh female perspiration; it told of emotions, of agitated hormones. Of a woman capable of great passion.

He was weighed in the buff and returned to the ante-room. Alice returned – a little calmer.

'We'd just like to take a couple of blood specimens to verify some results.'

'Oh – OK.'

'And we'll need to weigh you in five days' time.'

'Oh – alright.'

'You currently weigh roughly the same as when we first saw you.' Her face softened and the old Alice returned. 'We were so sure we were on to something – now we just don't know.'

David was still confused but cautious about asking for likely explanations.

Alice read him.

'How have you been feeling?'

He explained how his regime of taking it easy had left him less tired.

'And what about the painkillers etcetera?'

'Well, thinking about it, I don't need quite so many.'

'And you said you're eating well?'

'Yes.'

She smiled gently.

'It's early days. We call it remission.'

'Does that mean I—'

'Yes, David.'

After donating two fingers of blood he was winging it back to The Rillington. And trying to assimilate Alice's words.

'Afternoon, boss.' Mohamed beamed from the concierge desk. 'Letter came for you, sir – Renée left it on your bed.'

'Oh! – err ... thanks, Mohamed.'

'No sweat, boss.'

Letter? Maybe from Wrightman, or the bank.

Addressed in an infantile scrawl the contents set David back. A composite of words cut from newsprint read: 'We know you are the friend. We want $8,000 to keep quiet.'

It went on with instructions – put the money in an envelope and throw it out of a taxi window whilst passing '4-Hour-Foto' on West Fifteenth at 11.00 pm tonight.

'No cops or else.'

It was an almost childish attempt to extort money. Who, though? Wrightman was whiter than white. But his staff? Surely not. Fritz had helped him upstairs on his return, but there was no connection.

Ferdi? Drop-off was only two blocks from his office and he claimed to need 10,000 bucks for research. A possibility.

Red? Never in a million years.

Events of the morning replayed. 'No malignant cells detectable'. What was the significance? Was it an oversight of his body? And would some reappear? He desperately wanted to enjoy hope – real hope. He'd 'accepted the worst and anything less would be a bonus'. But for now the only certainty was 'the worst'.

Which he'd long accepted.

At 6.00 Maria lit up the screen looking like the cat who'd just devoured a very large saucer of cream.

'We now have in our possession evidence that leads us to believe the "Friend" is staying in a hotel on West Thirty-fifth, not far from Eighth Avenue.'

Was this speculation or did the Manhattan Roundup team have something on him. David started to see Maria in a different light. For all her beauty and charm, she was probably as ruthless as any other media hound. After all, she'd made it as anchor for the MR team. And with her talent, experience and sheer charisma, most likely without help from the casting couch.

Her smugly delivered message appeared as a veiled threat to David. Was she taunting him? From strolling along West Thirty-fifth he knew of no other hotels in the vicinity.

No idle channel hopping tonight. And 'The David Jenner Story' was shelved until further notice. Instead he decided to brave O'Banion's. Arriving at seven, Ifeoma ushered him to a table, which ironically was where he and had Roberta had shared poignant moments. Ifeoma was a sweet, very attractive young lady. Intrigued by her strong African dialect he ventured to ask, 'Which part of Africa are you from?'

She smiled. 'Enugu in eastern Nigeria. People there are from the Ibo tribe.'

'Have you been in America long?'

'Nearly eighteen months.'

David nodded in acknowledgement.

'I hope you don't mind me saying but your name is very appealing and unusual.'

She looked deep into David's eye. 'Ifeoma means "All is well".'

It was a strange, sibylline moment, from which David drew a self-serving interpretation.

Soon he was tucking into peppered rump steak followed by Death by Chocolate. And visions of he and Roberta chatting over dinner filtered back. Going solo just wasn't the same.

After, a stroll to the shop. Imagination perhaps, but he sensed being discretely observed by the hotel staff. On passing 'Coffee Confidential' a woman arose from one of the large red leather settees and walked towards him. It was Jennifer York.

Dressed casually and with a relaxed smile she discretely accosted him.

'Hello Mr Jenner – how are you today?'

Guardedly:

'Oh, I'm um ... OK.'

Her easy demeanour persisted. There was no inquisition, no aggressive clamour for 'the truth'.

She spoke softly, gently. 'Did you see the Roundup tonight?'

'Well yes, actually.'

'And what did you think?'

Mentally, David responded with, I've been rumbled, Miss Nosey.

'Well, it's all a bit speculative.'

'Maybe, Mr Jenner. You know what the media's like.'

She winked – easing the tension.

'Maria enjoyed meeting with you yesterday.'

'Oh, err ... well it was very nice meeting her.'

'I've come here on her behalf to ask a favour – Maria is hoping you might help her with something. Could you come back to the studio with me for fifteen minutes?'

It sounded ominous.

'You're not going to put me on TV – are you?'

Jennifer laughed. 'Absolutely not, Mr Jenner. We're not quite that bad.'

'I should tell you I'm not very well at present.'

'Mr Jenner we'll take great care of you. The studio's only six blocks away, and if you start to feel unwell, we'll bring you straight back – I promise you with all my heart.'

'You're not just going to ask me more questions, I hope?'

Jennifer could see David's resistance dropping and seized the opportunity. 'Definitely not.' Gently taking his arm she assured him, 'If we go now, you could be back by seven forty-five.'

David was still a little hesitant.

'Maria would have come here, but she has some preparation to do for the late slot.'

Mention of Maria's name tipped the balance.

'Oh, alright then.'

They were whisked away in the large black 4 X 4 from yesterday – with Dominic at the wheel.

The 'interrogation' room was a small hospitality area in Maria's office. And she got up to greet David, affectionately taking his hand between hers.

'Mr Jenner, thank you so much for agreeing to come here.'

Dominic called out from the bar, 'What would you like to drink, Mr Jenner?'

'Oh, err ... well, fizzy water if you have it.'

A clear head would be needed.

The team sat round and close to David.

Maria asked, 'Are you comfortable?'

Swathed in the large blue fleece, now his standard 'uniform' he felt very comfortable – as it concealed his 'condition'.

'Yes thank you.'

'May we call you David?'

'Of course.'

'David, I know you have said you had nothing to do with the Kwi-Megei refugees and we take you at your word.' Her smile was soft but it had a hard centre as she continued, 'We approached you initially on the strength of a tip-off and naturally we've investigated all angles to this. We have found evidence that conflicts with your claim but out of respect we wouldn't want to press you further.'

'I see.'

David didn't really see. Why then was he here?

Jennifer cut in, 'David, we would like to say that we think you are a very, very wonderful man.'

David aped puzzlement.

Over to Dominic. 'You probably realised it was me following you yesterday. Sorry if I alarmed you. I had three of the refugees with me and they claimed to recognise you – and also your coat; it's quite distinctive. And that badge on the lapel.'

Ah, yes – his *BoyZo* train spotter's badge. It was all conjecture though. Dominic probably saw the badge yesterday. He was still ahead.

David retained composure.

And it was back to Maria. 'This might interest you David.'

She produced a small brown envelope – that he instantly recognised.

'This is one of the envelopes given to the refugees.'

'Oh, that's interesting.'

Proceedings took a slightly more serious turn.

'I owe you an apology, David – I used your champagne glass from yesterday to get a DNA sample. I'm sorry to have deceived you.'

He just knew what was coming next.

'However it matched the DNA on the envelopes. Quite a coincidence.' With a patronising smile and a knowing glance at her cohorts she breezily she added, 'Of course, DNA testing isn't infallible.'

Whatever Maria and her cronies were thinking they sustained a friendly, passive front. Moreover, true to Jennifer's word, there were no inquisitions. But they were pros and David knew in one way or another they'd squeeze him 'til the pips popped out.

Slipping beside David, Maria took his hand.

'We're worried about you. There are some pretty unpleasant news people out there. And they're not interested in how generous you've been.' She was working the voodoo, but everything rang true. 'In the end, David, they'll get it out of you. You'll be better off giving an exclusive story to one of the papers or television networks to get the mob off your back.'

Now Maria was scare mongering – and it was working.

He'd had enough, though.

'I'm not feeling so good.'

'I understand – Dominic will take you back right now.'

Marie and Jennifer bade him sugary goodbyes.

'Stay in touch, David.'

Back at The Rillington, Dominic slipped him a card and urged him, 'Call us when you're ready.'

'When' – not 'if'. Having run him to ground the MR team were far from done. Their evidence was conclusive. They'd hooked him. And when he tired they'd land him like a prize sea bass.

Cutting a swathe to the lift he sensed being observed more blatantly than before – staff noticeably striving to make smiling eye contact.

Word was getting around.

What to do? Over a cup of loganberry tea he reviewed the options.

Deny: the relationship between his tongue and forty-nine envelopes posed a problem. However nothing prevented systematic denial, as after all, he wasn't on trial.

Come clean: it would defuse the situation. Albeit the ramifications of that action would catapult him into the public eye.

Do nothing: seemed simple enough. But how long would the media onslaught persist. Most likely they'd chip away relentlessly, winkling out every atom of evidence.

As regards the blackmail letter David chose to ignore the threat, assuming it to be based on nothing more than speculation. Besides, it paled against the MR team's DNA evidence.

The decision was easy. He'd order a Rillington burger and Bud, and have another crack tomorrow.

Nine o'clock was upcoming and he still felt reasonably bright. And he cautiously indulged himself a smidgeon of hope that remission was in hand.

Edwin arrived – his face loaded.

'Story's goin' around you helped the refugees.'

Through a mouthful of burger David managed a surprised 'Really?'

'Yeah – we heard about Maria Arabella visiting and stuff.'

Washing the residue down with a slug of Bud David explained. 'Someone must have tipped the news people off in error.'

Edwin thought about this one.

'Yeah, but Fritz says you came in at twelve. An' Maybelline says y' came by just before 'leven.'

'That's right, Edwin, I went to Walgreen's for some med and had a snack before coming back.'

Not convinced, Edwin countered that. 'Fritz says you was really bad and needed help.'

Lowing his voice David confided in him. 'Quite honestly Edwin, I wish I was rich enough to give away that amount of money.'

After more word games Edwin departed reasonably happy, but a little miffed, perhaps, by smoke without fire.

By 10.00 David was glad to conclude the day and crawl into bed. Just as dreamy *BoyZo* reveries took him off his mobile rudely jazzed into life with 'Lullaby of Broadway'.

'Hello?'

Husky, smoky, wheezy – overpolite.

'It's Ferdi – just thought I'd see how you're doin'.'

'Not feeling too bad at all thanks, Ferdi.'

'Err ... that's good.'

As before, David sensed Ferdi was scene setting. And his suspicions from earlier started to solidify.

'So, err ... David, are you doing anything this evening?'

He played along, explained he'd got to drop something off in West Fifteenth at 11.00.

Ferdi responded with a nonchalant 'OK', but his voice subtly intoned relief and anticipation. Clues that a trusting ear would have missed.

'Here for you David, twenty-four seven.'

Click.

David powered down his mobile and instructed the switch – 'No calls'.

And rolled over into position one – to sleep like a baby.

23

The Theatre of Life

Fresh, and having enjoyed a full English David took his mobile and got comfy on the settee. Switching on the phone, he placed it on the armrest.

And waited.

Within five minutes it piped up, four beats to the bar. A very agitated Ferdi.

'David, err ... just checking to see how you are – err ... worried about you having to turn out last night. DID YOU GO?'

'Go where? OH YES, of course.'

'So you dropped off the mon— err ... whatever it was?'

'Yes I did, West Sixteenth as req—'

'WEST SIXTEENTH!' It must have been raining yellow saliva on Ferdi's mouthpiece. 'But weren't you supposed to drop it in West Fifteenth by the Twelve err ... I mean where they told you?'

'Well, I opened the taxi window and a man came up to me, so I said is this for you? and he said yes.'

'YOU GAVE IT TO A STRANGER?'

'That's right.'

'But, but, your were supposed—'

'Must go, Ferdi.'

Click.

Turning his mobile off again, David called the switchboard. In anticipation of media calls, he advised approved names – Ferdi not being one. And calls did come – Babette kept a list. More difficult to fend off were the aggressive reporters and paparazzi who infested the lobby and foyer. Once in the street, he was fair game – saved only by Carl's whistle.

After two more ragged days and no place to go, David wearied. And the prospect of visiting the MR team's confessional took on a different complexion.

The 6th of January arrived, along with the conclusion that change for the better wouldn't occur spontaneously. And his Workaday 3-Size Pants now only stayed up courtesy of a belt. Sliding out of the staff entrance David made it down to Isaac Gerome's emporium and picked up two pairs of 40-44 inch Workadays. Isaac, bless him, found it all very amusing.

'Vould you like to take some stock vith you to sell to your friends?'

Back at the hotel David found himself running not only the gauntlet of reporters et al., but the growing curiosity of staff. And from the relative safety of Junior Suite 1738 he got strategic. Moving accommodation was an option – though he suspected it would only be good for a week or so. Staying suite-bound until the story reached its sell-by would be a long road. Adopting a disguise had some merits.

A very real prospect to be faced was potential lack of funds. If remission persisted for more than a week a cheap boarding house would warrant serious consideration.

David sculptured some interesting scenarios, none of which addressed the core problem. However, coming clean was still an option and he tried to get his mind round the likely consequences. Moreover it was becoming clear that by staying in denial he was only deferring being 'outed'. And when that day came, it would be on the media's terms, not his.

Being savaged by a news machine that cared not whether he was glorified or vilified tipped the balance. A call to the MR team was imminent. But before that there was a need to bring Don Rodriguez into the picture. Babette promised to get back when she'd got Don on the line. It took nearly twenty minutes.

'Hi, this is Don Rodriguez.'

'Oh, Mr Rodriguez, I wonder if I could talk to you in private?'

'HEY, yeah, sure Mr Jenner – is it urgent, sir?'

'Well, it's probably better sooner than later.'

'Shall I come to you, sir?'

Knowing the perils of traversing the lobby he happily agreed.

'Fine buddy, err ... Mr Jenner – be there in five.'

Despite being one of Don's many Paymaster Generals, he couldn't help but feel like an employee waiting to ask for a rise.

Two firm raps signalled Don's arrival.

'How can I help you, sir?'

'Well,' began David a little awkwardly, 'I wanted first of all to apologise for being the cause of all the reporters hanging around the hotel.'

Don smiled knowingly and his voice softened.

'OK bud— err ... Mr Jenner – let's take this little by little. Firstly, trade's up forty per cent on account of the action here. So don't you fret, sir. It's called free publicity. Secondly, we've all been wondering about the "Friend" thing. And thirdly, I know you've not been too well, but if I may say, Mr Jenner, sir, you seem to have gotten some colour back.'

'Oh, thank you.'

David braced himself for the big one.

'Well, the other thing is that I am the so called "Friend". You see I—'

Don clapped his hands and stood up.

'HEY, Mr Jenner, SIR! I had my suspicions. YES SIR! Put it there buddy.'

It was another knuckle cracker, but warmly intentioned.

'Well, MY MY! So we really HAVE got the "Friend" staying at The Rillington. WELL, I'll be a hot dog! Son of Gun!'

Finally managing to get a word in edgeways, David explained his decision to give an exclusive to MTV.

'They've got DNA evidence that it's me, and frankly I can't handle being hounded much longer. I wanted to tell you first, Mr Rodriguez, so that you'd know what was going on.'

Don was touched.

'Why thank you, Mr Jenner, sir – I value such consideration.' Opportunities loomed in Don's mind. 'I presume you'll be interviewed?'

'I'm not sure. I really don't know what their reaction will be yet.'

'Suggestion, sir. The camera crew come over ... see what you can do?'

'Of course, Mr Rodriguez.' And he asked Don if he would please, 'Hold off telling the staff until it's official with MTV?'

'Sure thing, buddy.' Don was smiling like a tin of worms. 'You must be hungry – I'll get someone to take your lunch order – this one's on the house!'

Turning back at the door he pointed at David in mock accusation. 'One more thing, Mr Jenner SIR, from now on ... y' call me DON!'

Tap, tap, nod, 'Yeah!' – gone.

David's mid-afternoon sugar-low responded well to the Rillington Chef's Special – delivered by a curious Jomayra. Not wanting another 'Friend' inquisition, David smoothly switched her attention to modelling.

'College starts next week – I'm so excited.'

'Wonderful Jomayra, I'm so pleased for you.'

Fortunately the sight of a 10-dollar bill flipped her into 'goodbye' mode. All sweetened with a request to 'Tell me all about it before your leave.'

Post food, he slipped into the impressionable settee and speculated the next day's headlines.

'Dying Brit gives last penny to Refugees'.

Or: 'Wealthy limey saves Kwi-Megei people'.

Maybe: 'Rillington Benefactor comes to the rescue'.

David pulled back from the edge before Zachariah Lightning took over. He decided against a sickly image. And *BoyZo* love would play no part. It would simply be a simple story of kindness and generosity.

Ringing Dominic's mobile number got a businesslike 'Hi'.

'Err ... this is David Jenner calling from th—'

'OH, hi David – great to hear from you.'

'Well I—'

'So you'd like to give us the exclusive.'

'Yes, err ... if that's—'

'Shall we come to you?'

He gladly accepted. Although feeling strong enough for the trip to MTV, wading through a sea of curious and aggressive humanity appealed not.

'Good – I'm tied up at present, but I think Jen's free to pop over – just check.'

A muffled enquiry and 'Jen' was lined up for 5.00 pm.

'She'll discuss all the interview detail with you.'

On entering the suite Jennifer glanced at David's coat. And with a broad grin confided, 'You had us fooled for a while.'

They settled in the lounge and he and Jennifer sipped Rillington black currant and mandarin tea.

'Err ... Miss York I—'

'Jennifer.'

'Yes, err ... Jennifer, my story's very simple – I saw the plight of the Kwi-Megei refugees on Manhattan Roundup and—'

'AH! On Manhattan Roundup – that's good.'

She scribbled away.

'And, well, I had some money set by and decided to try and help them. You see I could have donated it to an international charity. But then, one never knows quite what it's used for or how efficiently it's used.'

Jennifer smiled and nodded her head.

'So I decided to use the money in a way that would bring a known benefit to a situation I had personal knowledge of.'

'So you just happened to have half a million bucks tucked under the mattress?'

She winked playfully.

'Yes, Jennifer, something like that.'

'What brought you to Manhattan, David?'

'Well, err ... I just thought I'd take a long break from work and see New York City. I used to read about it in comics and see it in films, and always wanted to visit.'

'So what about the money, David. The truth, now.'

'Hmm, the truth.'

'Yes David, the TRUTH.'

Her smile broke into laughter.

'Well, Jennifer, I decided some months ago to give away my money during my lifetime so that I could enjoy seeing others benefit. You see, I have no relatives to pass it on to.'

'So, you woke up one morning and thought I'll go to New York and give away all my wealth?'

Even David had to see the funny side.

'And will you go back to Thompson Wigs?'

'How did you know about THAT?'

'We're news people – it's our business to know about things.'

'Well, it's unlikely.'

'So what are your plans?'

He had to stop and think about this one. He planned to go and see Alice the next day, and find somewhere cheaper to live – little more.

'The truth is, I don't really have any.' On a more serious note he added, 'I've got personal issues at present, but nothing I want discussed in the interview. Please, Jennifer, can we just keep it very simple?'

'Of course, David – we're only concerned with your immense act of kindness to these people.'

Remembering Don's request, David asked, 'Could the interview be conducted at the Rillington?'

'Oh, definitely – it's the ideal venue. When would suit?'

'Sometime tomorrow afternoon?'

'I'll check with Maria.'

After a brief mobile consultation Jennifer announced that, 'We can have the crew here at two.'

'OK, I'll tell Mr Rodriguez.'

With the smile of someone in the know she advised, 'No need – we'll talk to Don.'

The business done, Jennifer bade him well 'until tomorrow'.

From wanting anonymity, the notion of being cited as a local hero started to have a modicum of appeal. And although it wasn't in David's nature to seek attention, he quite liked the idea of being compelled to own up as the 'Friend'.

By 7.00 hunger drove him to O'Banion's. Staff curiosity was unchanged. But conspicuous by their absence were the legions of reporters and photographers who had also disappeared from their street-based encampments. David reasoned that either Maria had sent them in the first place, or she had the right connections.

At just after 11.00 the next day he was starkers and on the scales again. Alice had sweetened up.

'You're actually putting ON weight.'

'But my waist size is getting smaller.'

'Hmm.' She thought for a few seconds. 'David, I suggest we get another CT scan done to find out if there's been change.'

And so he bounced and heaved once more in Katz's rusty investment. In sequence Alice placed the large negatives on a light box and overlaid them with the analogous images from five days earlier.

'David, can you see how much your tumour has reduced since the last scan?'

David tried to make sense of the strange shapes, shadows and curves, but his eye could interpret nothing.

'Oh yes, Alice, I see what you mean.'

'There were no irregularities in the blood samples we took last time.'

'Oh.'

'I would go so far as to say that you appear to be moving towards a significant degree of recovery. But remember, David, you'll always be in remission.'

'I understand, Alice – thanks for taking such an interest in me.'
She smiled warmly.

No longer was Alice mad that her warm cadaver had other plans. And David finally allowed himself the luxury of controlled elation. If he didn't run yelling and screaming down the street it was because he'd truly accepted the worst. And the worst had expanded his intellectual horizons as could no other experience.

In two weeks he'd return for 'Final checks and closure'.

He alighted at the gold canopy. And sweeping his gaze through a complete circle saw Manhattan for the first time.

Don was bustling around the Coffee Confidential area – a seriously happy bunny.

'Hi Mr Jenner, sir – thought we'd do the interview on one of the leather settees. We'll cordon off the area and keep the noise down.'

'Sound's like a good idea, Mr Rod—'

'DON!'

'Err ... Don.'

Up in his suite David showered and spruced up for his first and probably last TV interview. On went the XXL fleece and a splash of Magnetique aftershave from Macy's sale.

Don called just after 2.00. 'Best come down, sir, make-up need to get started.'

MAKE-UP? A little nervous he hit the lift – and was taken in tow by a sweet young thing who marshalled him to a chair seconded from O'Banion's. And she not only prepped him for the camera, but also pandered delightfully to his bourgeoning ego.

Lights, cameras and boom mikes had converted one of the red leather setters into a studio set. Whilst the crew adjusted and fiddled, assistants with clipboards managed the curious faces peering from beyond.

Once seated there were last-minute touches to his make-up. And then excited voices.

A flunky opened the roped barrier and in strode Maria Arabella looking heavenly. She swivelled and dropped down besides David. They shook hands.

'It's lovely to see you again, Mr Jenner.'

Before he could respond, Maria looked away to confer with crew members. Turning back to David she asked, 'Ready?'

He nodded nervously and Maria signalled proceedings to start.

A loud voice bawled 'SILENCE' and the floor manager commenced his finger countdown.

Maria looked away, and then slowly brought her smiling countenance face on to the camera.

'Staying here at The Rillington Hotel on West Thirty-fifth is a very special person. Over the past week he has become known as the "Friend". It's through his generosity that the forty-nine Kwi-Megei refugees can look forward to a life in America and financial assistance to help them on their way.

'Our investigative journalists finally located the "Friend", a man who turns out to be a shy, modest individual. And his inspiration came from watching our story on Manhattan Roundup. I can tell you now that he is David Jenner who is on an extended visit from Britain. Better still, he's very kindly agreed to an interview.'

She turned regally to David.

'Good evening, Mr Jenner, we appreciate the opportunity to talk to you.'

Maria went on to ask David the obvious, who in turn articulated his syrupy story. Never once did she stray beyond the agreed limits, instead asking benign questions about his past life and future plans – questions, though, that gave him every opportunity to add some polish.

Nervous at first perhaps, David was soon lost in Maria's hypnotic aura, and the rest of the world appeared to evaporate whilst they enjoyed their intimate tête à tête on the red leather settee.

In conclusion Maria thanked David as only an interviewer can. And she went on to ask for money to support similar causes, instructing viewers, 'Please send your donation to MTV, care of The David Jenner Fund.'

DAVID JENNER FUND? He managed to suppress any surprise, later philosophically accepting it as part of the media game.

The floor manager announced, 'It's a wrap' and Maria bade David farewell. As her shapely derrière receded the crew moved in to clear up. With their interview in the can David ceased to be the subject. Nevertheless, he treasured the experience for what it was – a brief but memorable moment of glory.

By 6.00 Maria was back in front of the camera with the interview seamlessly spliced into their evening story board.

Now free to roam The Rillington David sauntered to O'Banion's. Immediately singled out by the maitre d' he was led to a table in the Premier dining area – complete with 'Mr David Jenner' engraved on a large brass place name. And every encounter with restaurant staff triggered a loud 'Yes Mr Jenner – SIR!' leaving diners in no doubt as to his identity. After three courses of bowing and scraping, and pleasantly weary, he welcomed the seclusion of Junior Suite 1738. Where, from on high, he observed Manhattan's vibrant populace, fascinated as always by the city's restless spirit. It usually left him feeling a wistful outsider – the sickly kid watching his friends through the bedroom window, yearning to join in their games.

But tonight was different. Sounds, light and energy from the street formed an ethereal mist that drifted up and into his suite. Invisibly and gently it suffused his mind, uplifting his spirits and inviting him to 'come out and play'. And no longer did he feel alienated from the throb of life below.

As he gazed reflectively through the window, Alice's encouraging prognosis spontaneously came to mind, prompting him to ponder what might have precipitated his reversal of fortune.

A romantic notion suggested it was somehow the act of giving away his material wealth. Whilst a more likely scenario pointed to unspecified fluids decanted into his veins by the Holbrook under the guise of 'diagnostics'.

Then there was Red's 'Brew'; to which he ascribed a modest likelihood that it had successfully ejected the bad boys down and back to a watery grave via a mechanism hitherto unknown by conventional medicine.

Though he cycled through a whole raft of realistic explanations there was one theory David felt he simply couldn't dismiss; that as the flame of his self-indulgent life flickered and dimmed, so the hand of the Almighty had reached down and touched him.

And given him a second chance.

24

Start Over

The 8th dawned bright and crisp. No more the unwieldy sequence of manoeuvres to struggle out of bed. Today David flung back the duvet and slid to his feet, stretching his arms and gulping in a lungful of Rillington perfectly conditioned air. From tick-over his pulse accelerated to a lively bossa nova, promoting a wonderful flush of well-being as billions of healthy red corpuscles pleasured the walls of his veins and arteries.

In the bathroom mirror he studied his shrinking midriff. Alice's good news had been met with guarded optimism. But nothing could more powerfully convince his inner psyche that recovery was in hand than the hard evidence before him.

And for the first time this year David was able to enjoy the seasonal buzz he usually got from January. Because analogous to September bringing the blues, so January came with lengthening days and a loaded anticipation of good things to come.

Quietly confident his life was being resurrected, time now seemed right to think beyond The Rillington. In calculating the living bequests, he'd held back sufficient contingency to cover a lingering demise. But with his changed circumstance this now translated to another week in Junior Suite 1738 and maybe a month in cheap digs. Money would be tight and he kicked himself for not screwing a few thousand bucks out of MTV for the exclusive interview. But with all the indicators pointing to sunny, David started the day optimistic that a new life would bring new opportunities.

The room phone belled up.

'Where will you be taking breakfast today, Mr Jenner, sir?'

This was a first.

'Oh, err ... well actually I think I'll come down to Rebecca's Patisserie.'

'Very good, Mr Jenner, your table will be read for you – sir.'

His table? Yes, his table – complete with the brass place name.

'Good morning, Mr Jenner, how are you today, sir?'

He liked Roz. Sixty going on twenty, blonder than blonde, cuter than cute, husky voice, pert butt – had a walk-on part in *Ben Hur* – 'knew' Victor Mature. And a smile that would melt a bar of Bournville in three seconds. She normally called him 'Sweetie-pie'. Though it wasn't just Roz. He'd got well enunciated 'Mr Jenners' all the way through. His full English wasted no time in arriving, and part through, Don stopped by to bid him a knuckle cracking 'Good morning Mr Jenner – SIR', in a voice aimed at the gallery.

And to pointedly note, 'We are proud to have you staying with us, MR JENNER – SIR.'

It wasn't quite the moment to seek an audience with Don. But back in the suite he enlisted Babette's help.

'Don Rodriguez here, Mr Jenner, how can I help you, sir?'

'I wonder Mr R— err ... Don if I could talk to you briefly.'

'I'm on my way, sir.'

Click.

Don bustled in, moustache all a-twitch. David sensed the topic wouldn't be a good fit.

'Err ... Don, I shall be leaving on Saturday as I—'

'LEAVING?'

'Yes, err ... I've—'

'But, but—'

Even Don was stuck for words. Though graciously he shut up long enough for David to explain.

'The fact is, Don, staying here has been wonderful. But my circumstances have changed and I need to move to lodgings more suited to the longer term.'

Whatever Don's inner thoughts, his response was instant. 'HEY buddy, err ... Mr Jenner, hadn't I told you? You're now our house guest – 'cos we at The Rillington would like to show our appreciation for your kind generosity.'

Now David had to think quickly. And with trepidation replied, 'That's very kind of you, Don. Err ... how long do you think I will be staying on?'

Don shrugged evasively. 'Well, I mean HEY! How long's a piece of string?' And hands on hips, lips pursed studiously, he strolled around peering at the shabby detail. 'Yeah, might change a couple of things.' Then, 'Oh, yeah, Mr Jenner, sir, could Art Phillips – he's our security manager – get a photo of you sometime today? It's for an initiative we're running. Sure you'll approve.'

Don slipped away before David could express curiosity.

He understood the basis of Don's offer and decided to take each day as it came – ready to leave rather than be pushed. Later, whilst mentally scratching around for funds, he recalled the nine grand investment with Eternal Slumbers. Could it be redeemed?

He phoned 'Michael'.

'Hello, this is Mr Jenner – I bought a Serenity-Plus package several weeks ago. I, err ... have a small problem. Would it be possible to see you?'

'Of course Mr Jenner, it would be a privilege to see you again. But is it something I can help with over the phone?'

David realised his only chance was a face to face.

'Not really, it's rather personal.'

'That's fine, Mr Jenner – when would you like to visit Eternal Slumbers?'

Now would have done. But Michael inked him in for 10.30 the next day.

He got whisked away for the photo call early afternoon, a smiling head and shoulders in front of the Rillington. If he did know the purpose Art kept shtum. But ventured, 'We all admire you, Mr Jenner.'

Somehow the solitude of Junior Suite 1738 no longer bred isolation. Seeking now to ramp back up to an active life, one with a future, David welcomed the restive atmosphere. It helped nurture creative thinking – figure the way forward. And quietly absorb the full realisation of his good fortune. There was no question of backing up into his former lifestyle. Three months before he had been a young head on old shoulders. Now he had life skills and a maturity that only comes from reaching the brink of death – and returning to tell the tale; wiser for the experience.

There was no grieving for the money. David had long since

reasoned it as worldly goods passed on ahead of time. But for circumstances, it would have simply remained as equity. And in the long term
there'd have been little impact on his material life either way.

He now felt complete. And if loneliness momentarily struck, a
stroll through the hotel's public areas provided pleasant, if slightly
patronising contact with staff only too eager to engage him in conversation. For now he was a Local Hero, a small fish in a rather small
pond. And he took pleasure in knowing he'd distinguished himself in
a modest way – albeit at a considerable cost.

But cheap at the price.

Later that afternoon Jesse arrived. She was tickled pink at hearing
about David.

'Well my, my Mr Jenner – so YOU is the Friend.' She sank onto
the bed and smiled fondly at David. 'You is deep down good, son –
your time WILL come.'

They chatted and Jesse explained she was leaving for her cruise in
the middle of February – that Simone would 'do' for him in the
interim.

Manhattan Roundup didn't seem the same. Today's *Mercury*
linked Maria Arabella with Vincent Del Lombardo, a porn king from
the West Coast. Which put her out of circulation again. And neither
the refugees nor David got a mention. He accepted being yesterday's
news, as such was the volatility of this business.

Nevertheless, his interview inspired letters from many viewers.
Most expressed admiration – both with words and money. Others
begged for handouts. Then there were the predictable offers of
marriage from women seeking a mail order husband. And some simply
wanted to meet up in a cheap hotel. Women – and men. David was
fascinated by the photos.

A downmarket local rag had sought to get some mileage out of
the story and had organised a beano in China Town for the Kwi-
Megei folk, with David invited as guest of honour. But he declined,
preferring to remember their silent, needy faces rather than endure
hyped-up smiles bought by the paper.

On the way out to O'Banion's he glanced at his elusive love.
And mused on the button. He'd often wondered if in death they'd be
united. But in life he knew dreams were as good as it would get.

By ten the next morning he was heading south to the lobby, en route to Eternal Slumbers. The receptionists chorused and Mohamed gave his usual salutation. Mounted on a flip chart stand by the revolving door was a large poster – 'The Rillington Hotel David Jenner Appeal'. Just visible below in small type was 'Not to be confused with the Manhattan Roundup Appeal'. And bang in the centre was a large smiling mugshot of himself. Whatever his initial reaction, David eventually allowed himself a wry smile. This wasn't a nickels and dimes tin rattle. It took in Visa donations, bequests and wads of the green ones – all in support of the Manhattan needy. Don was certainly milking this one.

Michael's welcome mimicked his last. Was he a robot?

'Mr Jenner it's so good to see you.'

Today, he was ushered to the 'Reconciliation Chamber' – a small, softly lit room, with a hint of Liszt's *Leibestraum* giving mood. And fragrant with the sharp essence of pine needles. In one corner a miniature Flame of Eternal Slumber softly hissed. Michael sat at a very large pedestal desk, the top laid with beautifully embossed red leather. David sat directly opposite.

'How can I help you today, Mr Jenner?'

'Well, umm, I've changed my mind.'

As before, he waited for Michael to falter. But he could never have predicted what came next. Michael's face lit up with a full joyous smile and he took David's hand between his own. They were small, white and clammy – nicotine stained.

'OH Mr Jenner, that is so, so beautiful – you have decided not to die – I am deeply moved.'

It stumped David for a few seconds.

"Err ... well, what I'm really trying to say is can I sell the package back to you? You see, I need the money.'

Michael's joy became more intense.

'Mr Jenner I would love to.' Relief washed over. 'BUT, Mr Jenner I can't. You see, your money is at this minute being employed in taking another of our dear members on their final journey of peace and love.'

David pondered the logic. 'Surely though, you have other members whose money will in theory pay for my final journey of peace and love?'

Michael sat back and clasped his hands, his face still in raptures.

'We have to have an exact match between your package and the one that will replace the gap that yours leaves.' Making reference to a computer screen he regretfully informed David, 'Sadly at this time your package is unique.'

David wondered if he'd ever get past this dude.

'Can I sell my package to someone else?'

Michael's wondrous smile persisted, and he waited for the counter argument.

'Of course you can, Mr Jenner – we will simply charge a reassignment fee of three hundred dollars.'

'Oh good, err ... thank you, Michael, I'll try and do that.'

'Wonderful, Mr Jenner, and may I say how deeply moved we all were on hearing of your generosity and kindness.'

David grunted some acknowledgement. He'd tired of Michael's sickly sweet delivery. And was tempted to scream 'Bollocks' in his face to find out who or what lurked behind the mask.

Flogging a nine grand prepaid funeral in Manhattan wasn't going to be easy. He did wonder about getting one of the lesser funeral outfits to sell it on a commission. Then eBay came to mind. His account was still active and details were loaded up on a $3000 reserve for a five-day auction.

Junior Suite 1738 appeared to have acquired an enhanced inventory. A mini-bar fridge sat next to the settee and the telly had grown into a 42-inch flat screen model. An array of designer products for men had found their way into the bathroom. And on the coffee table was a pile of topical magazines and papers. On the bed, a Platinum Membership card to the Rillington health and fitness club.

And wherever David went in the hotel staff loudly acknowledged him. Guests who recognised him from the appeal poster, or who simply knew of him through the 'Friend' story, would turn and speak. Some were just in awe. Others wanted the story, chapter and verse. Initial versions were simple and factual – recounted with an unassuming spin. But each iteration saw minor embellishment and the inclusion of 'forgotten' detail – all packaged in a stylish delivery that got smoother by the dozen. By now David welcomed the attention and on several occasions, nonchalantly hovered by the appeal poster waiting to be 'discovered'.

If, in the latter years of his life, he'd fretted over lack of achievement, the balance was swiftly being redressed. Jesse's proclamation was just words at the time. But having waited, his time had truly come.

Five days on a redneck from Alabama bid up nearly $6,000 for the 'Serenity-Plus package'. He and his ninety-six siblings and cousins had clubbed together for their 'Grand Maw' who'd ascended to redneck heaven two days earlier. 'She always did wanna ride in one of them posh Cadillacs.'

Nine grand had seemed small beer at the time. But now it paled against the auction proceeds.

Occasionally Wrightman's name would drift through David's mind. In theory LawServices4U were out of the picture – since the terms of his will held good whatever the timing of his demise. He nevertheless felt a compulsion to call the big man and tell him 'I'm alive and well'. And perhaps even pay a final visit that for a change would end on an enduring high note. The notion eventually spun into orbit.

'Err ... Mr Wrightman, it's Mr Jenner, I err—'

'MR JENNER! Sir, it is so good to hear your voice.'

'Well, err ... I appear to be almost better and I just wanted to say Hi to you under happier circumstances.'

'Sir, I was aware that you were still with us but to know you've conquered your illness is the most wonderful news.'

It was emotionally delivered.

'I, err, wondered if I might see you at some point when you're not too busy.'

'It would be my pleasure, Mr Jenner, let me have the privilege of buying you lunch!'

And they met, and ate, and talked and laughed. Now and then sitting in brief silence when darker days were unintentionally touched on. Their parting was easy and congenial – like old friends bidding goodbye 'til the next time.

'I'm here for you as always – please stay in touch.'

By the 14th, both pairs of Workaday 3-Size Pants 40-44 inch had been binned – probably finding new ownership before they hit the trash. In their place was a pair of Eazy-Fit 38-inch slacks. Tight at first but fast living up to their name.

Though not vain, a certain preoccupation with image had gotten a grip. His road show now on the up, baggy combats were seriously 'infra dig' – the Eazy-Fit slacks only a marginal improvement. David sought to adopt Ed Razaadi's stylistics, a feat not achievable with the shabby tat humped over from West London. Don Rodriguez's thinking was on a parallel strand. He got his point across the American way.

'Forgot to tell you, Mr Jenner, the men's outfitters three doors down are doin' a free pro-mo – asked if we'd send a selected guest along. Sure would be delighted if you'd take up the offer – you'd look swell in some of their suits an' stuff.'

David graciously accepted. He'd rather bought into the notion of free board in recognition of selfless generosity. But nothing is for nothing and it quickly dawned he'd have to sing for his supper; though no great imposition to be a smartly dressed Rillington Ambassador. Giovani's sorted him out with some slick attire and said to pop the trousers back as and when his shrinking waistline dictated. Budgets for the pro-mo appeared unlimited.

Without any prodding, David took the initiative to steer clients in the direction of the hotel's products and services. And he became a familiar face around the lobby and foyer. From playing down a previous life that was bland and uneventful, his biogenesis was creatively re-engineered in line with a persona that now oozed worldly charm – truly 'à la Rillington'.

Don was quietly complementary whilst slipping in a few tips here and there.

'Always look 'em straight in the eye and smile.'

'Agree with 'em first, then come in with the "but".'

'Look for something about 'em you know they're proud of and complement them on it – works every time. Putty in your palm.'

And he'd wink at David. 'Proud of y', buddy.'

One morning Lynndah from the Rillington Health Club called. 'Like to try our new sun bed?'

She had a face that took two hours to put on and five minutes to take off. Nevertheless she was very sweet and got David hooked on a ten-session course. He also came away with a snappy hairdo – now looking the part.

Occasionally Don would arrange for David to address groups of people in the Shangri La suite. It was a small but elegant meeting/dining facility, beautifully restored to its former art deco glory. He would talk to them about community projects and how they might receive public recognition for their sponsorship. On other occasions he'd regale them with deluxe versions of the Kwi-Megei story and spout amusing anecdotes he'd conjured from nowhere. As now, he was becoming a polished raconteur. It was all about earning a crust for the hotel. And David enjoyed it – living in style on the back of his new-found vocation. Both he and the staff played their parts like true thespians. It was the Rillington Theatre of Life.

Early in the last week of January he made his last appointment with the Holbrook Institute. From Alice's look, he sensed she now beheld a very different David Jenner.

'You're looking really well, David.'

'Thanks, Alice, I feel good as well.'

They left it at that, and with her arm affectionately slipped through his she steered him around the new Blood Analysis facility whilst explaining how each piece of equipment functioned.

At the front door they stood face to face searching for an appropriate goodbye. Alice held her arms out. 'Shall we hug?'

They slipped their arms around each other in a goodbye that quickly became hello. With cheeks softly touching and firm frontal contact they remained locked in a fond embrace. And just before they drew apart Alice whispered something very softly to David. It was almost inaudible but registered clearly.

'Thank you.'

He knew exactly what she meant and smiled in shy acknowledgement.

She assured David, 'We're here if you need us.' But her eyes were more truthful. 'I'm here if you need me.'

The encounter lingered in David's mind. And he teased himself with some pleasantly erotic thoughts of Alice. It was now her turn to be on the operating table. And he was in attendance – complete with stethoscope and a wonderful bedside manner; and wearing little more than a smile.

January became February, and the bleakness of winter persisted. When

David wasn't strutting his stuff around the hotel, he'd take a stroll around the shops, or ride the subway to more distant places. Sometimes he explored cultural venues – took in the odd show. Evenings were never dull. Invitations to join guests at their table cropped up frequently. And the restaurant staff were always looking to pair him with suitable female guests.

Often though, after a day of vigorous socialising, he was happy to curl up with a room service menu. And fed and watered he'd gaze out at the night-time vista and lapse into sentimental thoughts of people and places. More and more during these reflective moments he'd dwell on a life written off over four months ago.

And he frequently thought about Roberta – her card was still on the dressing table. Many times he'd been on the verge of phoning, only to hold back for fear he'd suffer a relapse and break her heart again. But each day improved his confidence of a happy ending.

By now his waist was back to 34 inches and he looked and felt well. Towards the middle of February David detected a slight decline in the demand for his attention. Don had removed the lobby poster as the David Jenner Appeal had reached maturity. For Don, the next brownie points would be awarded for distribution of funds. And so the traffic fell and David sensed autumnal melancholy as The Rillington summer faded.

One afternoon, whilst chatting to Mohamed, Don bustled up. 'There's someone waiting to see you in the Shangri La Suite.'

Traditionally Don deposited people there if they shaped up as likely beneficiaries. As David entered, his prospect stood up and came towards him – a lady. And she carried herself with an elegance that spoke volumes. Around David's age, she had darkish hair and attractive looks that would never desert her. Her youthful size ten curves were encapsulated in a beautifully tailored beige suit – visible through an unbuttoned brown leather coat. A sweet fragrance filled the room.

They shook hands. She smiled softly, cautiously.

'I'm Natalia Millar.'

David went to introduce himself with the charm and confidence befitting an insurance salesman. But something stopped him. Her eyes told of a different mission. Eyes that had smiled at him before. In one millionth of a heartbeat the blinding realisation saturated his sentimental soul.

'It was a photograph of me you saw in *BoyZo*.'

David stood transfixed as every facet of his *BoyZo* fantasy distilled into solid reality. For here stood the darling girl of his dreams, safely delivered through the enigmatic mists of time.

His head swam with climactic elation.

'I, I, err … can't tell you how wonderful it is to meet you.' And sighing in amazement he asked, 'How did you know about me?'

Natalia explained that. 'A lady called Roberta Johansen contacted me – she was very sweet and—'

'ROBERTA!'

'Yes, she is one amazing woman. It took her just three days to track me down – I live in upper west Manhattan. In 1958 I lived with my family in a tenement on the east side near the Brooklyn Bridge. Anyway, Mr Jenner, she—'

'Would you like to call me David?'

She smiled that smile.

'Yes, David – please call me Natalia.'

'Thank you – Natalia.'

They laughed and any awkwardness faded away.

'Well, David, Roberta told me about you and why you had come to New York. And that you were very ill. I was very touched by all I heard.'

David listened quietly, still in shocked amazement at what was happening.

'Roberta begged me to come and see you – I think she felt you'd find it comforting. I was given Mr Rodriguez's number. Such a helpful man. And partly out of a sense of duty, and partly out of intrigue, I rang him – this was about seven pm on Christmas Eve. My plan was to try and see you the day after Boxing Day. But Mr Rodriguez tried to tell me in a kindly way that it might be too late. He was in touch with a Dr Schwartz who said he was surprised you'd made it this far.'

Natalia's unfolding story blew David away. 'I had no idea about all this.'

'Well, I wanted to come over straight away, but for personal reasons I couldn't leave until nearly ten thirty. And by the time I arrived at the hotel, amazingly you weren't there. It all seemed so bizarre to me.'

'Looking back, Natalia, it was bizarre – I was high as a kite on some incredible cocktail given me by Dr Schwartz, and off to find the Kwi-Megei refugees. I don't know how I got back.'

Natalia shook her head in amazement. 'However, Mr. Rodriguez very kindly let me sit in his office until you returned. Just after twelve, his night porter came in and said that you were in a very bad way. I was advised to see you straight away should you take a turn for the worst.'

'It must have been awful for you – I'm really sorry.'

'It didn't matter, David. By then I was determined to see things through. Anyway, I was taken to your room by Mr Rodriguez. He opened the door sufficiently for the hall light to filter in. I just stood at the foot of your bed for less than a minute. You were lying on your back with your arms stretched out either side. I thi—'

'I was flying.' David grinned mischievously.

'You were flying?' Her pretty eyes sparkled with amusement.

'I promise you, Natalia, I was flying.'

'You were mumbling things – you might have been hallucinating. And then, David, you opened your eyes and gave me the most beautiful, beautiful smile. It was as if you knew me. It unsettled me terribly – I kept dwelling on it.'

David nodded. 'I saw you alright – you were so real.'

Perplexed, Natalia asked, 'But you didn't recognise me straight away this afternoon?'

For a few seconds David struggled for words that might explain the paradox.

'I know it sounds strange, perhaps I saw you in more of a spiritual sense – I'm not sure. But yes, I saw you at the foot of my bed.'

It left question marks for Natalia, but they moved on.

'I had brought one of the buttons from my Rockette's uniform – which my mother had kept for me. I'm not sure what inspired me do to that. I think I just wanted you to know I'd not deserted you.'

David shook his head and smiled. 'Natalia, you have no idea how much that button intrigued me. But it gave me hope that somewhere, in a dimension I might not even understand, you existed.'

'I'm glad, David. I kept in touch with Mr Rodriguez, and it seemed you were hanging in. And then the story about the refugees broke and I was told you were now recovering. And I felt I had to see you one more time.'

Such words were pure music to David's ears. 'I still can't believe I'm having this conversation with you. I'm so glad you came to visit me.'

Natalia nodded and smiled. 'Me too.'

For David, the inquisition wasn't quite over.

'So, how long were you a Rockette?'

It was Natalia's turn for the mischievous smile.

'Well actually I never was a Rockette.'

In one fell swoop the very fabric of David's nostalgic crusade was swept away. But slowly it filtered back, like salt water seeping into footprints on a sandy beach. As within the emotional lobes of his mind the dream was already immortalised as romantic Radio City Music Hall folklore.

But a surprised exclamation had already been dispatched to his mouth. 'Oh?'

'I had a bit of a stage mum, and she took me along to Phoebe Western Photographic next to Penn Station – I was fourteen. Anyway, they created a portfolio for me and six weeks later I was called in for an assignment to do the *BoyZo* photo. I was supposed to be eighteen, so they made me up quite heavily. We didn't get paid much. And it was my one and only assignment.' She laughed. 'I had quite a bit of 'fan' mail forwarded from London.'

David smiled shyly. 'I think every *BoyZo* reader fell in love with you.'

And with the coyness of a fourteen-year-old girl Natalia asked, 'And what about you, David?'

He grinned awkwardly, admitting, 'Yes, I suppose I did.' And added, 'Yes, I did.'

A wicked twinkle in her eyes, she egged him on. 'So, David, you came here to find me?'

Embarrassed, he looked down. And then with a submissive nod conceded, 'Yes, I came here to find you.'

With the smugness of a young girl who'd just got one over the boy next door, she announced, 'Well, David, you were looking in the wrong places, so I came to find you.' She mused thoughtfully at some arbitrary point in space and then turned back to him. 'You know, the story of how you came here hoping to find me – it's so beautiful. I was very touched when Roberta told me about it.'

For a moment they shared an affectionate silence whilst their hearts sorted out the detail.

Looking at her watch, Natalia appeared a little concerned at the time.

'I have to leave soon.'

For David, the prospect of not seeing Natalia again was as devastating as a relapse of his illness.

A little awkwardly he asked, 'Err ... will I ever see you again?'

'I hope so, David.'

Her answer seemed more like a question.

Then her face clouded over a little. 'I'm going through a very difficult personal situation at present and will not be able to be in touch for a while. Would you be able to wait?'

David's answer came easily, and with Rillington aplomb. 'Natalia, I've waited forty-six years, so a little longer won't make any difference.'

Her face lit up. 'Thank you, David – that was a lovely thing to say. I won't be able to contact you directly – do you think I could leave a message with Mr Rodriguez when the time comes.'

Nodding, David assured her, 'I know Don would be happy with that.'

From her bag she drew an envelope.

'I brought this to give to you.'

They went to shake hands, but somehow managed to end up with a wonderfully tangled ball of sixteen fingers and four thumbs.

Suddenly Natalia was gone. And save for the fragrance that lingered it might well have just been a dream.

25

Life Goes On

David walked slowly across the lobby whilst replaying every word, look, smile, expression – in fact anything to which he could ascribe an atom of hope. And holding the envelope he'd open in the privacy of his suite.

He felt someone squeeze his arm gently – it was Don.

In soft, knowing tones he asked, 'Everything OK, buddy?'

From David's dreamy expression, the answer was obvious.

'Yes thanks, Don.'

'So you had a good meeting?'

'Oh yes. It was someone I'd wanted to meet for a long time.'

Don nodded and smiled. 'She seems a lovely lady.'

Just as they broke away David remembered to ask, 'Oh, Don, err ... would you mind if Natalia, I mean Mrs Millar, occasionally contacted me through yourself?"

It sounded a strange way for David to be in touch – but whatever Don construed he gave no outward indication.

Instead he flashed the Don Rodriguez winning smile, assuring David, 'Yeah, I'll be pleased to do that for you, my good friend.'

Back in his suite David sat on the bed and carefully opened the envelope. It was a photo – the very photo used for *BoyZo* page 6 – a high-quality original measuring around 7 by 5 inches. He gazed at it for quite a few minutes, taking in detail that never made it past the murky half-tone printing process. On the back, stamped in dark-blue ink, as was the custom: Phoebe Western Photographic, 25 Sep 1958.

For the time being it stood next to *BoyZo* page 6, propped up against the table lamp. But tomorrow it would be installed in a silver frame. And by the photo lay the button. As David sipped a cup of apple and black currant tea he wondered how long it would be until Natalia's situation was resolved. Days, weeks, months? Hopefully not years. He knew Natalia was real – they had touched. But love is just emotional energy. Without it, physical presence can be meaningless.

Roberta's card caught his eye. It was time. And even more so now. A little nervous he dialled her home number.

A voice answered 'Hello' – soft, low, measured. It threw him.

'Oh, err ... this is David Je—'

'DAVID! Oh DAVID. I'm so glad to hear your voice.'

They shared a good minute of emotional exchanges before managing any rational conversation.

Roberta was tearful – and David felt emotional fingers squeezing his throat.

'David honey, I knew you were getting better – Don kept me informed. But I cried for days after I left and prayed something wonderful would happen.'

'Thank you, Bobbie – now I've got my life back I won't waste it.'

For an age they reminisced and exchanged news.

Then David broke step. 'Err ... Bobbie, I had a visit from Natalia Millar today.'

Silence at first. Then 'Yeeees ...'

'Bobbie, I will never ever be able to thank you for finding Natalia. I don't know how you did it, but today I became the happiest man alive.'

'David, honey, it was a strange dream you were chasing, however I so wanted you to be at peace with yourself.'

'But Bobbie, how ever did you manage to find Natalia?'

Roberta laughed – the wonderfully infectious laugh that went with her infinite personality.

'Well, honey, it wasn't easy. I took a liberty and asked Don to copy the *BoyZo* comic page you had in your room. Then I enlisted the help of all the people of influence I could muster. Being married three times to well-known, well-heeled businessmen has its merits, David, honey.'

Peels of laughter issued from the earpiece. It even got David going.

'My London moles managed to get hold of the relevant archive and they also found an ol' timer who'd worked on the editorial side. From that we established it was Natalia Ginetta who lived on the east side. Then my helpers trawled all manner of public records. It was fast and furious, David, but when we found Natalia I felt like I'd won the lottery. I couldn't believe my luck that she was still living in Manhattan.'

David recounted his meeting with Natalia. And after they'd talked some more, and levelled the emotional humps, they bade each other love and goodbye. And made a promise to meet before September.

Tonight was room service menu night. After showering off the nervous sweat of the day he pulled on the Eazy-Fit slacks – by now an extremely easy fit – and admired the photo some more. Before devouring another Rillington Chef Special.

As the last week in February shaped up David knew a change of direction was imminent. There was a time to enjoy a free ticket at The Rillington. And a time to step off and say 'Thanks for having me'.

He'd recently got curious about life beyond The Rillington. Celebrity status had given him to believe another career was in the making. Though fortuitously common sense kicked in before perception became a reality he couldn't sustain. Besides, the pleasant suspended animation of Man about The Rillington would soon give way to real-world bump and grind. And he didn't want to get caught with his pants down.

Though David was sustained by the inner glow of *BoyZo* love, practical aspects of living called the shots. In theory he was still employed by Thompson Wigs, and still the owner of a large musty Edwardian semi in West London. But most importantly – richer in wisdom and intellect.

The nucleonic beginning of life's next chapter came into being – and grew. Just as a particle of dust attracts molecules of water until it falls as rain. And David knew he must bid adieu to his stateside family and take up the reigns of a life for which he was now well equipped.

He assumed that Dr Schwartz had keep Dr Bharani informed of his situation. But having met the inimitable Ferdi he wondered if this was actually the case, reluctantly opting to ring. A dull continuous tone came through. After several more attempts, Babette tried for him.

'Number's unavailable, honey.'

A trip over to Ferdi's seemed imminent, but in the meantime he arranged to see Don – whose office was something to behold. Full of tasteful memorabilia, it presented a fascinating timeline of the hotel's history – 1926 through to the present day. As Don jokingly pointed out – the collection started long before he was a twinkle. Furnishings were in plush leather with Don resplendent in a captain's chair at a desk that could seat a baseball team.

There was a warm welcome.

'HI! C'mon in, buddy, err ... Mr Jenner. One of the guy's git you a drink or somethin'?'

David politely declined.

'Well. Err ... Don. First I want to thank you for looking after Mrs Millar on Christmas Eve and for keeping an eye on me when I was so ill.'

Shaking his head, lips pursed Don looked down for a while.

"Man, we were worried about you. There was quite a bit of stuff goin' on behind the scenes – but you got there.'

Broaching the main topic David started to articulate his thoughts of the future. 'Umm, well, Don, I've enjoyed being at The Rillington, but I feel I need to get back into a normal lifestyle.'

Don smiled with an almost fatherly depth of understanding. 'I know exactly what you mean. But we'll miss you – you've been an inspiration to us all. So, Mr Jenner, sir, what—'

'Please call me David.'

'HEY! Right – so David, what will you do next?'

Do next? Hmm ... 'Well, Don, I need to tidy up the loose ends of my life here and then get back to where I was three months ago.'

'If I can help, David, let me know. And there's no rush – a few more weeks ain't gonna dent The Rillington finances.' And grinning he added, 'You're still doing some good stuff for us out in the lobby.'

Ferdi came to mind. 'Err ... Don, I tried to contact Dr Schwartz today but his number was unobtainable, do you ha—'

Don lowered his voice. 'Seems Doc Schwartz is in a little trouble – got caught dealing dope. He could be off the scene for a while.'

David was surprised, but not surprised. And in a sense was grateful that Ferdi had eluded the law long enough to keep him primed with the necessary.

'And Don, if you hear from Mrs Mill—'

'David, my good friend, you will be the first to know. I said I was here for you, and Don Rodriguez keeps his word.'

Back at base, there was much to do. First on the list, though, was to call the kindly doctor who'd felt so helpless and saddened at his plight. Though only mid-afternoon, time zones were against him. It would have to be in the morning. And it would be via Dr Bharani that work would hopefully recommence.

Now the compass was pointing firmly east, David got seriously into the implications of a return to the UK. He'd enough money to re-establish himself, but getting back into harness was paramount. In lieu of knowing otherwise, he assumed there would be a job waiting, if not a decent redundancy package. And either way, after nearly thirty-five or so years at Thompson's, there was a healthy final salary pension to look forward to. Depending on Edith Rogers's take on things, there could also be some sick pay to add to the pile.

Keen not to overstay his welcome, David planned to make tracks by mid-March. With the major decisions in hand he felt settled and happy, and after a cold Bud from the complimentary mini-bar, made off to the lobby to earn his keep. The loud 'Mr Jenner' salutations had been phased out, and instead staff signposted guests to David, who in turn helped expand their final accounts through his astute suggestions. Had they tried the health club – the massage comes highly recommended. Or how about a Rillington Wedding – if appropriate. Perhaps the 'Banquet in your room' dining experience. And business visitors found him helpful, listening with great interest as he praised the conference facilities he'd found so efficiently run – personal recommendations have no equal.

His great strength was the ability to float around, taking on the characteristics of a staff member or visitor as suited the occasion. And it worked every time. On some occasions he'd wear his David Jenner badge for an air of officialdom.

As planned, he called Dr Bharani – who had no idea of David's current situation. But was overcome with the news of his recovery.

'David, we assumed you had di ... err ... become too ill to contact us.'

David on the other hand had assumed Ferdi was feeding back to

Dr Bharani – which wasn't the case. But nevertheless, he gave a glowing account of Ferdi's helpfulness, which to a greater part was true. Importantly he outlined his plans to return and asked Dr Bharani if he could let Edith Rogers know that medically he was now fit for work.

'Oh, of course David, I'll be very glad to do this for you.'

Over the next two weeks David waded through the administrative clutter necessary to transfer his life back to West London. And during the last week he progressively cleared his room of redundant possessions. In particular delighting in ditching the shabby apparel of David Jenner, old world. All supervised under Natalia's watchful eye.

A one-way ticket to Heathrow was tucked into his cabin holdall: 15 March – departure 16:30. Tired, old hand-me-down luggage back from under the bed got junked for new kit. And his carefully selected 'going home' outfit waited patiently in the wardrobe.

It bothered him that a visit to Roberta was going to be difficult. He phoned with a suggestion of training it down for a day. But she begged him not to worry himself at this time. 'I have a photograph of you in my heart David, honey, and knowing you're well and happy fulfils me. And may everything have a happy ending for you and Natalia.'

They parted on a poignant note, as true friends do. With promises of Christmas cards and a resolve to keep in touch. And meet again one day.

With two days to go and now marking time, David took a sentimental journey around the locale that had now become home. It was one of those walks that stimulates mental activity and resolves any backlog of emotive issues. He thought of Natalia, seeking to convince himself that distance wouldn't compromise love; that their meeting wasn't just a cruel confusion between real and surreal. He so yearned for *BoyZo* romance to flourish with the simplicity of a comic strip.

Thoughts of the transition back to a large empty Edwardian house weighed heavily – there being no vibrant hotel life beyond the bedroom door. And he struggled with the prospect of reabsorption into West London suburbia as plain old David Jenner. Whilst his brain laboured away on full capacity, so his feet pounded the Manhattan sidewalks – with busy streets and avenues floating by unnoticed.

Until abruptly he was snapped to attention by two strong hands grabbing him firmly by the shoulders. And a gruff voice asking, 'How y' doin', buddy?'

He might have recognised the reddish, greyish beard, and the tanned leathery skin and beady eyes. But memory recall from smell was nanoseconds ahead.

It was Red!

Before David could react Red was off into his routine. 'Can you spare a man a buck or so?'

Cocking his head to one side, lips pursed and eyes wide and expectant, Beard Man waited – for a moment. And then threw his head back with a raucous laugh.

'Thought you was in the business of dyin', brother.' And with mock seriousness affirmed, 'Y' musta' drunk the brew – I told you, cures everything.'

By now David had found his tongue. And amused at this unlikely but enjoyable meeting confirmed, 'Yes, Red, I drank it – every drop, and it definitely did the trick. Thank you so much.'

'Taste good?'

David saw the funny side. 'Well, Red, it's the best drop of python piss I've ever had.'

Red's face screwed up with mirth. And then a serious note took over. 'Heard aboucha', good buddy – may y' be blessed for your kindness.'

David nodded in silent acknowledgement. 'Looking back, Red, I wish I'd thought to set something aside for you.'

Shaking his head Red explained, 'M' dearest friend, I thank y' for such thoughts. But it woulda' killed me in no time. See, I'd go soft an' lose the survival instinct – need the challenge.'

'Understand, Red.' He didn't completely understand. But accepted Red's choice of street life. 'So, do you feel a malt coming on?'

Red gave one of his wide-eyed, lips-pursed looks. 'Sure do buddy, BUT, tucker's on me today.'

David's protestations fell on deaf ears, and he was escorted to yet another greasy spoon where a tramp and a well-dressed Englishman could slide in unnoticed. And whilst David enjoyed the chef's unhealthy dish of the day, Red got serious with the malt and watched his friend demolish a morning's takings on Fifth Avenue.

'So, good buddy, where does life take y' now?'

Invoking a modicum of dry humour David informed him, 'Well, I've given away all my money so I suppose I'll have to get a job.'

Red grunted and ah-hmm'd several times – then winked at David mischievously. 'Tell y' what, brother, this work thing's not good for y' – Shufflin' Bill's movin' on to Atlantic City, so we gotta spare place if you're interested.'

They parted as two kindred spirits, and David continued, his stomach full, though not necessarily well fed, but feeling more positive about repatriation.

With one day to go, he pottered about and mentally rehearsed his homecoming. A couple of hours were spent browsing the shops around Fifth and Sixth Avenues where he bought a few mementos and snapped up a half-price winter jacket at Lord and Taylor. His old red-and-blue quilted zip-up Thermo-Warm jacket had seemed trendy seventeen years ago. By current standards it lacked sophistication, giving him the appearance of a two-tone Michelin Man.

A message came through from Babette – could he see Don in his office at 10.00 the next day to finalise a few details.

In the lulls between activity, Natalia would always come to mind – and David mentally listed any number of 'personal problem' scenarios. He could think of none that would prevent some level of communication. Accepting the worst – that he may never hear from her – was difficult. If not impossible.

For the last time he made tracks for O'Banion's. Deliah must have been laying in wait.

'Oh, Hi David.'

He turned to see her get up to come over. In the time he'd been at The Rillington Deliah had always been glued to a seat. In red 4-inch mules she stood 6 foot 7 inches and sported the Rubenesque figure of a Greek goddess – legs that could halt the traffic in Times Square.

Walking provocatively up to David she cooed, 'David I won't be here tomorrow to say goodbye, so let me wish you the best now.'

With that she engulfed him in her powerful arms and crushed his face into her colossal bosom. His Gino Bertolini jockey briefs strained happily confirming all was well below. And he now knew without any doubt:

That Venus was a black woman.

Shaken, but not stirred, he continued to O'Banion's. Company was available, but he preferred to eat in a brown study. And afterwards enjoy a Southern Comfort and fresh orange juice in a dark corner of the Broadway Bar. From whence he tinkered around aimlessly upstairs with the TV for company.

Recently, thoughts of Pauline had surfaced, their half-cocked friendship still in limbo. Departing West London a sick man appeared justification at the time for an open-ended withdrawal. On returning David knew Pauline would meekly accept his shallow explanation and a wasted twelve years without challenge. And he felt uncomfortable knowing she'd quietly bear the hurt. And still hope when all hope had gone.

Sleep was fitful and by nine David was in Rebecca's Patisserie getting value out of his last free meal. Per Don's request he fronted up at 10.00 – and walked into a dozen familiar, smiling faces, being greeted by a collective 'Hi David!'

Don was grinning like a tin of worms.

'We just wanted to drink your health, David, and wish you the best.'

With glasses charged, David was toasted. And there was more. Don presented a gift-wrapped item about 10 inches square.

'It's a small memento, David, to make sure you don't forget us.'

The small memento was quite heavy and removing the gift wrap revealed a polished aluminium miniature of The Rillington Hotel, mounted on an oak plinth.

David was enchanted.

'I found it in one of the store rooms in the basement. It was made for the original opening ceremony in nineteen twenty six – had it cleaned and polished. Knew it belonged with you rather than gathering dust.'

Don went on to quip about excess baggage and there were kisses and handshakes. And then some rather contrived small talk took over – until the phone rang and Don gave a non-committal 'OK'.

He shook David's hand once more. 'Good knowing you, buddy – stop by now and then.'

Clutching his prize David arrived back at Junior Suite 1738 to find that in bright brass letters it had been renamed 'The David Jenner Suite'. On the surface he felt a pleasant flush of delight. Deeper down, though, was a more enduring reaction – the realisation he'd finally made a small dent in gaining some self-worth.

With goodbyes said he stayed suite-bound, ready to slide away unnoticed. At the curb Carl bade him a warm farewell. 'Boss says for Wesley to take you to JFK in the limo.'

Within fifteen minutes they'd been swallowed up by the Queens Midtown Tunnel, shortly to be discharged into the faceless urban sprawl either side of Highway 495. At JFK David went through the usual check-in rigmarole. And then did himself proud in duty free with the purchase of a large bag of jelly beans AND some ear plugs for the flight.

In the distance from the departure lounge window he could see the Manhattan outline. He'd come to New York City to die, but instead had found life and love.

Already pangs of withdrawal were paining his sentimental heart.

26

An Old Life – A New Outlook

With a jolt Flight 1176 hit the cold, damp tarmac at Heathrow. Still dark, the myriad lights from working situations around the airport gave a soft glow as their collective lumens amalgamated in the early morning mist.

David welcomed not being an 'alien', and the fast transit through passport control it accorded. Within twenty-five minutes he was outside, savouring the chill of early morning mid-March – revelling at the sight of London black cabs. The sheer thrill of standing on English terra firma after three months away elevated his weary being.

He'd phoned a Riverside Taxi whilst waiting to disembark, and managed to locate it 'by the Coca Cola machine just past the last pedestrian crossing'.

Now it was the Heathrow Tunnel that swallowed and disgorged David's taxi to join earlybird motorway commuters. M4 became A4 became A306, and they rumbled across Hammersmith Bridge to the first knockings of a grey dawn. Finally coming to rest outside Number 69. For David it was a strange and poignant experience to see the dimly silhouetted house that had known him, man and boy. As he opened the gate a familiar shadowy shape ascended the gate pillar – Victor. He stopped and announced, 'I saw you, Victor.'

Victor said little but responded by gently rubbing his round fluffy face against David's.

Three months could have been three years. As crossing the threshold was like revisiting a childhood haunt that now seemed smaller and shabbier when beheld through adult eyes. It was a measure of David's intellectual rebirth. But the house felt good, as it embodied happiness and fond memories, sunny days and loving parents. And it had not a single bad bone.

A mountain of mail lurked within, swept back like deep snow on opening the front door. Providing a forwarding address had made no sense. In truth David had ceased to care when he pulled the door shut for the last time. And it was cold and dark – no gas or electricity. Or telephone. But for whatever reason mains water was still available. He'd preferred to manage the reconnections post return, happy to accept that firing up the domestics would take a day or so.

Daylight was slowly giving form to the rooms and for all the downside David felt good just to be home again. As here he was, healthy, fit and tanned, and full of resolve for a new crack at life. Within fifty minutes most shops would be open. Whereupon he could get on with the basics – and do justice to an all-day breakfast.

At around 8.40 someone knocked – Mrs Pewsey, who 'was worried there might be burglars'. But who smilingly observed, 'It's nice to see you back, David.' She quickly figured his situation. 'Would you like a nice cup of tea?'

Gagging for something hot and sweet he accepted.

'That would be lovely, Mrs Pewsey.'

She almost turned to go. 'Hungry?'

'Well, err ... I'll probably eat out.'

Mrs P was undeterred. 'I've got some lovely smoked back bacon and large ducks' eggs.'

At this juncture he caved in. It would be the Spanish Inquisition but he'd already cobbled up a story to feed the neighbourhood town criers.

Triumphant, she smiled sweetly, and with a wink asked David to pop round in ten minutes. Time enough to lug in some anthracite from the coal shed and get Ideal Boiler No. 1 back in business. At least hot water would be on tap.

Mrs Pewsey – Lydia – and he, went back a long way. When David had moved in with his parents in 1949, she was living alone in the house, bequeathed her by an aunt. And then along came Jack, a lovely man, who'd responded to Lydia's ad for a lodger. He was working at the Osram light bulb factory in Shepherd's Bush. They filled a need in each other's lives and eventually married. Sadly Jack died of a heart attack soon after – he was a lot older – and she never remarried.

Lydia's house was the mirror of his. But the clock had stopped in 1955. As a young boy he'd sometimes been invited round to watch television on the proverbial 9-inch Bush TV. In June 1953 he and his parents had spent all day watching the Coronation.

There was a warm welcome. 'Come through, David.'

Her kitchen was cosy and lived in. But gone was the pretty solid fuel stove, replaced years ago with a gas boiler.

Breakfast never tasted so good. And Lydia waited for the first egg and two of the four rashers to go the way of all food before commencing the exploratory.

'So, David, you must have been away for about three months.'

He was ready, though, and without further prompting spouted a glitzy account; of how he'd surveyed the hair industry in New York, the new partnerships he'd forged, techniques and fashions he'd studied, new business generated – opportunities galore.

Lydia's eyes glazed over on several occasions as she strove to comprehend David's buzzy marketing jive. There'd been whispers before he left – none of them consistent with what she was hearing. Or his tanned, healthy countenance. Her face echoed bemusement, but she managed an unconvincing 'Oh, I see.'

Clearly Lydia didn't 'see'. And David wondered with inner mirth how she'd articulate his story to her cronies. And just how much it would be corrupted as it passed from pillar to post.

Lydia was still struggling to iron out some of the contradictions. 'When I saw the Simmonds Brothers I thought perhaps you were moving.'

Leaning forward a little, David took her into his confidence.

'Well, between you and me, Mrs Pewsey, I did have thoughts of moving to America. And so I stored my possessions in readiness. My agent would have sold the larger items and dealt with the house sale.'

He leaned back in mock thoughtfulness, sipping the best cup of tea in three months, adding, 'Of course, what I've told you is confidential – my employer has no inkling of this.'

Lydia's eyes were getting bigger. 'I understand David – I wouldn't tell a soul.'

He smiled sweetly. 'I knew you wouldn't, Mrs Pewsey.'

Now with the last piece of the puzzle nearly within her grasp she asked, 'Why did you decide to return?'

David sucked his breath in pensively. 'Well, Mrs Pewsey I—'

'DO call me Lydia – after all, we've known each other for a long, long time.'

'Oh, thank you, Lydia – well anyway, I enjoyed America, but one day it dawned on me that I had a lovely house in West London, wonderful neighbours and a job that's heading for a directorship. And I just pulled up stumps and came back.' After a reflective silence he added, 'You know, there were some strange rumours about me when I left. But then that's folk for you.'

Nonchalantly thanking Lydia he returned to the tasks in hand. Culling the mail mountain came first, with 90 per cent sacrificed in the name of hot water.

After that it was a taxi ride to Hammersmith for food and another PAYG mobile phone. Red letters had arrived from the utilities and BT. But debit card arrears payments and a good sob story got next-day reconnection promises.

With luggage upstairs and unpacked, David made a room by-room inspection for no other reason than to refamiliarise. Ideal Boiler No. 1 grumbled, roared and gurgled, simply glad to be wanted again. And the kitchen became warm and inviting – as if nothing had happened. Whilst Natalia had pride of place on the high mantelpiece. By late afternoon frenetic activity had backed off to a gentler, more sustainable level, as a house once more became a home. And the hot water WAS hot and eased away the grime and fatigue of David's transatlantic journey.

Fading light was overcome with an old hurricane lantern that had hung in the coal shed since time immemorial. And something resembling tea was made by heating water in a saucepan placed on top of the boiler.

By 9.00 lack of sleep and the tedium of travel caught up. Armed with a hot water bottle and torch David wearily climbed the wooden hill to crawl between cold, unaired bed linen. And curling into a ball, waited for body heat to make a more sociable environment. Once warm and unfurled he lay on his back and gazed at the intriguing shadows and striations on the bedroom ceiling cast by street lights –

and the silhouette of poplar tree branches as they danced around the wall to the tune of a gentle breeze.

It was a far cry from his cosy room at The Rillington. But cocooned in the single bed that had delivered him safely through the night since childhood, he felt secure and happy. And he drifted off to join Zachariah Lightning in saving the world.

A jet-lagged brain got David up and about just before 6.00. Within three-quarters of an hour he had the boiler roaring away like a blast furnace. And with the small round lid at the top removed he found it possible to heat the frying pan fat into a frenzy. Thus a rustic meal was enjoyed. Even toast was managed, albeit with a few casualties, by carefully lowering slices of bread on a fork into No. 1's fiery belly.

As the day progressed normal service was resumed. Natalia took a trip to David's bedside table, and the Rillington miniature took over the kitchen mantelpiece.

By the following day he was able to consider the wider implications of returning. Thoughts of Pauline hung around uncomfortably at the back of his mind. He felt guilty at how casually he'd used her giving nature, had kept her on tap. Looking back, he wondered what had motivated such insensitivity. It prompted him to reach for the phone.

'Hello?'

Her voice was gentle, a little vulnerable, unpretentious – working class with the smooth edges chipped off.

'Err ... hello, it's David, err ... David Jenner – I know you must have wondered—'

'I'm married now, David.'

The words smacked into his eardrums like a bucket of ice cubes. And he rather inanely aped her reply.

'Married?'

'Yes David, I married Geoff Higgins six weeks ago. I realised we wasn't goin' nowhere. Geoff has always liked me and I finally said yes.'

David knew Geoff Higgins had been lurking around on the periphery of things but always smugly rated him as a no hoper when it came to Pauline's affection.

'Oh, I see, Pauline, I'm very happy for you.'

'I've got to go – Geoff wants his lunch. Best not call again David.'

It left an unpleasant taste. He was off the hook, but not before toying with the illusion that Pauline was waiting by the phone. And now she had turned to someone whose simple qualities won the day. It dulled his mood for an hour or so until he finally convinced himself that providence had come up with a sensible solution.

In order of importance, the next phone call would be to Edith Rogers.

'Oh hello, David – I've been expecting your call. Dr Bharani's been in touch and we're all so glad that you're better.'

Her voice was pleasant, reassuring – a euphonious blend of professional and personal.

'Thank you, Edith – I'm calling about returning to work.'

'Well, we thought perhaps you could come in for a couple of hours before you actually start back. I'll need to see you regarding your sick leave and then I believe Emily would like to discuss your role with you.'

'Emily?'

'Yes, Emily – I'll bring you up to speed when you come in. Now, how about this Thursday at, say, eleven o' clock?'

It was a done deal. But Emily? Hmm. With her offspring now adults it was likely she'd returned to help 'The Captain'. Two days hence gave him plenty of time to prepare. He wondered how they'd perceive the new improved David Jenner. And how he'd cope with returning to a murky MoD grey office. Work appeared an attractive option when living came back into vogue. But he was fast normalising to having a pulse – though eternally grateful.

Since leaving Thompson's he'd rubbed shoulders with the highs and lows of humanity, enjoyed his brief claim to fame as the 'Friend' and a pleasant interlude as Man about The Rillington. And suffered the slings and arrows of an outrageous Cupid. All of which had raised his expectation of life. To resume the preordained daily drudge and endure the Rikkis and Raymondes was a depressing prospect too far.

And it set him thinking.

For although his Rillington stardom wasn't portable, the slick persona he'd developed and honed for working the lobby floor had made it back intact. With a smile he recalled Don's simple but effective advice and realised there was latitude for some smooth talking at Thompson's.

David's next call was to Simmonds Brothers. They could return the five tea chests on Thursday.

'Can you make it after three pm?'

Then he spoke to the HSBC and arranged to go in the next day and rationalise his accounts.

Finally he organised an audience with Mr Paine at Paine Procter and Pratt. It was about tweaking his will a little and taking them off Red Alert as regards his now deferred passing.

Mid afternoon crept up with daylight on the turn. But it was dry and a sociable 12°C and David slipped into the street for a break from the domestics. Strolling through the pleasant Edwardian neighbourhood, he was thrilled not to be looking at everything 'for the last time'. And he just followed his nose, which steered him along by the river and up the high street – much as before. At Mulligan's News he bought a pad and envelopes having felt the need to write a long letter to Roberta. Email would have been a simpler option, but he wanted to send something she could curl up with on her plush settee whilst sipping a Jack Daniels. And read over and over – hopefully.

He arrived home in darkness welcomed by a warm glow from the hall light. And at the kitchen table let rip to Roberta. Much of what flowed onto the paper had little relevance to their friendship. However she'd proven a good listener and he needed to exorcise an assortment of mental clutter. Though David copiously penned his heart out, no amount of therapeutic letter-writing could alleviate the emotional impasse of *BoyZo* love. His completed tome ended up a mixed bag of rambling thoughts – wide of being a simple affectionate communication. Re-read the next day, the letter would almost certainly have been binned as pithy and inappropriate. But he sealed the envelope, and hence his mind, against any change.

After a microwaved meat and two veg, he relaxed in the sitting room and soaked up heat from glowing chunks of lookalike coal. Flames flickered and danced with that characteristic 'blupping' sound – and the gas softly hissed. It lulled him into wistful daydreams that gently teased out sentimental memories.

It's Never Too Late was still on the coffee table next to the settee, and David idly thumbed through it, still struggling with the logic of Eloise Goodridge's central axiom: 'Don't bemoan the failings of yesterday's yesterday, enjoy the rewards of tomorrow's tomorrow – today'.

But its by-numbers approach no longer appealed. He concluded the wisdom gleaned empirically from his recent awakening surpassed any self-improvement messages from Ms Goodridge. And *It's Never Too Late* provided a light supper for the boiler.

Wednesday came and went, and shortly after 8.30 on Thursday David was padding around in his undies, showered and shaved. He'd decided to wear the beige Eduardo Cabeleira suit with Marcos Le Monde tan shoes and a very visible tie bought on Eighth Avenue, featuring an art deco schematic of the Empire State Building. His wardrobe for the most part paled in comparison, most of it being earmarked for the Humana recycle skip.

Ninety minutes later he was heading for the bus stop. A few curtains twitched. And he said a few Hi's to people with whom he'd never got beyond 'Hi' in over fifty years. Some of the older folk in his road were parents of the kids he'd known at primary school – they all knew him. And their houses were family homes – people stayed for a lifetime. It was easy to pick out the many long-term residents. Peeling paint, original gates and front doors, milk bottles well washed, a pleasant, easy decadence.

For all his new-found bluff David felt apprehensive as Thompson's came in view. He'd last departed a nondescript, unstylish individual who'd blend into any crowd – complete with a sickliness his colleagues must have detected. Now here he was, fully refurbished mentally and physically, and dressed to kill.

He slipped in past Gwen on reception. She was on the phone but raised her eyebrows in bemused amazement, mouthing a silent 'WOW'. He managed to get close to Edith's office undetected. But the door to Wages was open and although he slunk past quickly a loud 'DAVID!' stopped him in his tracks. Celia Clarke dashed into the narrow passage, her face flushed with delight at his spectacular reincarnation.

'Gosh! David, you look fantastic – where have you been? We didn't know what had happened to you – Gosh! You look really good.'

And whilst her mouth verbalised delight, Celia's eyes busily undressed him.

'Must go – got to see Edith.'

'Will you be around at lunchtime?'

'Should be finished by one, maybe one-thirty – I'll come by and pick you up.'

Celia flashed David a smile full of disgusting promises and disappeared back into Wages.

'Come in!'

Edith was probably as surprised as Celia but she kept a professional lid on things, venturing, 'David, you're looking very well and it's good to see you again.'

He reciprocated with similar pleasantries as Edith went on, 'You have a wonderful tan, David. Have you been somewhere hot and sunny?'

It was the trigger – and his face clouded over. 'Oh, no, Edith, it was the machine.'

Her eyes narrowed quizzically. 'Machine?'

'Yes, the one they used for the treatment.'

'Oh, the treatment.' Edith knew David had been away for some unspecified treatment. 'Oh I see. So you used a sunbed as part of the treatment.'

David gave his knees a long, controlled look and then looked up at Edith. 'I'd like you to know the truth about my absence, Edith, but of course I tell you this in complete confidence.'

Now he had her full attention.

And she learned of his terminal condition – and how he'd surfed the Internet and found a small clinic in New York City that offered revolutionary treatment.

'I stayed in this small boarding house and travelled there each day. It was touch and go at one stage. My tan was due to the side effects of using this machine – some sort of stray radiation. The machine was in a lead-lined room and the staff observed me using closed-circuit television for safety.'

Edith's face was a picture of compassion. 'You poor man – what you must have endured.'

But David wasn't quite done. 'Each day I had to drink a bottle of this black oily medication – the staff called it The Brew. It made me feel so ill.'

Edith was now mentally living David's ordeal.

He smiled gently. 'But it worked, Edith – I'm completely cured.'

For a while she could only shake her head. 'It must have been terribly expensive, David — were you able to claim through your medical insurance?'

He shook his head. 'My insurer wouldn't have paid because of the experimental nature of the treatment.'

'So you paid—'

'Yes, I paid for it myself — it meant mortgaging my house but it was worth every penny.'

Edith was pensive for a few seconds. 'Forgive my being curious, David, but are you able to say roughly what your treatment cost?'

'Between you and I, Edith, nearly thirty thousand pounds?'

'Thirty thousand pounds?'

'Yes, but it was a drop in the ocean to get my life back.'

Edith was right on cue. 'Do you have the receipts?'

'Not any longer, Edith — once I was better I threw away everything that reminded me of being so ill.'

Edith thought aloud. 'Hmm — I'll talk to Emily.' And to David, 'Of course, you will be paid in full for the sick leave taken.'

It was a question he'd hesitated to broach.

'Thank you kindly, Edith — it will save me taking out another mortgage.'

She smiled sweetly. 'It's the least we can do.'

Cautiously he asked about Emily.

'Oh yes, Emily. Well, all I can really tell you is that Captain Urquart left rather suddenly. And Emily is now running everything.'

Edith stood up signalling David's departure. 'Emily's expecting you now — she's in The Captain's office.'

David made his way up to the first floor. The rooms upstairs were originally built as offices, unlike the converted workshops and storage areas on the ground floor. It was evident when Thompson's first took over the building that a strong blue-collar/white-collar demarcation had existed. Old Man Thompson took the largest office for himself. But he made it a working situation that staff could freely visit to discuss any problems or issues in fulfilling orders. It would be festooned with trial products and machine tools, sketches of new lines and all manner of paraphernalia associated with the business. For all his strict regime, Harvey Thompson never forgot that his company was made of people, not masonry and equipment.

The Captain viewed life differently. His hands remained clean whilst supervising operations from an ivory tower. And the office slowly became a shrine to his ostensibly distinguished career. There was no doubt he'd steered the company to a more contemporary image. But in recent years he'd started to cream off quite large dividends in recompense for investing his army gratuity. Now mysteriously he was off the scene.

David arrived at The Captain's office and afforded himself a wry smile at the regimental shield and polished brass nameplate – CAPTAIN MICHAEL URQUART. There was a bell-push and a green or red light would illuminate depending on The Captain's availability.

It was a spacious office with a large conference table extending down from a king-sized oak desk. In the old days the door was always open. And Harvey more often than not would be playing around with a new product. There was always a cordial greeting of 'Come in son and have a seat'.

It was a far cry from The Captain's high-ranking approach to staff.

Ringing the bell on this occasion met with a pleasant 'Do come in'.

Emily's sweet little hamster face nearly popped at David's snazzy appearance.

'David, you are looking well! – I DO like your suit. You've really benefited from having some time off.'

More than you'll ever know, mused David.

She waxed delight for a few minutes more in her rather matronly way – whilst he graciously acknowledged her compliments with a winning smile.

Delicately she broached the subject of his absence. 'I'm so glad that you've overcome your health problems – the treatment you received must have been very effective.'

David looked down as painful memories dulled his face. 'It was a long road, Emily, but I got there.'

There was no need to elaborate – healthy cross pollination between Edith and Emily was guaranteed. And besides, he needed an upbeat bias to the conversation.

'Yes, of course David, that's all that matters.'

Now Don was standing behind him. 'C'mon buddy, find something about her to compliment.'

He searched Emily's tired features, detecting nothing to be proud of. Except that her hair was possibly less grey than six months ago. And a bit more stylish from when she wore a low-maintenance bob cut. He gave it a shot.

Engaging her eyes with a sincere smile he cooed, 'Emily, pardon me for saying, but your hair is looking very pretty.'

Bingo! Flushed with pleasure she cupped the palm of her hand against her remodelled barnet – as women do.

'Oh, I'm so glad you like it, David – you think it really suits me?'

'Definitely Emily, and it makes you look so young.'

Now he was motoring, with Emily perched on the edge of her chair and fast rediscovering him.

'You know, Emily, when I was at the clinic in America—'

'America?"

'Err … yes, I had to go there for the treatment.'

'Oh, I see – I didn't realise – so sorry to interrupt you.'

'Well anyway, I met this guy who runs a large company in, err … I think it was Oregon, making a range of hair-based products for the fashion market. And would you believe it, he'd heard of Thompson Wigs!"

Emily's face was a picture.

'REALLY? That's amazing.'

'Yes – he was charming – Phil. He gave me a card but I've since lost it. And besides, I was too unwell at the time to be that interested. Needless to say I turned the job offer down.'

'Job offer?'

'Oh, err … yes, he wanted me to join him as Business Development Manager – my thirty-plus years at Thompson's really impressed him.'

'Hmm.'

It was highly thought-provoking for Emily.

'So what sort of business would you have developed?'

David was shooting from the hip and enjoying it.

'Well, Emily, it would have been about tapping into the wealth of new markets that require hair products, services or equipment.'

David could almost hear Emily's brain ticking. Thinking aloud she asked, 'Wouldn't it be rather expensive to pay someone just to develop new business when there are already sales people getting orders?'

Coming in with the punchline David replied, 'YES, of course it would, Emily. BUT, you see, the Business Development Manager is there to identify new opportunities and ensure the company evolves strategically with changing demand. Their salary is small beer compared to the additional sales revenue they generate, and it assures the company's future.'

Having regurgitated a few definitions from 'Business Development without tears', fortified with patter soaked up from Rillington business clientele, he casually switched topics.

'When did you envisage I should recommence, Emily?'

Emily's brain was still embedded in the world of BDMs. 'Oh, err ... start – err ... let me see. Well David, if it's alright with you I think Monday would be fine.'

'I assume I'll pick up where I left off?'

Emily was a little uncomfortable with that one. 'Well, David, technically ... yes. Peter Spinks has been looking after your work in the interim. Of course we didn't know how long you'd be absent for. And I have to say he's managed the role admirably.'

An uncertain future appeared to be shaping up.

'Keith Welsh in Film and Television is retiring in six months time, and we wondered if you might welcome a change.'

Film and Television were being run down due to poor demand. And David had no intention of being the tail-end Charlie on that one.

Emily waffled on about other 'options' – which he read as either an incentive for him to leave or take early retirement at sixty. But it was clear she'd never expected this smooth manifestation of David Jenner to walk through the door – it was throwing her plans into disarray.

Thoughtfully she noted, 'You know, David, you're right – you've been with Thompson's a long time ... and you know all about the business.'

With Rillington cool he purred, 'It's been my life.'

Emily's little face puckered up and she hmm'd a few times.

'David, I really would like to talk things over with some of the directors before we take any decisions.'

He nodded in quiet agreement.

'Anyway, David, we'll see you on Monday as planned.'

David got up to leave. With a smile that was truly James Bond he replied, 'I'll look forward to that, Emily – and may I say it's been wonderful to see you again.'

And Emily smiled back – as she used to, over twenty years ago.

Celia was hovering outside Wages. 'How did it go?'

David shrugged his shoulders. 'OK, I suppose – back to the grind on Monday. Anyway, where shall we go?'

'Well, the Pony and Parrot's going to be full of Thompson people.' And somewhat salaciously, she added, 'There's always the Monk's Hole – it's not too bad on a Thursday.'

In a corner of the lounge bar they sipped their respective tipples. Celia sat slumped back in a small brown leather club armchair – her large shapely legs crossed provocatively. The meat was on display and David wondered what was in the offing.

'So where have you been? We've heard all these different stories.'

David spouted pure hyperbole.

"Well, I had a medical condition that eventually needed treating. It could have been done on the NHS but the waiting list was five years. So I opted to go private and got recommended to a specialist clinic in New York. Anyway, everything's fine now – it was just a bit of a lengthy process.'

Celia's curiosity persisted. 'So, are you going to tell me what the treatment was for?'

Furtively David leaned forward. 'Promise you won't tell anybody, Celia, but it was a sex change op.'

Celia stuck her tongue out. 'OK then, what about the perma-tan?'

David nonchalantly explained, 'It was all part of the aftercare therapy.'

Not wholly convinced she concluded, 'Anyway, you look really good David.'

Inspired by Celia's large thighs, David's groin returned the compliment. 'You're looking pretty good yourself.'

Her smile deteriorated into a smirk. 'Want to hear the gossip?'

'You mean The Captain?'

She nodded.

David was more than curious. 'Sure do.'

It turned out that Emily had found texts of a highly explicit nature from 'Rikki' on his mobile phone. And after a heated showdown he'd left her and also resigned from Thompson's.

Though David sympathised with Emily, deep down he felt a thrill, as it wasn't such a bad situation in the overall scheme of things.

'So how did you find out?'

'Well, Emily came in to Thompson's very upset. And apparently she blurted everything out to Pam – you know what a gossip she is.'

'So Emily's taken over?"

'Yes – but I think she's struggling.'

'So where's The Captain?'

Shrugging, she raised her eyebrows suggestively. 'Probably shacked up with Rikki.'

After some more catch-up he got home in time for delivery of the tea chests – deposited back in the dining room by two chrome-domed hunks from Simmonds Brothers.

'Everyfing alright, Guv?'

David nodded. 'Yes, thanks.' And quipped, 'It's been a really moving experience.'

Which was greeted with a blank look, followed by a cheesy grin at the appearance of a crinkly tenner.

It was a novelty to see the five chests again – a poignant reminder of the mood four months ago. They'd been packed in a sentimental stupor, with David perceiving the contents as physical evidence of his life; treasures to be lovingly preserved for a faceless posterity. But now he had a future. And with a few exceptions these sacred artefacts had reverted to being just possessions – many on a return ticket to the loft.

The weekend was spent boning up on sufficient Business Development theory to pass Thompson scrutiny. Though it would be relatively easy – as their current business practice was a derivative of Harvey Thompson's simple home-grown formulae. And in the main this catered well in managing repeat business from a loyal customer base. It was all about cranking the sausage machine handle. Thus with little need to compete for orders, Thompson's business methods had remained somewhat parochial.

From a trading angle their Profit and Loss account appeared healthy. But for the wrong reasons. No money was being expended on advertising or promotions for new business – a major revenue cost for any successful company. In its heyday, Thompson Wigs had enjoyed perpetual motion, their reputation alone filling the order book. Now investment was needed to bring in new accounts. Amazingly the Board of Directors remained in denial on this issue – thanks to corporate arrogance that assumed repeat orders would repeat. To his credit, though The Captain had injected money and ideas into the company, his main contribution having been to stream-line the operation and introduce new lines to existing customers. But alas, he'd also wanted his pound of flesh.

However, the company offered a sound and stable financial shell for potential redevelopment. Asset-wise, they owned the building freehold and had no borrowings. Labour costs were well contained as most long-serving employees had traded job security for modest salaries. And Thompson's credit worthiness was second to none, with the company name ranking highly in the industry.

In recent years David had sensed the incipient decline in demand for traditional products – and he'd noted potential threats from cheap imports and changing trends. But any initiative on his part to act on these realisations was killed off by extreme apathy. Instead, he'd nursed dreams of a plumb pension in the event of Thompson's demise.

Now he was enjoying a total personality inversion. An intellec-tual awakening infused with strategic wisdom. And it served him well. It provided the tools to visualise Thompson's for its warts-and-all worth; to usefully recall and deploy decades of company experience that had been absorbed by his idle subconscious. Taking up the theme of 'give me solutions not problems' David extended the breadth of his thinking to innovative ideas for Thomson's to trial. It was a stimu-lating exercise. And his brain cells throbbed to the beat of complex harmonics – creating an imagination more fertile than a newly pubes-cent maiden's womb.

He'd originally planned a return to Thompson's sufficiently versed to talk his way up a cog or two in the organisation. But by Sunday night a crusade to lead the stodgy outfit to glorious new horizons had been crafted. Getting Emily on board was the first hurdle. A few suitable cracks in her professional veneer had appeared on Thursday. They just needed prising open a little to get at the simple soul who lurked within. With a sly grin, David pondered whether he could sweeten Emily.

With a bag of Maltesers.

27

The Wind of Change

It was the same drill. Edith first – then another audience with Emily in her regimental suite. David was resplendent in a grey double-breasted number, another of his snappy suits from Giovani's. Courtesy The Rillington. It harmonised with his tan, maintained with a sun lamp from Boots. Edith didn't say anything, but she rather obviously sucked in the detail. After all, his appearance was so 'non-Thompson'.

Emily was more on the surface, her smiley face bobbing around like a nodding dog.

'You're looking very smart today, David – gosh! How many suits do you have?'

Three didn't seem such a big deal.

Whilst counting an imaginary collection of suits on his fingers he replied coyly, 'Oh, a few.'

Emily popped off a few mechanical pleasantries. Whilst David slid back smooth responses. Today he was treated to tea and biscuits from the managerial silver service trolley. Hopefully a good omen.

Contemplating her clasped hands pensively for three or four seconds, Emily finally looked up – her neutral expression giving nothing away.

'Over the weekend I spoke with our directors.'

For what seemed an eternity, Emily looked away at an invisible central vanishing point.

Then came Part 2. 'And we feel we'd like to listen to your ideas on generating new business with a view to possibly implementing them.'

David managed to suppress any muscular inflection that might blow his cover. But within, everything fell into a limp, sweat-soaked heap of relief.

His reply was paced to the slow tick of a cerebral metronome. 'Emily, it will be a pleasure to cooperate with you on this exciting initiative. And may I say that I believe a very bright future exists for Thompson Wigs.' With a gentle, wistful smile he added, 'I know your father would have been proud at what you're wanting to achieve.'

Emily assumed the texture of pink Plasticine. And David felt a pang of unease that he'd so easily manipulated her. It was a welcome reality check and he vowed to exploit the burgeoning opportunities with her interests very much at heart in future.

They discussed how and when David would present his ideas and then turned to the domestics.

'Now David, I though for the time being you could use Arthur Mackendrick's old office.'

Arthur had retired the previous year as the Chief Buyer. With the ease of on-line procurement his role was deemed redundant. It was a smaller office for David, but at least sported a window. And importantly it was upstairs on mahogany row. He was to present to the directors a week hence – long enough to rationalise his entrepreneurial thoughts and translate them into business speak.

For several hours David tinkered around getting the office sorted. A little apprehensive he realised that sooner or later he'd need to bite the bullet and get 'seen' by the rest of the crew. By 12.00, the time seemed right and he took a slow hike to the blue-collar loos. Over and over the 'official story' got aired. Nash was right back on form. Those delicious Moroccan eyes giving him a full body search. But she was now pregnant. Father unknown. Vera ribbed him mercilessly, pinching his cheeks and backside.

'David Jenner, you really are a flashy bugger!'

Frank Weller failed to show with the passing trade. Jack Waterfield claimed he was in and David moved on to Dispatch.

The big man grabbed David in a brotherly bear hug. It was an emotional reunion with damp eyes.

'Davy, where y' bin? We was so worried.'

There were no punches pulled. 'It's a long story, Frank.'

Surrounded by ogling packers, it was neither the time nor the place.

'Locomotive, one o'clock?'

'See you there, Frank.'

In the pub they sat quietly servicing their pints for a moment.

'We was wonderin' what 'ad happened to y', Davy. There was all sorts of stories goin' around. I fort y' might 'ave got in touch.'

David played around with the condensation on his glass before explaining. 'Well, the fact is, Frank, I was seriously ill. But no one here knows the real truth.'

He winked knowingly at David.

'Gotcha, mate.'

Whatever careless words got spilled to Frank, they'd never see the light of day again. And for twenty minutes or so he filled in with the convoluted facts of his absence.

'You know, it must all sound rather bizarre, but somehow I'm better off for the experience. I didn't realise what an aimless individual I'd become – just wish I'd done more with my life.'

Frank shook his head slowly and grinned. 'Don't punish y'self, mate, you're a decent geezer. An' I'm just relieved it's the same ol' Davy under that posh whistle.'

Frank's easy beer, fags and football ethos never failed to suck David's personal misgivings into a black hole.

'Nice of you to say, Frank. I suppose it is the same old me. I thought I'd changed, but really I've just wised up to myself.'

He waxed philosophic for a while longer. And Frank listened patiently, slumped in his chair like a partially deflated bouncy castle. When David finally surfaced for air, big boy quickly took his cue. 'Well, there y' go, bruv! Nuvver pint?'

Old times kicked in and Frank kept his pal in stitches with an irreverent account of The Captain and Rikki, punctuated by the occasional raucous fart. A couple or two Thompsonites stopped by to marvel at David's appearance, ask the same questions – and be regaled with the same spiel, now polished to perfection.

Back at his desk, and over the hump of reacquaintance, David cracked on with the master plan. Emily popped by several times to 'See how you're getting on'. Now all smiles she was clearly relieved another hand was steadying the tiller. Whilst David, having shot his bolt, knew he'd need to meet her expectations. But it was a challenge and his pulse quickened at the creative possibilities. During the next few days he viewed the company through fresh eyes: accommodation, floor space, services, staff skills, equipment. He arrived early, left late –

packed in additional hours at the kitchen table. By Friday the magic spell was taking shape in the form of a graphic presentation. He was on a serious roll – a man possessed.

On Sunday, with the last bells and whistles installed, David trialled his delivery – to Natalia. Who smiled with sweet approval.

There were six directors on the board – all heavyweights in running medium-sized organisations. And all from diverse commercial backgrounds. In the early days the Old Man used to drink at the Astorian Club in Jermyn Street. It became a popular venue for business-to-business socialising. And over time Harvey and his drinking buddies started to coalesce into a fraternity of like-minded businessmen. They recognized the value in pooling their varied skills and resources. With no conflicts of interest it worked superbly and the Astorian became their board room surgery. They were truly a league of gentlemen.

But then something happened that forged an incredibly enduring bond. Cecil Robinson mentioned he was looking for directors, and Archie Lancaster jokingly suggested, 'You know, chaps, we should all be directors on each other's boards.'

There was a deathly hush as the profound wisdom of Archie's jest sank in. And with not a word spoken it became law. From that moment on they closed ranks and stood by each other with unfaltering loyalty.

The green light came on and gingerly David entered The Captain's office. Presiding at the desk was Emily, the tips of her praying hands propping up her pointy chin – head cocked to one side with a twee smile.

She tinkled a welcome. 'Hello David – thanks for joining us.'

Six heads turned to observe David's entrance.

There was Reg Frith, still a ladies' man at eighty-two. Dogtooth suit, silk Beardsley tie and handkerchief, handlebar moustache and dyed brown hair. For many years specialising in performance sports car sales from a showroom on the Great West Road at Brentford. He found fame getting his rocks off with a blonde astride him whilst doing a hundred and fifty in an AC Cobra round Brands Hatch one night after a drunken race celebration. His son from that liaison now ran the business.

James Bowman – small, dapper, sallow features, bald, morning suite, bow tie. Made a fortune selling aluminium rivets to the aircraft industry. Wisely converted to adhesives to match the evolving needs of aerospace manufacturing. Still an active director on various boards, though now enjoying retirement with his sixth wife at their Hendon home.

Les Hummerstone – portly, jovial, red faced, very obvious thick combover. Sports coat, immaculate grey flannels. Red suspenders holding up his socks frequently visible. Les owned a string of wine merchants throughout South London. Though recently bought out by a conglomerate, he remained a major shareholder. On his third liver transplant.

Good old Archie Lancaster, still going strong at eighty-eight. Round animated face, bright mischievous eyes, bald dome save for an incorrigible tuft of hair towards the front. Glasses like twin TV screens, grey pinstripe, regimental tie, shoes shinier than black patent leather. Did moderately well selling on bankrupt stock. Switched to buying scrapped buses and rolling stock. Made his money by hoarding the items for a few years and then selling to nostalgia junkies world-wide. Had done well out of Dr Beeching's closure of the branch lines in 1962. Still had extensive stock 'maturing' in sheds, sidings, warehouses and fields. Borrowed heavily to begin with – now seriously cash rich.

Joan Robinson, Cecil's widow – very large, grey-blue hair, perceptive eyes, long-skirted black business suit, a warm charismatic lady with razor-sharp judgement. Cecil and Joan had run a printing works in Woolwich, their main revenue coming from stationary and knocking out some of the lesser rags and journals. But with Desktop Publishing systems available to the masses, demand had dropped. However, Joan spotted the growing trend for printing on tee shirts and sporting merchandise. Sadly Cecil was taken by emphysema as they retooled but Joan successfully completed the transition.

Finally there was Keith Somersby – eighty going on thirty. Jeans, pink trainers, tee shirt, black double breasted jacket. Long brown hair, equine face, skin like distressed leather. Plus all the usual jewellery. He'd started off selling dirty mags on a stand in Soho and then gradu-ated to a clip joint in Wardour Street. One became three. And he eventually sold up, using the dodgy proceeds to buy a disused flea pit in North London. Six months later it reopened as a highly successful dinner club with a busty chorus line-up. Keith took on directors to keep a respectable spin on the joint. In return he was good for advice when colleagues stumbled into the foggy zone that separates legal from illicit.

After the hellos David got alongside the overhead projector. To get a few positively charged ions buzzing around he briefly aired the Thompson Wigs success story. Subtly his pitch curved round to changing demand, cheap imports, smaller client budgets – they might want a Rolls, but could only afford a Mini. Pie charts, bar charts and stats galore were flashed in front of his audience. And he boldly displayed trends that forecast a trading loss within six months – if no action were taken.

So far, so good. David's material was well researched, and lucidly presented. It was punchy, concise and honest – negative facts were portrayed in a positive light. And clearly it had grabbed the directors' full attention, their facial expressions in synch with the changing content. At the back of the class was Emily, who viewed proceedings through her designer horn-rimmed specs, nodding astutely in the right places.

But at this stage, David had little more than stated fact. Now it was time to promote the theme of high overheads and a worn-out tradition. Wisely, he ramped up gently, alluding to poorly utilised or wasted space, labour-intensive methods, old-fashioned materials, creaking machinery. And in-house services that could be more cheaply outsourced. It was all about a company ripe for redevelopment.

His audience prepped for cultural change, David got down to the nitty-gritty. Apart from theatrical wigs Thompson's had concentrated on making up the shortfall of natural hair – products that at best were functional.

With confidence and panache he bridged across to the future vision. Hair had never been more fashionable than at present. It had been the lifeblood of Thompson's for nearly fifty years and history was poised to repeat. But now they'd tap into the lucrative world of hair fashion products – with a difference. Rather than vie with established competition on a like-for-like basis, they'd develop their own synthetic hair fibres, materials, attachment methods, equipment, techniques – and a unique range of styling options.

From being silently plugged in to David's every word, the directors became reactive. Joan Robinson cast him an approving smile and genuflected with her chin. She was on board – heavyweight support at that. Les Hummerstone was busy scribbling. Keith Somersby was solemnly nodding – the word 'fashion' had struck a chord. Reg Frith's left leg was all a frantic dither. And Archie Lancaster's glasses were steamed up.

David was poised to expand his ideas but question time broke its waters early. Having anticipated most of the key hot potatoes, he fed back convincingly. Raising money was an easy one. In fact the company should have re-invested its collateral a long time ago in a programme of continuous improvement instead of accruing assets. Reg Frith got hung up on new fashions – how could they compete with top designers? Simple. A study of hair adornment within tribal communities around the globe would provide inspiration.

And wouldn't it be a reinvented wheel to develop fibres when proprietary materials were available? It was a chorused question, with David laying in wait. He expounded the idea that developing new materials with unique properties and qualities would be the key to getting a significant marketing edge. From inception, Thompson's had run a small Research and Development function managed by Herbert Penningfeather – 'Hairbert' to his friends. With the proliferation of off-the-shelf materials available, R & D was due to be phased out. But in his idle moments Hairbert had developed experimental fibres, seen at the time as little more than novel. And it was this boxful of dusty bobbins and whatever else lurked in his sinewy imagination that held the answer. R & D would rise out of the ashes to be a leading light. And Hairbert could once more wash, style and polish his goatee in readiness for the new challenge.

Temporarily satiated the directors slipped back into repose and David added the finishing touches. The large wig Steam and Press workshop would be converted into a salon to showcase new products and styles. Paid models would submit to experimental processes. There would be an observation gallery – a coffee shop. Buyers would be entertained in a new corporate suite. A massive picture window would broadcast to the outside world. And Reception would be beautifully remodelled. A tasteful neon sign would grace the entrance.

But one last detail remained – small but sticky.

The name – Thompson Wigs; for nearly half a century synonymous with quality products and services, it would no more suit the hip new image than a ballerina wearing clogs. Tactfully, David introduced the idea of changing the company name to give a contemporary look and feel.

'I've agonised long and hard about dropping the traditional name, but I truly believe that it is paramount to a successful change in direction.'

He drew a flip chart up to the table.

'I have a suggestion – and it is only a suggestion; I've taken the word "hair" and the Italian for "love" and created a possible trading name, together with a brief caption. I hope you might like it.'

With an artistic flick of the wrist, David revealed the suggested name.

TressAmorë – The Hair you'll L♥ve©

Fourteen eyeballs locked on to the target. And the proverbial pin could be heard. For a few seconds seven pairs of lips silently mouthed the words. Archie was the first to verbalise his thoughts. 'You know chaps, I rather like it.'

Joan concurred. 'I agree, the name has a lovely ring to it.'

James Bowman was still getting comfortable with the idea. Deep down he was still a rivet man and struggled with artistic judgements. 'It could have some merits.'

Keith Somersby was at the other end of the spectrum. 'Bleedin' brilliant if you ask me.' And turning to David he asked, 'Mr Jenner, you've been with this outfit for quite a while now?'

'Yes Mr Somersby, nearly thirty-five years.'

'So how come we've not heard from you before?'

David quickly cycled through the possible sentiments, and chose humility.

'Well, Mr Somersby the company has done well to date and I didn't like to interfere.'

'Interfere! You can come and interfere with my business anytime you like – well done, mate.'

Though glowing with pride at David's creative presentation, Emily had one small reservation.

'Err, David, if we adopted your ideas, what would happen to the company name?'

Sensitivity to rebadging was understandable. Though she had nothing to fear if David's assurances had any credence.

'Thompson Wigs Limited will remain as the holding company and TressAmorë will become a new trading division.'

Now Don Rodriguez was tapping David on the shoulder.

'OK buddy, time to go — leave 'em hungry.'

David thanked his audience and slipped away to the sound of appreciation.

Slumped at his desk, he felt pleasantly limp, but with energy to spare. Intuitively he knew the presentation had gone well — it was quite a defining moment in his life.

Celia appeared like a female genie. And draping herself across the desk like old times enquired, 'How did it go?'

Noting her large thighs carelessly splayed with great precision, his answer got queued behind a five-second fantasy that lasted fifteen minutes.

He pushed Celia roughly down onto the desk and they hammered away until the creaking structure gave up and they crashed to the ground amid a shower of wooden debris, laughing and screaming with delight.

But it was an old chestnut and David knew if he stoked the fire, he'd never be able to face the mantelpiece after — though his Marks and Sparks Y-fronts egged him on. It was a seminal moment that usually got dispatched by hand.

'Oh, err ... fine, thanks.'

'I suppose you're teacher's pet now?'

Seeking inspiration from the ceiling, he finally conceded to being temporarily in vogue.

They headed for the Pony and Parrot, scooping up Frank and Pete on the way. Celia had patently planned a one to one, but David just wanted to slurp a pint in easy company.

Mid-afternoon Emily asked him to stop by.

She was still enraptured by his smooth delivery, though winning her over had only achieved first base.

'The board expressed great interest in what they heard today, but you never quite know what they really think. We've agreed to meet in a week's time to make a decision.'

David smiled philosophically.

She went on to cite a number of instances where the board had enthused over ideas but lacked the balls to proceed. To David it spoke volumes about why the company was heading for free fall.

With girlish sweetness she professed, 'But I think your ideas are wonderful, David, and if it were up to me I'd proceed straight away. Anyway, I'm seeing our Financial Controller later today to find how we stand in terms of raising capital.' Assuming a slightly naughty but very endearing smile, she added, 'I'm going to work on Joan Robinson – she believes your ideas would be very successful. Joan's a real go-getter. Hopefully I'll get her support in convincing the others.'

It went quiet – and Emily peeked at him coyly whilst toying with a biro.

'Gosh David, I didn't realise what hidden talents you had.'

'Well, you know what they say, Emily,' he announced with a cheeky grin, 'still waters run deep.'

It amused Emily, but invoked a more personal note than he'd intended. And after fiddling with her biro some more she caught him off balance. 'So, David, you think the way I do my hair is nice?'

There was a price to keeping Emily sweet and he knew he'd have to cough up at some stage. But not now. And his response was calculated to counter any amorous intent with an equal and opposite force. But alas the words fell out clumsily and uncensored – like the nightmare occurrence of accidentally sending an explosive email to someone, knowing it couldn't be retracted.

'Yes Emily, it really suits you – does your husband like it?'

It was a cruel, cold slap in the face, and David waited, horrified, for his callous reply to annihilate Emily's radiance.

And he was almost equally horrified when she retained total composure. Instead, squirming around in her chair to achieve a more relaxed and perhaps slightly artistic pose.

Slowly and deliberately she spelled it out for him. 'Well, David, the fact is, what my husband thinks is no longer of any consequence.'

David tried a nonchalant but rather unconvincing 'Oh, I see.'

Emily revisited the biro; and without raising her head, slowly looked up at him with what could only be described as a seductive smile.

'David?'

There was a husky edge to her voice that ruffled his nerve endings.

'Yes ...?'

'Do you remember the first time we went to the pictures?'

Instinctively David attempted to blur history.

'Oh, err ... yes – let me see, it was *Doctor Zivago*.'

"NO David, it was *Tootsie*.'

This wasn't part of the plan. He'd unwittingly been playing around with a hand grenade and the safety pin had just dropped out. Where was Don when he needed him?

With an artificial smile he 'remembered'. 'Ah yes, of course.' And lightly smacking the table with his right palm he got up to go, announcing in a matter of fact way that, 'Anyway, I'll have a fully costed proposal ready for Friday.'

Emily saw David to the door and he left briskly, avoiding any eye contact; and back on seat contemplated the unexpected force majeure. He theorised that some trapped sentimentality had stirred Emily's emotions as it vented to the atmosphere. Though deep down he sensed worse would come before better. And he'd learned not to underestimate the tenacity of an amorous female. Men considered themselves hunters, but women were the true predators.

From the safety of his office David eventually managed down his apprehension and pigeon-holed Emily as a situation to be contained.

And he joined the swirling masses to Marylebone Station.

28

Momentum and Emotions

At a slow canter the Hammersmith and City line bumped and ground along the undulating track. A few days earlier the clocks had gone forward and travelling home in daylight was still a novelty. Resplendent in his Gabrielle Valentini dark-blue pinstripe David felt good. Today had been his best day ever at Thompson Wigs. Even if his proposal was not adopted in entirety, there was every likelihood of his playing a major role in turning around the company's fortunes. And besides, he was well on the way to ascending the organisational strata.

David's carriage comprised the usual assortment of human life, none of which exhibited body language that invited spontaneous conversation. He missed the easy chit chat with strangers that came so naturally in Manhattan. And if he did venture a 'Hi' it got reciprocated with suspicion.

From Hammersmith he walked. Though still fresh the penetrating cold had gone. It was seasonally reminiscent of the chilly early October day when terminal news had redefined his life. Stopping on Hammersmith Bridge he took in the same upstream vista so poignantly surveyed six months ago. On this occasion it was enjoyed with a warm sentimentality. And David fondly recalled encountering his primary school pals on the tow path.

On his flying visit when the air was warm and sweet.

Arriving home as dark descended Victor and he bid each other silent hellos. Within minutes Lydia was at the door clutching a small packet. It was from The Rillington. With a racing heart and trembling hands he got to the contents, only to find it to be two pairs of Gino Bertolini jockey briefs beautifully laundered. And accompanied by a sweet note from Tania in Housekeeping.

Since returning David had tried to exercise a realistic expectation of seeing Natalia again. Though slowly she was reverting to being almost as mythical as when he frantically searched Radio City Music Hall for some vestigial evidence she existed in body or spirit. Emotional sores festered again and he spent the evening in a dismal *BoyZo* fug.

But he managed to bury his aching heart under the mountain of effort needed in producing the costed proposal for Monday hence. Presenting an idea was one thing. Making it work on paper was something else. For the directors to sanction his proposal it needed to demonstrate a by-numbers approach that left no question marks around implementation. It was another week of long hours and sessions on the kitchen table. He avoided Emily as much as possible – but subtly. Though the more intensely he worked the greater her fascination in him became.

Now she smiled at him differently. A designing smile. And whilst most of his creativity went into the task in hand, a small residue worked relentlessly on the means of keeping Emily in her box. He felt a certain vulnerability whilst the cake was in the making. Rather like a delicate bridge made of many spars and struts. And which assumes maximum strength only when the last strut is fastened in place. Metaphorically the last strut would be board agreement to proceed and a commission for David. At full strength he'd no longer need to appease Emily.

Rumours of impending change were circulating – mainly insti-gated by Vera who quietly sniffed around at meetings with her teapot. Though she usually got it wrong. There was to be a takeover. Thompson's was in receivership. Redundancies were on the horizon. A switch to making erotic underwear was in hand – they were to compete with Ann Summers.

Celia tried to pump David – to no avail. But she didn't miss a trick when it came to Emily's extra-curricular interest in him. And Celia was becoming a little hostile, regularly brushing her full curves against David in unspoken communication; on one occasion pinning him up against the wall by the Coca Cola machine with her right thigh firmly thrust between his legs.

'So, little Emily's got the hots for you, has she?'

It was pitched as a playful taunt, though her knuckles were white from grasping David's lapels. Imprisoned behind her impressive bosom and fearing for his nuts, he'd sweetly talked her out of the tree.

To boot, a subtle change in Emily's dress code was in the making. Tights had been abandoned. Her heels were a little higher – skirts a little shorter, lips a little redder. And more than a hint of cleavage was on the way. Half of David – the top half – was quite appalled at the emerging vamp. But the bottom half welcomed each incremental departure from decency. Now the stuff of fantasies, Emily was in danger of a virtual boning on The Captain's table.

Over the weekend David sorted out his personal transport as a lack of wheels was localising his activities. He trekked over to a trade car supermarket that flogged ex-fleet vehicles and came away with a high-mileage Ford Mondeo. It was cheap, but better than the rusty Ford Escort junked four months ago.

On Monday the three-suit rota stopped on the beige Eduardo Cabeleira kit. By 10.30 he was waiting apprehensively to be summoned before the board. Nervous sweat had struck earlier – fortuitously quelled with a squirt of Celia's nether region spray. And it was nearly lunchtime before the phone warbled. In and out in ten minutes, his proposal was briefly tabled and added into the pot.

Now it was a serious waiting game – on call with little to do and nowhere to go. Vera kindly rustled up coffee and a roll – and the usual ribbing about his appearance. And the afternoon dragged by, punctuated by regular loo trips to break the deafening monotony. By 4.00 every crack in the ceiling and walls had been memorised. And by 5.00 low blood sugar was inducing drowsiness. Shortly after, the internal telephone brought a rude awakening.

Whatever the decision, it was hard wrought. Jackets were off, ties slackened and the smell of human endeavour hung around. Clearly the board was relieved at having decided which way to jump. Though there were no clues. And if the overall mood appeared positive to an observer, it signified only that the right decision had been made. It was a hard-nosed process concerned only with serving the best interests of the company. And David had philosophically accepted that the right decision in the board's eyes might well be to simply do nothing.

Emily looked exhausted, but managed a weak smile and after

getting some inspiration from her clasped hands delivered the verdict.

'Well, David, we've discussed your proposal in great depth and I'm pleased to tell you that we have voted in favour of implementing everything you've put forward.'

The directors nodded in solemn assent. It was a moment of intense inner elation for David and one by one the board gave assurances of their confidence in his ability to deliver, pledging also their support. And for his part he eloquently thanked them and vowed to meet all their expectations.

Timescales would be aggressive – just three months to turn things around. 'TressAmorë' would be trademarked ASAP and incorporated as a business name.

There was a parting shot from Emily.

'One more thing, David, the board has decided to create a new role – 'Business Development Manager' – and we'd like you to assume this role with the proviso that it will become your permanent title on the successful introduction of TressAmorë.'

It was the icing on the cake. Post final thanks and assurances and David took his leave.

Pleasantly wearied once again, he shut up shop and trundled downstairs. Celia suddenly appeared as he passed Wages. With hands clasped behind her back she slumped up against the door post provocatively.

'Long meeting, David?'

It was meaningless patter, since her 40-double-D cup was doing all the talking. But for the sake of keeping his three-piece suite intact David kept objective.

'Err ... not really, Celia, I was only on for a few minutes – but had to wait my turn.'

His words fell on deaf ears. Slowly and deliberately Celia slipped her right foot from its shoe and stroked her pointed toe up the inside of David's calf.

'Coming in for a chat?'

They'd teased each other before – playfully enacting the theatrical moves of erotica. It was a game. But the rules appeared to be changing.

Though he burned for a detached encounter of the flesh there was no mileage with Celia. They were a horrible miss-match – he frustrated, she fixated. He started to bluster on about needing to get away but got cut short.

'Oh, it's ALRIGHT, David, you'll be quite safe.'

Reluctantly he ventured into the small room and defensively glued himself into a visitor's chair. Whilst Celia sat on the front of her desk, legs wide apart.

'When are we going to know what's happening?'

'Well, I think Emily's going to make an announcement soon.'

They shadow-boxed for a while with Celia getting none the wiser.

Outside, heavy footsteps on creaking wooden stair treads signified the board's departure. Noisily the gaggle made its way past the slightly ajar office door. Five minutes later a lighter step descended the stairs. It was Emily. Her approaching footsteps were barely audible – almost as if she were tiptoeing. Subtly David monitored the slender gap between the hinged side of the door and the door post. Light from the corridor gave the appearance of a thin white vertical line. Silently someone passed across, blocking the light momentarily. And through the narrow aperture he saw something that glinted. It was an eye! With equal stealth the voyeur moved on. David struggled with the notion of Emily having a sly peep through the crack. But deep down he knew it was her – a chilling indictment of her current state of mind.

Sweetly bidding Celia goodnight and resisting an invitation to regroup at the Monk's Hole, he struck out for Marylebone Station.

The more he dwelled on the 'eye', the more it spooked him, overshadowing the boardroom success feel-good.

Meeting with Emily the next day was an uneasy experience. Had her eye seen his eye looking at her eye? Or was she looking at Celia? Whatever the scenario her interest was keener than ever. Normally primly posed in her executive chair, Emily was today slumped back, side on to the table – legs stylishly crossed.

'We did well yesterday, David, didn't we?'

The 'we' grated a little, but he graciously went with the flow.

At twelve midday the entire cast would be summoned to the refectory for a full debrief. Emily would give an intro and David would infill the detail.

There were the usual questions – job security being high on the list as expected. David gave convincing assurances, though he knew some of the older lags would never make the cultural transition. But he took comfort knowing that in the rundown of traditional manufacture, redundancies and retirements would maintain the balance of nature.

Jack Waterfield struggled valiantly to air his concerns but only succeeded in making some strange farting sounds as he vainly attempted to break the seal of his thin lips.

Nash asked about voluntary redundancy. It suited her to leave as, having chosen a likely 'dad' for her unborn child, she was off to marry into a life of luxury, ever hoping there'd be no DNA test.

A few of the staff were indifferent. And out of that group one or two would be perfectly happy as long as they could ogle the Page Three tits during their tea break.

On all fronts David creatively allayed fears and insecurities, skilfully drawing on his apprenticeship at the Rillington Academy of Cool.

Towards lunchtime Edith came round. She looked different – delightfully different. And it suddenly dawned on him that she wasn't wearing glasses. Or stockings. Her shoes were more strappy than usual. And her M & S fitted grey business skirt was a tad shorter. A little of Emily appeared to have rubbed off.

Teasingly David noted, 'Edith, I don't think I've ever seen you without your glasses.'

She smiled coyly, for a while stepping out of formality. And sinking gracefully into one of the tubular steel visitors' chairs told him, 'I'm trying out some contact lenses, and it's all a new experience for me.'

David realised he'd always looked at Edith through a mental filter. She was schoolmarmish Edith Rogers with the specs in Personnel. Now he saw her for the first time – and was enchanted.

'Edith, you look really good.'

She laughed. 'Thanks David, I wish I had tried contacts years ago.'

And, mused David, you should have tried short skirts and bare legs years ago.

Then it was back to business.

'Emily discussed the circumstances of your illness with the directors. They all agreed that given your long service and value as an employee they'd like to see Thompson's making a contribution to your treatment costs.'

A few quid wouldn't go amiss. His undrawn sick pay had helped get re-established but the house was still a little spartan. And keeping things sartorial had its price.

'That's great, Edith, how much wi—'

'Emily will tell you the exact figure – can you see her sometime between two and two-thirty?'

All done and dusted she headed for the door. Turning the handle to exit she looked back and gave him a cheeky wink. David pondered, with bemusement, what the real Edith Rogers was like when she'd showered off the dust and grime from a day at Thompson's. And just as she'd started to tease him in a pink baby doll nightie and 4-inch stilettos the internal phone rang.

'It's Frank, Davy. A few of us is goin' darn the Parrot at twelve firty – see y' there?'

'OK Frank.'

By the time David arrived, Frank and his cronies from Dispatch had got the beers in. And two tables had been pushed together to accommodate the drip feed of Thompson bods; Phil Appleby from Production, Pam Brewar from Finance, Ajit Patel and Rodney Peppercorn from Steam and Press, Jenny Murgatroid from Design and Harry Briginshaw from Goods Inwards – plus Celia. Then Pete Spiller arrived with Joan. Now permanently off the booze she looked pale and vulnerable, though more like her old self – curvy, busty, blonde, gold 4-inch sling-back mules. And still oozing the 'je ne sais quoi' that attracted the wrong sort of bees to the right honeypot.

A little later 'Hairbert' ambled in. To the uninitiated he was the bald bof with the dickie bow working in R & D. But his sparkling wit made him a must at Thompson socials.

The conversation started and ended with TressAmorë; it was an extension of the morning's briefing – plus humour. David was in the hot seat fielding questions with smooth abandon – the focal point of an arc of eager faces.

Poe faced, Frank asked, 'So, this retraining fing, Davy, what will I be trained as?'

Assuming a serious demeanour David explained, 'Well, Frank,

your skills haven't gone unnoticed and you're to become a hair stylist.'

'AN 'AIR STYLIST?'

'Yes,' purred David. 'And you'll need to wear pink Lycra cycling pants and have your hair dyed yellow.'

The penny dropped.

Frank slurped his beer with relief. 'I'll stick to packing, mate.'

Jenny piped up – dark, pretty, slim, late forties, red toenails – fabulous butt. 'Right, David, what about me?'

He spent a few seconds in mock contemplation and chin stroking. 'OK Jen, you're going to stand in the salon window and model the new TressAmorë collections. TOPLESS!'

As David progressively lowered the tone, so the laughter got bawdier.

Smugly Celia cooed, 'What do you have in mind for me David?'

"Ah, Celia, special retraining for you. You'll be working in the coffee shop serving coffee and crumpet.' And with a smirk he added, 'Only you're going to be the crumpet.'

It got a hoot from everyone except Celia, who managed only a wry smile.

Hairbert burst into life. 'What about me, old chap?'

'Hairbie, you're going to be a sandwich man and walk up and down in front of Thompson's advertising TressAmorë products. And you'll wear a hair design that explodes every ten minutes and releases a cloud of confetti – just to get people's attention.'

'Hmm.' Hairbert nodded approvingly, and with a wicked grin announced, 'I'll get on to that one right away.'

So the banter continued, with David lording it as the grand patriarch to his close-knit bunch of workmates – their acquaintance measurable in decades. Whatever status or position separated them within Thompson's the humble Pony and Parrot engendered a classless society.

Back at base David pushed the button and got green. Emily was enthroned as before. She seemed a little incoherent, though there was no mistaking the sexual innuendo of her body language.

'I've persuaded the directors to reimburse part of your medical expenses – we can claim it back from our insurer.'

Still none the wiser as to the amount David thanked her,

delicately enquiring, 'How much were you thinking of, Emily?'

She leaned forward on the table, folded arms creating a suggestive vignette around her bust – which seemed to have acquired pneumatic qualities since his hands-on experience of twenty years earlier.

'How does ten thousand pounds sound to you?'

He humoured her. 'Sounds great, Emily, but what's the real figure?'

Laughing, she flopped back into her chair, crossed her legs, allowing her skirt to carelessly ride up.

'Just told you, David.'

'You mean—'

'YES.'

Subliminally, a flashy set of wheels zoomed past.

'Thanks very much, Emily.'

Ten grand seemed an excessive unsolicited contribution towards his 'treatment'. Two weeks ago it might have amounted to a small token payment. Upping it to the big bucks was a subtle thanks in advance for commercial leadership. With an underlying expectation that he'd deliver.

Edith had instigated the windfall. But he knew for sure Emily would want her personal pay day out of it – currency to be advised.

As David went to leave Emily leapt up and quickly moved ahead, thrusting her arched back against the door, and seductively announcing, 'If you want the money, David, you'll have to kiss me.'

Her breath stank of booze unspecified, and metaphorically, another thigh was jammed up against his goolies. There didn't seem much latitude for making a break. Besides, Emily was spoiling for some physical rumpy-pumpy. He decided on a respectable peck on the cheek. And, stepping forward to pay his dues, stumbled and clumsily fell against her. Their faces collided with a dull thud and Emily yelped, instinctively clutching her bruised mouth.

Beholding her bloodstained fingers she screamed, 'You've cut my lip! You BASTARD, David!'

Mortified, he searched for befitting words of apology. But as the first garbled syllable emerged Emily lunged forward, clamping her hungry, wet, bloodied lips over his, and he felt her small delicate tongue search into his mouth. Instinctively pulling away he failed to break the connection, his neck grasped by hooked fingers – nails dug in like barbs. Release finally came. And Emily sidled away from the door sporting a jubilant smile. With a hastily muttered 'Excuse me' David slipped away before things got any messier.

Edith passed him in the corridor and giggled. Catching his arm she lightly touched the side of his mouth.

'Better check yourself in the mirror, David.'

From the safety of the executive loos he quietly admired his battle scars – an interesting combination of blood and lipstick. Far from being rattled the idea of rough handling by an amorous female gave a buzz. She was surprisingly strong – and firm and wholesome. And she smelled good – the sort of smell exuded by women whose brain cells are on heat. In the days of *Tootsie* Emily was mousy and domestic – demure and docile. And when he'd kissed her she'd pucker up her lips like a cat's sphincter. Now there was a tiger in the tank. David wondered if The Captain had provided her with an exotic sexual awakening. He envisioned Emily submissively cowering on the bed clad only in her husband's regimental jacket whilst he stood over her in just his cap, menacingly brandishing a riding crop.

But he quickly binned the notion. More likely Emily had spent twenty years gagging for a good sorting out. He could just imagine The Captain's by number's approach.

'Right, my dear – foreplay at twenty hundred hours, penetration at twenty hundred plus sixty seconds – climax at twenty hundred plus one hundred and twenty seconds.'

'Any questions?'

Grinning, he cleaned up, marvelling at life's rich tapestry. Though he wondered the means of maintaining a working equilibrium with Emily. It was akin to the earth's journey around the sun. Increase the separation and another Ice Age sets in. Get too close and the planet becomes a glowing meteor. Now free of the warpaint David admired himself in the bronze-tinted mirror. Still partaking of the ultra-violet rays his tan appeared almost continental. And he wondered how he'd ever managed without the Rillington makeover.

As the afternoon wore on he got to grips with the vast job in hand. But his concentration faltered. Not through any anxiety – more on account of his brain, in background, brokering a solution to keep the tiger at bay. Frank, bless him, agreed to lend an ear over a quick half in the Locomotive at 5.00.

Pan faced he considered David's plight.

'Err ... well, mate, I fink the best fing to do is tell 'er y' got the pox.'

David dissolved in fits. He'd not really expected a solution from Frank who served best as a king-sized sounding board.

Another suggestion was filtering through Frank's porous grey matter. 'Tell y' what, Davy, I could fix you up wiv' a blonde and you could be seen snoggin' 'er outside Thompson's.'

They laughed – but on a serious note it did seem to have some merits. Though flouting another woman in Emily's face was probably a recipe for disaster. Discreetly hinting that there was someone else would be better. But then, there *was* someone else. And that small glimmer of hope kept David's mind closed to any other emotional attachment.

29

On and Up

The journey home separated day and evening shifts, David's kitchen now a makeshift office. It was a warm, inviting family room incorporating hallmark Edwardian spaciousness and design; built-in cupboards and sideboard, large pantry, high ceiling and a hearth that would accommodate an inglenook fireplace.

Evidence of family life lay ingrained in the kitchen table's seasoned oak timbers; circular marks left by over-hot plates, scratches and cuts from building Meccano and balsawood models, discolouration from solvents and adhesives, ink stains, spattered paint from decorating, indentations from ballpoint pens on thin paper, oil and grease marks from repairing a moped engine – there were a few nuts and bolts left over when the engine was re-assembled. David never did figure where they went, and the moped went better than ever.

But for the immediate duration, it was a desk. And David beavered away happily each evening to the comforting rumbles and gurgles of Ideal Boiler No. 1. For company he'd taken to bringing Natalia downstairs and his illustrious efforts would unfailingly win her approving smile. TressAmorë saturation point usually came around 9.30, and he and Natalia would retire to the lounge. Whereby he'd contemplate the glowing gas-fired coals or catch the back end of prime-time TV. On the floor by his chair was the reinstated pile of *BoyZo* comics – all 229 editions; ready to transport him back to sunny days should the enigma of *BoyZo* love re-ignite the blues.

At this time David rarely felt the need to go out. Work was all embracing and the three-month implementation challenge absorbed any emotional slack. And though a typical workday drew heavily on his resourcefulness, with Celia and Emily never far off the boil, he was able to temper manic productivity with some light relief. Thompson's was work and play – his surrogate family.

Unable to settle one evening he'd taken a spin over to Richmond on a long shot that the Jeanette d'Arcy Dance Studio was still a going concern. Predictably it was now a night club with bald men in black searching handbags.

On another occasion he met up with 'Chunky' Matthews, one of his unconventional pals from way back. They'd made acquaintance at the dingy 101 Club in Twickenham around 1971, and thereafter frequently teamed up to go on the pull. Forever pursuing a career in music of one sort or another, Chunky remained on the periphery of even moderate success but stoically kept at it from bedsit land. Entering The Half Moon pub in Putney David quickly spotted the 'uniform' – tight jeans, Cuban heals, navy blazer and scarf. But whilst his standard kit remained timeless, Chunky had aged within, his hair long and white, walrus moustache yellowed from the weed, weathered face and ragged fingernails. In his aimless days David happily co-existed with the lowest common denominator. But for the first time he saw his geeky friend in a different light – though it made not an iota of difference. And from the depths of his heart he pondered the vagaries of providence.

Following a sheepish apology from Emily, all in the garden was sweet – for a day or so. As a new tactic was now in force; the deployment of charm. She was now 'interested' in everything David did. Could she be actively involved in the TressAmorë project? A willing pair of hands eager to be put to work. And where did he learn all these professional skills? Could he mentor her in the fundamentals – after hours? Each morning Emily would perch at the side of David's desk and listen with intensity as he outlined the day's task.

'You're so clever, David – I don't know how you do it.'

On one occasion, Emily came over 'faint' as she went to leave. And whilst David held her waist she clung to him like a limpet as they made a laboured journey to her office. Where she quickly recovered.

All in all he managed to progress reasonably unfettered in bringing TressAmorë to the masses. Steam and Press was now gutted. And brickies, chippies, sparkies and plasterers milled around transforming the grubby production area into a space-age salon. Reception would be next. Then the coffee shop.

Hairbie stayed locked in his lab. And occasionally strange smells and the sound of minor explosions filtered into the refectory. When things had gone well Hairbie would emerge smiling triumphantly, sometimes with singed eyebrows, or peppered with strange substances.

Ajit, now a displaced wig steamer and presser confessed to being a wiz with website design – and got the job. Vera would manage the coffee shop and wear a hip new uniform. It would be based on the 1936 Lyons Corner House waitress styling, but slicked up for modern times. And there was no shutting her up.

Jenny Murgatroid had jetted off to darkest Africa to study hair styles of the folks in grass skirts. To date she'd established that they had satellite TV, mobile phones, wore Diesel watches and supported Man United.

Though everyone at Thompson's was wading around in muck and bullets, the anticipation of things to come kept spirits high. Those with the practical trades happily applied their skills in support of the metamorphosis. And the business and marketing brains re-engineered the commercial detail to fit TressAmorë branding. It was a wonderful renaissance. Just like the pioneering days when Harvey Thompson and the 'family' worked all hours building success in their basement beginnings.

A week into May David arrived home to an airmail letter. It was another false start, but nevertheless a heart-warming reply from Bobbie. As always she proved a big woman in many ways, tenderly responding to the thoughts David had spoken out loud in his therapeutic outpouring a few weeks back. Though he'd waxed excessive Bobbie distilled his emotive ramblings down to the prime mover – love and a sweet lady who was still fourteen in his heart.

On the 16th of May David's 60th birthday unceremoniously came and went. Apart from qualifying for cheap public transport little else changed. And he certainly felt no difference.

By the third week in May all of the structural alterations were complete. High ceilings had allowed for the coffee shop to reside on a mezzanine balcony overhanging the salon area. And the observation platform was a raised area on the other side bounded by a Greek themed balustrade. Closed circuit television would relay close-ups of salon activity to large screens in the observation area and also

Reception. Fitting the plate-glass shop window took three days and dramatically changed the front elevation of Thompson's. Regular passers by were getting curious and the plate-glass window was fast becoming soiled from snotty noses.

Reception was wide and spacious and bundles of wires emerged from the floor in readiness for connection to the receptionist's desk and console. And the entrance was remodelled from being square and functional to a wide arched portal with automatic doors. Metal studs to support the illuminated TressAmorë sign were already in place over the entrance. And both the entrance and plate-glass window would have attractive awnings.

It was exciting times.

June quietly arrived and by now most of the fixtures and fittings were in place. On the seventh Hairbert was presenting the new products. Time was tight but marketing had already previewed the lines to enable advance preparation of the sales and promotional material.

Celia was still dishing out her roll call of smutty come-ons. And David was responding sufficiently to keep the meat warm. It was a game. Whilst Emily stuck to her regime of subtlety – with winning ways that proved quite difficult to resist. Having believed he'd be set like a jelly when TressAmorë got the nod David now trod carefully, knowing Emily's hormonal blips could transcend reason and logic.

After a long grimy day on the 4th, David walked from Hammersmith to enjoy the warm balmy early evening air. Half an hour later Lydia was on the doorstep with yet another small package.

'This came for you and it needed signing for.'

Thanking her he hurried inside, his heart on the double once more.

It comprised a small brown mailing bag. Inside was a Rillington Hotel compliments slip and a small brown cardboard box around the size of two matchboxes side by side.

Inscribed on the slip was: 'Hi David, passing this on to you as requested by the sender. Best wishes, Don.'

It didn't strike any chords. And he certainly wasn't expecting a piece of wedding cake from anyone. The box was well sealed with Sellotape and inside was an envelope. With great anticipation David opened the envelope and out dropped a small item that sent his spirits soaring through the roof. A button identical to the one Natalia had left by his bed. And steeped in the same fragrance.

Natalia's words came back in a flash: 'I think I just wanted you to know I'd not deserted you.'

It was the same message and there was no questioning the lack of any other communication. Freshly infused with sweet memories this small velvet button delivered a thousand unspoken words. And David knew it was no idle gesture. To send a fond memory from 1958 bathed in romantic essence was a conscious decision of the heart.

When the habitual etceteras of early evening were done David relaxed by the fire. He delved into the pulp pile, joining Zachariah Lightning, Fists Malone, Hoss Maguire, Professor Inventor and Inspector Hero, and was lost in *BoyZo* happiness.

Arriving at work the next day around 9.30 he was in time to witness two workmen offering up the illuminated sign – nothing akin to the garish flickering neon of a burger bar. Instead, stylish individual letters crafted in red and gold relief with soft internal lighting. At work on the plate-glass window, a signwriter was applying the TressAmorë name and caption in artistic script, with a light drop shadow to add depth.

Reception was now functional pending the final decoration and clean-up and Gwen was receiving instruction on using the elaborate console. She'd been reared on the old Telecom PBX switchboards and Bakelite handsets, so the new array of buttons was her big challenge.

Everything was taking shape with increasing momentum. As with decorating a room, nine-tenths of the effort is in preparation. And it's only on application of the shiny overcoat that everything falls into place.

Meanwhile Jen Murgatroid was now in Amazonia and being ferried around the steamy backwaters in a wooden dugout. The main evidence of her visit was photos of her holding sloths, pythons and baby crocs.

Emily glowed with delight as David's vision progressively became reality, her affection now tinged with reverence. In much the same way that charm had superseded overt flirtation so her appearance mellowed to the bounds of decency, whist still being wide of frumpiness. Heels stayed high but stylish and hems came down – a smidgeon.

She switched to woollen tops that on a good day tastefully displayed a 2-inch cleavage. Whilst lips softened to pink and nails assumed a designer elegance. And her make-up and hair acquired the sophistication of a TV makeover.

David no longer felt threatened. Though he should have done. As when Emily had plagued him like an irritating fly he'd only to brush her off. But unlike a fly she was quietly getting under his skin and his guard had been dropped, confident there'd be no physical stand-offs. Occasionally she'd lightly touch his arm as they talked, or rest her hand on his shoulder whilst he sat and she stood. One day as they passed on the stairs Emily tripped and 'fell', and was masterfully caught by David, his hand inadvertently grabbing her right breast. Whilst he recoiled with embarrassment, Emily calmly smiled and assured him, 'It's alright, David, you saved me from a nasty accident.'

With her gentler approach he was able to develop a certain fondness, reminiscent of 1982, and tempered with whatever testosterone levels prevailed at the time. For the most part he found Emily's sycophantic attention to be a pleasant adjunct to an already vibrant day.

Hairbie's big day dawned and the refectory was crammed with expectation. Equipment stood at the ready and product samples were skilfully hidden from view. His presentations were legendary – more like a magic show. In fact some had featured a few tricks. Hairbie liked nothing better than a live audience and the opportunity to reveal his new babies with arcane flamboyance. Today was no different and the static electricity crackled and sparked in his goatee.

Featured first was the TressAmorë range of hair fibres. With deft legerdemain befitting any Magic Circle member he plucked the first fine product from behind a screen and presented, 'Magno-Tress'

This beautifully natural-looking synthetic hair fibre was available in any colour. And it could be colour matched to a user specification – as with paint.

But the most exciting feature of Magno-Tress was its ability to be styled. A demonstration was given. Hairbie selected a lady from his audience – Vera as it happened. She was seated in the hot chair and a wig comprising long chestnut hair fashioned from Magno-Tress was fitted. Hairbie explained at this juncture that the hair was available as a wig or attachments.

For the sake of the demo he quickly styled the hair using special rollers. And then a large beehive-shaped hood was lowered over Vera's head. He flicked a switch, the hood glowed and a magnetic field was activated, harmless to humans but which set the hair as styled. After five seconds the device was switched off. And with a majestic flourish Hairbie whipped away the hood, extracted the rollers and, Hey Presto! The curls stayed put.

Hairbie bowed and his devotees clapped.

And to prove the amazing ability of Magno-Tress the hood was quickly repositioned, the switch thrown again for five seconds and the curls dropped out rendering the hair completely straight.

Bowing again to rapturous applause Hairbie announced with the style of a music-hall master of ceremonies, 'I give you – Magno-Tress!'

Next to be featured was 'Chameleo-Tress'. This intelligent hair gently changed colour to match its surroundings. And it could be adjusted instead to assume the complementary colour of its surroundings or a mixture of the two settings.

Then there was 'Thermo-Tress', a remarkable product that changed style according to the ambient temperature. The audience watched entranced as the hair slowly curled and twisted and skewed in response to warm air from a hair dryer. In very hot sun it would darken and assume an Afro style.

There was more: 'Sonic-Tress', that curled and straightened to sound; 'Marquee-Tress' – dynamic colour changes slowly traversed each strand.

Vera returned to her seat to clapping and a few raspberries.

Equipment came next. And Hairbie prepared to demonstrate his star invention: Tress-O-Fix – patent applied for. This called for clinical conditions. Now 'Doctor Hairbert', he donned a white coat and for good measure, a stethoscope. His 'model' comprised head and shoulders fashioned from foamed polystyrene, and wearing a short-haired wig.

Looking through twin high-power lenses he became a micro-surgeon. And with specially developed tools he demonstrated the process for attaching fine swatches of TressAmorë hair to the model's existing hair. It comprised using a minute elastic band made from Tress-O-Prene, the size of a pinhead, which would easily expand to fit his thumb. The band secured the attachments to the natural hair. Then came the magic – hot air from a hair dryer shrank the already diminutive elastic band to microscopic proportions. And in the process it assumed the strength of high-tensile steel, locking the hair extension to the natural hair.

He waited for the big question – and it came. 'Yeah, Hairbie, but how do you remove the hair attachments?'

As if producing a rabbit from a top hat, Hairbie whipped out a stylish bottle concealed in his jacket. 'Tress-O-Zolve, my friends.'

Adding a capful to a bowl of warm water he proceeded to 'wash' his model's hair. And one by one the attachments fell away. Holding up the released attachments Hairbie announced with theatrical grandeur, 'Tress-O-Zolve dissolves only the Tress-O-Prene band, leaving everything else intact.'

To a standing ovation, Hairbie concluded his demonstration.

In three weeks time TressAmorë would go live. Four freelance hair extension stylists had been engaged for six months. And having familiarised with the new products and equipment they'd be ready to get weaving when the doors opened at the beginning of July. In the background they'd train in-house volunteers who'd become tomorrow's TressAmorë expert operatives.

The salon buzzed with pre-launch excitement. Staff posed as customers in the coffee shop and learned a few exotic expletives as Vera did battle with the new Cappuccino machine. And a stream of students from Marylebone Art College submitted their barnets for experimentation in exchange for a coffee and roll. This could be upped to a main course and pudding if they would spend an hour touting their new hairdo around London, handing out flyers to the curious public.

Advertising was well in hand and each day on the hour, every hour, the TressAmorë jingle trilled out on all the popular local radio stations.

A week before D-Day, David happened to wonder into the salon. Janine, a young lass apprenticed to learn the trade had installed a white poodle in one of the plush new salon styling chairs. Seeing David she slid guiltily in front of her 'client' – which served only to arouse curiosity. In jest David adopted a mock look of austerity.

'And what are you up to, Janine?'

Her face fell like that of a child caught with their fingers in the cake tin.

'Oh, err … I'm sorry, Mr Jenner, I was just playin' around.'

David's countenance softened into a fatherly smile, and he winked.

'Our clients seem to be looking more like poodles every day.'

This client was called Oscar and belonged to Janine's mum. And Oscar had acquired a very illustrious coronet attachment fashioned in Chameleo-Tress. While sprouting from his tail was a long rainbow swatch of stylised Magna-Tress.

David's imagination fired up once more as he hmm'd a few times and looked at Oscar from various angles.

'You know Janine, I rather like it.'

She smiled with relief.

'I though you was goin' to tell me off.'

David slipped his arm around her shoulders.

'Far from it, Janine – but I'd like you to do something for me. Would you take Oscar in a taxi to Knightsbridge and walk him around for about an hour and see what reaction you get, if any?'

Janine's eyes sparkled. 'OK Mr Jenner.'

Nearly two hours later Janine and Oscar arrived back, face alight and with stories to tell.

'Loads of people stopped me and asked about Oscar.'

David gently debriefed Janine to elicit the true yield. And it seemed in the space of ninety minutes she'd fielded at least twenty-three serious enquiries.

'So what did you tell people, Janine?'

'Well, I just said that it was an experimental design being tried out by TressAmorë.'

'And?'

'And I told them all about TressAmorë and that we're opening in a week's time.'

David left Janine with a remit to exhort any further creative ideas she might have on Oscar, whilst he retired to Mahogany Row to formulate another proposal. The idea of fitting dogs up with arty hair extensions was little more than a variation on a the current theme. David grinned as he mused whether 'fur-extensions' was the correct term. And he saw no great obstacles in replicating the business model to cater for four legs.

It seemed mainly about dreaming up a catchy name. David cycled through most of the doggy type names, but they were basic and unsophisticated: doggy this, doggy that, Fido this, Fido that. Then he recalled Mrs Wallace's dog Rex, from when he was a kid. After playing around with the name he came up with RexArama. It had a pleasant ring and he realised no single word could possibly allude to the services on offer.

David spent the rest of the day figuring out the whys and where-fores of extending TressAmorë services to a canine clientele. He discussed it with Emily who hung on to his every word as if he were blowing her tender kisses.

'Oh, David, what wonderful idea will you come up with next?'

And she laughed with good-natured amusement but quickly signed on to the idea, as by now the smell of success appeared to filter out of everything David touched. Later she ran it past the directors who decided to pilot the idea with minimal outlay for a period of three months. The large store room next to the salon would be redec-orated and set up as an interim doggy parlour.

Life for David was busy, interesting and fulfilling. Each day at Thompson's was a blur. Evenings were invariably spent mentally planning the next day. And for the last month he'd added Saturday to the working week. Sunday was for reflection and long tramps around Richmond Park to recharge his imagination.

But during the tranquil hours of slumber, David returned to happy days and 1958.

30

Love Hurts

At nine o'clock on the 1st of July TressAmorë opened its doors to the capital. There was champagne for all, with reporters and camera crews, business-minded folks looking for a franchise opportunity and salon owners seeking to operate the TressAmorë system under licence. And of course a stream of excited ladies who'd later emerge with their magnificent TressAmorë transformations.

Hairbie was in his element, dinner-suited and dickie-bow'd, dispensing samples of his magical hair fibres to the curious public. And Oscar, now with a showing of plumage that a hen peacock would be proud of, was being paraded back and forth by Janine – who also sported a TressAmorë hairdo *à la fantastique*. From the former Goods Inwards entrance issued elegant hounds regaled in RexArama splendour.

David wondered around taking questions, encouraging the staff, slipping a cool line of patter to clients, extolling the virtues of franchise opportunities and patting the poor canine punters who must have considered the whole pantomime a bit of a bummer. It was the Rillington lobby all over again.

Emily was aglow with happiness. 'I wish dad could have been here to see all this.'

David mentally concurred. Harvey had been a lovely guy, always ready to give reign to other people's creativity. Today's activity would have brought a broad smile to the Old Man's face.

'Yes, I know what you mean, Emily. If it wasn't for Harvey we wouldn't be here.'

He smiled and slipped his arm fondly around her shoulders. And she melted against him, her eyes brimming momentarily. David couldn't help but notice how lovely she looked today – and how lovely she felt.

Success that day came in almost make-believe proportions. And within two weeks the salon and RexArama were booked to capacity. A growing trend was for Chihuahua-carrying ladies to leave their furry fashion accessory with RexArama whilst they got the treatment at TressAmorë. People jostled for a good viewpoint in the observation gallery. And the business fraternity jostled each other in the corporate suite to have their orders prioritised.

Hairbie worked relentlessly on second-generation products and equipment. RexArama had ignited his already white-hot imagination. Prototype products were starting to appear, Hear-Boy! and Hear-Girl! being the latest. Fido wore a set of earphones, similar to the small Walkman ear-buds. Their owner carried a remote control already pre-programmed with a recording of their familiar call, such as 'Here Reginald', or 'Here Fifi'. At the press of a button, Fido would hear their master's or mistress's voice and it would appear to come from wherever the remote was being operated. It was all to do with stereo-phonic sound. And an errant hound could stray up to a mile from their owner and still be directionally summoned back.

Then there was 'Bite-Guard' – at the push of a remote control button a muzzle would snap into place over Fido's mouth. And more ideas were on the stocks.

Far from being able to rest on his laurels David's workload maintained impetus, the exploitation of one opportunity unearthing many more.

August arrived amid a long heatwave. David sweltered on the oven-like Bakerloo Line, his office little better than a sauna. Emily was now in her skimpy summer cotton togs and sporting a healthy tan. And at their daily one-to-one's in her office she'd endearingly kick off her shoes and curl up in her chair – little girl style. Their working relationship was easy and productive – unhampered by emotional tensions. Managerial issues were often resolved over a lunchtime drink away from the usual watering holes. Or a working meal at the Regent's Canal Brasserie. David revelled in the belief he'd elicited Emily's cooperation without falling prey to her romantic voodoo. Though in truth he'd got Emily just where she wanted him.

Although confident of having successfully earned his tenure on Mahogany Row David still trod carefully around Emily, mindful not to rupture any emotional aneurisms. But his trepidation was soon to be dispelled. On the 10th of August the Board invited him to sit in on their quarterly meeting at which he received heartfelt thanks for his innovation and drive – and more.

Joan Robinson primed his ears with a warm smile. 'David, in every possible way you've fulfilled your promise to Thompson Wigs as acting Business Development Manager, and we would like to inform you that subject to your agreement this position will be made permanent.'

More than three months had elapsed since the first edict was announced, leading David to assume confirmation, if it was given, would be by letter.

Flushed and pleased he replied, 'Thank you, Mrs Robinson and members of the Board, I would be very happy to accept.'

There were smiles all round for a minute and then a sombre mood cut in. Archie Lancaster stood up and turned to David.

'David Jenner, you are formally invited to join the Thompson Wigs Board of Directors – do you wish to accept this Directorship?'

It was an unexpected bolt from the blue. Stumbling to his feet he managed a rather mechanical response.

'Ladies and gentlemen of the Board I would be proud to accept the Directorship, and I assure you of my ongoing loyalty and support.'

Solemn faces cracked into smiles and all and sundry filed past to shake David's hand and congratulate him. Emily gently took his hand, smiling affectionately.

'Welcome David, you've truly earned you place on the Board.'

Keith Somersby whipped out a bottle of champagne.

'This, my son, is how we welcome new directors.'

Glasses clinked and down went the bubbly.

Reg Frith gave David a king-sized wink.

'So you pulled it off, EH WHAT?'

Archie Lancaster tapped his bald pate.

'Do you think TressAmorë could help?'

David laughed. 'We're working on it, Archie.'

For half an hour or so he laughed and joshed with his fellow directors as they made him welcome to their close-knit fraternity.

As now, he was one of the boys.

A week later Emily dropped by. Sown into a pretty figure-hugging cotton dress amid a swirl of matching perfume she had the makings of a babe. Elegantly perching on the side of David's desk she surveyed him with her sweet little girl look.

'David ...'

His reply was slow, calculated – and apprehensive.

'Yes ...'

'Well, I've been thinking, David, now that you're a member of the Board and a senior manager, I'd like to take you out to dinner to celebrate.'

David hmm'd to maintain the continuity.

'Would you like that, David?'

With dinner invitations a little thin on the ground it didn't take too long to figure the answer. Though Emily's delectable appearance had already given a loud 'yes'.

'That would be nice Emily – did you have a particular restaurant in mind?'

She did; and a day and a time – the Riverside Steak House in Richmond at 8.00 pm on Thursday, two days hence.

David knew the venue – a far cry from the Wimpy Bars he'd taken Emily to in their heyday. Occasionally he'd treated his victims from the Jeanette d'Arcy studio to a meal there. If it seemed worthwhile. It was divided into cosy, intimate snugs, many with a panoramic view of the Thames as it meandered towards Petersham.

'One thing, though, you must let me treat you.'

After the usual playful insistences on both sides David got his way.

'Anyway, it's only fair, Emily – I need to make up for all those awful meals I used to buy you.'

She looked fondly into his eyes.

'Yes, I know, but wasn't it fun?'

From recollection it was more about economics than fun. Anxious not to descend into pithy nostalgia David 'remembered' with a breezy nonchalance. 'Oh, err ... yes, I suppose it was, rather.'

And drawing Emily's gaze, and hopefully her attention to the window, he followed on with some meaningless diversion about the hot weather.

On her way out she playfully waved a finger and cautioned him not to forget. Her perfume lingered. And thanks to the wonders of mental persistence of vision, so did an image of her size twelve curves.

Richmond basked in the warm balmy overrun of another hot day. Leaving his aged Mondeo hidden in a nearby street David arrived in the restaurant car park just before 8.00. Emily waved from her S-Class Mercedes and got out. Beautifully turned out in a long Wedgwood blue satin dress and matching everything, she was a seriously good sight – body and soul. Having normalised to her office wardrobe he'd assumed tonight that her appearance would just be a variation on a theme.

With her arm linked through his they strolled to the entrance. It felt right. Two people who, after a motley journey of friendship and affection, had at last found an easy camaraderie, a warm amity.

For a minute they absorbed the south-westerly facing Thames vista from their cosy, intimate vestibule.

'You choose the wine, David.'

Perusing the list he took advice from the wine waiter – who recommended Bin 27.

Charged also with selecting the food he confessed to not being au fait with Emily's palate.

But smilingly she cooed, 'If you like it, then I'll like it.'

After wading through some serious à la carte they sat back to enjoy coffee and liquors, and talked and laughed to the soft candlelight of perfumed tallow. Though Emily appeared happy and relaxed she must have been patiently waiting for an appropriate lull in the conversation – when it came she reached across, gently taking David's hand.

'David, I want to ask you something – but please don't give me your answer now; just hear me out and let me know in a few days when you're ready.'

He beheld her sweet, vulnerable face, dark pupils mirroring the candle flame. In the warm atmosphere of intimate friendship and Drambuie, David felt disposed to helping out Emily in whichever way he could.

'Of course.'

Her grip tightened a little.

'David ... please will you marry me?'

For a second his face went a little delinquent.

'Marr—'

Emily smiled. She was braced for the initial shock wave – a woman on top. Lightly she applied a finger to his lips.

'Don't say anything now, David.' Giggling with girlish amusement she added, 'I wondered how you'd react.' She read his puzzled expression. 'And yes, David, I do mean it.'

Emily had come of age. No pathetic, emotionally delivered plea for marriage that was dead on arrival. Wisely she chose to seal his lips and win him over with charm and staff benefits.

Her smile put David at ease. And she continued with the pitch. It was all about a relationship that would be based on practical values. Their long association gave a special bond, and she admired and respected him. Her father would have been so proud of his achievements. And he'd truly become a part of Thompson's – his rightful place being at the head of the table in Harvey's office.

'I could make you very happy, David. You're a good person and I so believe in you. And you needn't worry about not being in love with me because I have enough love for both of us.' She squeezed his hand affectionately. 'That's all, David – sales pitch over. I won't mention this again. But please give me an answer in your own good time.'

From recoiling at the initial bare-bones proposal David was able to see things in the intended light.

At Emily's car she turned to him with a slightly mischievous smile.

'You've heard this before, David, but don't be alarmed – will you kiss me – please?'

He obliged and Emily melted in his arms, her soft open lips gently pressed to his. This time she kept the lizard buttoned.

With his mind in mental overdrive David arrived back at Number 69, the return journey a vague blur. En route his grey stuff had critiqued Emily's proposal from both ends – over and over. It had merits. Love was, perhaps, out of the question. Leastways it had never been part of the action in 1983 – but love has many guises. All said, though, he'd felt very close to Emily tonight and she'd never looked lovelier. They'd come a long way together since the days of *Tootsie*, and recent events had somehow forged a relationship that was starting to acquire substance and some enduring qualities. He truly believed Emily's promise of marital happiness. And he knew then and there, that it would be a fulfilling relationship from every angle. Overall it was an attractive package, and he grinned at the prospect of clearing Harvey's office of all The Captain's military knick-knacks.

Victor ascended the gatepost as David approached. He sought advice from his furry ginger friend but made no sense of the answer.

From the bedside table Natalia's pretty eyes smiled at him, as always, sweetly approving his thoughts and actions – regardless. And for the first time it unsettled David, as the realities of life were becoming the cultural norm, overshadowing sentimental hopes and dreams that had once sustained an aching heart.

Discussing the daily business with Emily as if the previous evening's events lay on the cutting room floor was a little strange. Though Emily made no mention her face glowed – eyes sparkled. And her smile was knowing and full of wedding bells. On one occasion she accidentally called him 'Darling'. It was a loaded situation that simply didn't 'exist'.

By now Celia had backed off. She'd assumed David's close working relationship with Emily extended beyond the call of duty. Instead Peter Spinks, David's successor, was getting the treatment. From all accounts Celia was dumping her size 18 butt on the same old desk in the same old position and flashing the same old hot spots. Though unbeknown to her, Pete liked skinny birds.

Meanwhile RexArama was approaching meltdown, the interim facility more like a bad hair day at Battersea Dogs' Home. David reasoned with the directors to immediately sanction money for the pukka facility. Thus another large grimy room got the nod for change of use.

A temporary problem occurred when Westminster Council complained about the dogs' doos on the pavement outside RexArama's makeshift entrance. It was a challenge for Hairbie – who devised a self-service canine loo. But the owners got stroppy at the boys and bitches squatting together, some even having a sly hump. Messieurs' and Madams' made everything right.

Three days on from the Richmond experience and David was still on the fence. And he knew that without something to catalyse a decision he'd remain with a leg in each camp. On arrival he'd passed Emily, whose assumptive smile was expecting the final box to be ticked. And he knew that today he'd have to bite the bullet, if only in fairness to Emily. At 11.00, armed with sweaty palms and indecision he knocked on The Captain's door. There was no green light – instead Emily opened the door like a wife welcoming her weary husband home from work.

'Hello David, I thought it might be you.'

Her buoyant demeanour stymied any attempt at nonchalance. Door closed they stood facing each other.

In subdued tones David got to the point. 'I wanted to give you an answer to what you asked me in Richmond.'

It would have been clear to the average observer at this point that a resounding 'Yes' was probably unlikely. But for Emily the situation wasn't quite that black and white. Unfazed by any negative signals she brightly urged him to, 'Tell me what you've decided.'

At this point David had no more idea than Emily what would exit his mouth. But nevertheless words issued forth, and in a strangely detached way.

'I, err ... can't marry you, Emily.'

Immense relief washed over David, whilst once again Emily demonstrated a capacity to absorb bad news. Composed and still with a warm smile she replied, 'I understand, David – why don't we talk about things.'

Having deposited him in a chair she announced, 'I'll sit on your lap while we chat things over.'

Which she did – the down thrust of her shapely hind quarters pressing all the right buttons.

Stroking David's neck she softly invited him to 'Tell me all about it.'

Having delivered a 'No', he'd assumed declining Emily's offer would cut things dead, invoking tears and precipitating his fall from grace. Instead it honed up her tenacity.

Stark truth seemed the best ploy in defusing any residual hope.

'I met someone whilst I was in New York, Emily, and I'm hoping we will eventually get together.'

Bad move. Emily's eyes brightened – now there was competition to see off.

'Is she as pretty as me?'

They played word games for a while until finally in sheer exasperation David spelled it out for her. 'Emily, I just can't marry you, I'm in love with Natalia.'

She went quiet and he felt her crumple up in his arms. Then came tears and her shoulders heaved with silent sobs. It tore him apart.

For a long time he just held her, powerless to assuage her lachrymose demeanour. Until finally the tears eased and she raised her face, now an artistic array of salty mascara smudges, red eyes and unhinged lipstick. To David she looked more beautiful than ever before. And so vulnerable and adorable. In another existence he knew the answer would have been a heartfelt 'yes'.

'I'm so sorry, David, I don't know what you must think of me.'

He made all the right noises. And then stuck a wet finger in the air to test the water.

'Would you prefer it if I left the company, Emily?'

Her eyes brimmed again. 'OH NO, David, please don't do that, I'd be devastated if you left.'

Little by little he jollied Emily up, suggesting they have lunch somewhere in Covent Garden. It brought the colour back into her face, though just as he went to leave she slipped back to her old tricks.

'David ... when will you be getting together with your lady from New York?'

He smiled. 'To be honest, Emily, I just don't know, and it may never happen.'

Slipping her arms around David she lapsed into little girl mode.

'So ... perhaps we could go out together now and then UNTIL she arrives – IF she arrives?'

David laughed and tenderly kissed her forehead, nodding in affirmation.

'Emily, you really are incorrigible, but I wouldn't have you any other way.'

After spaghetti bolognaise and a glass or two of Chianti at Pasta City, the world seemed a better place. And a line was drawn under another full-circle emotional interlude that mercifully had dissipated without bloodshed. It left the pair another step closer to finding a compromise between friendship and love – Emily supplying the love, David the friendship.

A healthy afternoon's workload kept the grey matter engaged. But homeward bound David's thoughts defaulted to the emotional strands in his life. Fending off Emily's romantic overtures had kept him defensive – inhibiting any reciprocated affection on his part. And he'd allowed her matronly image from way back to tarnish current perception.

Emily however, like David, had shed a skin or two and quietly come of age. But true to gender, chauvinistic ignorance compelled him to assume she'd simply twisted herself way out of character to win his affection.

Immersed in thought, David emerged from Hammersmith Station and hit the pedestrian route home on full auto-pilot. As always those twenty golden minutes on the hoof served well to recall, reason, rationalise, reconcile – and resolve. Over and over he recalled how pretty Emily had become, how alluring she looked, how good she felt. And how sweet she tasted. In a supreme male moment it dawned on him that this was the real Emily. That she'd climbed out of her frumpy chrysalis to flourish as a pretty butterfly.

And it became apparent too that a deepening affection was bonding them – that a spiritual convergence was in the making.

In stark contrast was his tenuous link with Natalia; sustained by *BoyZo* dreams and smiling eyes David had been so sure he'd eventually find the rainbow's end. It was on the back of this conviction that his subconscious had finally delivered a 'No' to the offer of real love and a warm pulse. Now doubt set in, with depressing thoughts that elusive *BoyZo* love was simply retribution to punish his shallow regard for the hearts of others.

Victor was away working other gateposts in the neighbourhood. For the first time since returning David felt very alone in the house. He spent most of the evening agonising over love that was available and love that was, perhaps, no more than capricious expectation. Emily was the proverbial bird in the hand and her exotic plumage was becoming more attractive by the day day. Though at night, under Natalia's watchful smile, he remained captive in the world of *Boyzo*.

The next morning David worked with interior decorators hired to create a stylishly themed RexArama studio. But at the back of his mind lurked a growing need to behold Emily in all her sweetness, and for the first time to really 'see' her. Alas she failed to show at work.

However a day later, on the pretext of some minor detail he got the green light. Kitted out in a snug beige business suit and figure-hugging top with a tantalising degree of cleavage in view, she looked delicious. He received a smiling welcome – but something was different. Something akin to that almost imperceptible change when summer finally burns itself out and the first hint of morning dew appears

Two days before she had been determined to be David's interim companion. Now that spark seemed absent. Anxious to confirm her availability he suggested they might 'have a meal together one evening this week'.

Rather dismissively Emily explained, 'I'm going to be quite busy this week, David. Perhaps another time.'

Her answer served only to reinforce the intuitive vibes he'd sensed on entering. For weeks he'd lounged around on his laurels enjoying Emily's predatorial attention, never expecting the fall that succeeds pride. And now it seemed the pretty bird had returned to the bush. Overnight their affections had traded places leaving David hankering for what had been within his grasp.

Graciously he withdrew. And déjà vu blew a raspberry at him for screwing up twice with the same opportunity. Deep down he knew he'd had choices, made decisions. Being out of the running for something he'd probably never truly wanted was a bitter pill that thankfully had a relatively short aftertaste. It was a situation that illustrated how wonderfully faulted human nature can be.

For two days Emily went AWOL. On returning she asked David to stop by.

Pale and tired she explained, 'I'm going to be away for a while, David, and I would be grateful if you would act as Managing Director in my absence.'

David surmised personal problems and willingly agreed. Naturally the prospect of permanently taking on the MD mantle crossed his mind.

'I'll come in once a week to discus progress and any issues.'

There were no other instructions or requests. Emily simply wanted David to climb into the breach and take the reigns.

She smiled at him wanly, her mind seemingly elsewhere. But as he shaped up to rise she touched his arm.

'David, I want you to know what this is all about.'

She explained that a week ago Michael Urquart had called her begging for them to meet up. At first she dismissed him. But he seemed desperate to see her and she finally agreed. They'd met four days ago, and having talked all day met again yesterday and the day before.

'Michael has asked me to give him another chance. He's a much changed person and he really needs me, and I think perhaps deep down I need him. I was devastated when he left, but I feel, David, that I want to try and mend our marriage – and our children very much want us to reconcile.'

It seemed the Urquarts had opted for a quickie divorce but yesterday Emily had snatched the decree nisi back from the brink of absolution.

Within, David felt hollow. But he wished her happiness and walked to the door. Emily followed and shyly asked if he would 'Please hold me one more time, David.'

Their embrace was gentle and affectionate. And as they disentangled Emily kissed David on the cheek.

'My feelings for you haven't changed at all, David, and I shall always love you. But I must close my mind and give everything to repairing my marriage.'

They parted as friends who would always have a place in each other's hearts.

Business as usual followed and David had to appease a client whose Sonic-Tress hairdo had spontaneously burst into flames. Hairbie got a bollocking and more smells and muffled explosions escaped R & D as the problem was rectified.

Finding solace in *BoyZo* helped pass an empty evening. Whilst TressAmorë and RexArama challenges eased any solitude on Mahogany Row the following day. David declined a pint with Frank. He felt glum and didn't want any inquisitions. Nor even an opportunity to junk his woes into the dark, safe recesses of Frank's brain. Rather he preferred to quietly assimilate events of the last few days. Though a nagging thought persisted – that even if he'd accepted Emily's marriage proposal would she have been swayed by The Captain's plea for reconciliation? Eventually he managed to console himself with the rather contrived notion that he'd escaped the finite possibility of being unceremoniously dumped.

Working through until 6.30 truncated another potentially depressing evening. Tonight Victor was enthroned and anxious to engage David in eye contact. Articulating a silent meow followed by a strange gurgle from the back of his throat, he then gently patted David's nose with a fluffy ginger paw. It was a message in felineaze that succeeded, if nothing else, in bringing a smile to David's glum features. Opening the front door he scooped up the letters. One stood out from the rest – an airmail letter shrouded in a fragrance that was familiar music to his nose. Heart pounding to a frenzied ventricular fandango, his brain spewed an exotic chemical cocktail into his blood-stream that eclipsed any feel-good fix. Turning to close the door he caught sight of Victor. Perhaps it was a trick of the light. But he was convinced that:

Victor was smiling.

31

BoyZo to the Last

David's chest pulsed like the Super Woofer speaker of a 500-watt ghetto blaster. In the dark hallway he offered the thin airmail letter to his nostrils, savouring it like an expensive wine before consumption. In slow time he took a small sharp knife from the kitchen before getting comfortable on the settee. Cautiously he slit open the letter, careful to insert the knife between the correct folds of paper. It wouldn't be the first time he'd dissected an airmail letter in two.

It read:

> Dear David,
>
> I do so hope that after all this time there is a chance that we can still get to know one another.
>
> My unavailability must have seemed very strange to you, but I'm hoping the following account of recent events in my life will help you forgive such a long wait.
>
> For nearly a year I've been involved in an extremely acrimonious divorce. It had got to unbearable proportions around the time you were here, and I was being followed and monitored persistently.
>
> I so much wanted to be in contact with you, but we would have had to endure horribly clandestine conditions. Building a quality friendship would have been impossible, and thus I decided to wait, trusting that time wouldn't diminish our chances of meeting again.
>
> During the dark moments of the divorce when there seemed no light at the end of the tunnel I was sustained by your quest to find me after forty-six years of waiting. And not a day goes by

David read and reread the letter, occasionally savouring the familiar fragrance. And then flopped back in the settee to enjoy a pleasant reverie. He noted the time – nearly 7.45 pm. It would be early afternoon in the States. Unable to contain himself further he dialled Natalia's number. After the usual international pips and squeaks the dulcet single rings of a US phone number took over. A soft, composed woman's voice answered, 'Hello, this is Natalia Ginetta.'

The Super Woofer was hammering away again by now.

'Oh, err … hello, this is David Jenner.'

Warmth and emotion kicked in.

'Oh, David – it's so good to hear your voice.'

'And yours too, Natalia.'

Clearly neither party wanted to rake over the dreary coals of the last six months.

David got bold.

'Natalia?'

He could hear her smiling.

'Yes … David?'

'I think we should get together.'

'I agree, David, when did you have in mind?'

'Err … tomorrow.'

Her laugh was infectious.

'Fine by me – where shall we meet?'

'Well, I could come to you, or you could come to me – whatever suits you, Natalia.'

David would happily have packed his toothbrush there and then, but he wondered if Natalia might welcome a break from the grim backdrop of divorce.

'May I come to you, David?'

'Of course, Natalia.'

'When?'

'Tomorrow!'

More peels of laughter.

It was time for some Rillington assertiveness.

'Natalia, please, just buy a ticket to London Heathrow – I'm going to look after you.'

Her voice softened.

'Alright, David.'

'Now Natalia, I can organise a hotel for you, or I can put you up in my large spare room.'

His spare room was in fact the main bedroom that had remained clean and aired and cherished, but empty, since his parents' passing.

After some 'are you sure it won't be too much trouble?' banter they settled for David's spare room.

Finally they dragged themselves off the phone as 10.00 approached.

At work the next day there were numerous references made to David's silly smile. At lunchtime Frank and he finally got to having a pint together. Between gulps the big man smiled fondly at his effervescent friend as he rabbited on ad nauseam about Natalia.

Immediately after lunch David hit the Bakerloo Line. By 6.00 pm his parents' bedroom was fit for royalty. And the house shipshape.

Opening a Bud he ambled out into the garden and got comfortable on that old wooden sun lounger. Things looked much as they'd done exactly a year ago. A couple more brittle wooded slats from the fence had fallen away. And the wisteria was going seriously local. Wriggling onto his back he gazed into the misty blue of another warm summer's end day. Birds of every feather joined the evening chorus and a blackbird on the chimney pot sang 'Sweet Adeline' in a pretty mezzo-soprano warble. Harmonising with evensong was the smell of freshly cut grass as it mingled gently with dusk's sweet aromatic vapours.

Large silver birds from the east droned past, engines rising and falling in pitch as their on-board computers jockeyed the controls. David studied the brightly lit tailplanes with their characteristic designs and colours; Cathay Pacific, Qantas, British Airways, Lufthansa, Air New Zealand. American Airlines.

Tomorrow would be the 1st of September. But for all David cared it could have been the first of infinity – as now he'd found a universal cure for the blues. It was called 'Natalia'.

Armed with the empty Bud bottle he hit the scullery and shut up shop for the night. After a cup of tea and the usual flip through *BoyZo* he and Natalia were glad to get an early night in.

Emerging from the Heathrow tunnel David steered his five-year-old silver Mercedes towards the Terminal 3 short stay car park. Not a bad trade for eight grand and a knackered Ford Mondeo. In forty-five minutes Natalia's flight would touch down to the grey of dawn – enough time to figure the Arrivals gate geography and slurp a large sweet Costa cappuccino. He'd chosen the beige Eduardo Cabeleira suite to be smart without the austere formality of navy blue.

Still with an hour to kill he trawled the Departure Lounge shops upstairs and fitfully read the *Daily Mail*. Within ten minutes of taking up position at the arrivals gate a dribble of passengers from Flight 562 emerged. And suddenly Natalia was walking straight towards him. In an elegant powder-blue suite and delicate white heels she could have passed as a regal air hostess from those opulent days when Sunderland flying boats graced the empty skies and ladies in long evening gowns hoofed it up at the Ritz.

In no time they were in a tight clinch that lasted for eons, eventually disengaging to behold each other, as lovers do, and silently beam a million emotions.

Finally David found his tongue.

'You look so lovely, Natalia, I can't believe you're standing in front of me.'

'Nor me, you, David, and you look so handsome.'

Hands tightly clenched and with luggage in tow they strolled blissfully to the car.

Forty minutes worth of speed talking made a modest dent in getting acquainted as they sped along. And Natalia's eyes sparkled whilst observing the 'quaintness' of West London.

'I've never been to Britain before, David, it looks so different.'

Promises abounded. 'I'll take you to so many beautiful places, Natalia.'

To which she coyly suggested, 'We'll need a lot of time to do all that.'

David gave her a smooth side-on smile. 'Yes, but we've got all the time in the world.'

As they rumbled over Hammersmith Bridge Natalia remarked 'how pretty' it was.

David agreed, whilst silently recalling the defining moments in his life that had occurred whilst gazing upstream from the bridge.

Victor got the full treatment from Natalia and flashed David an 'I told you so' look.

Within half an hour they were sipping hot tea in the kitchen. Ideal Boiler No. 1 got jealous and threw a wobbly.

Natalia's face lit up with amusement.

'What ever's that?'

David laughed.

'It's the hot water solid fuel stove.' Hastily adding, 'I'm, err ... thinking of replacing it.'

Briefly studying the small black conglomeration of cast iron she granted a reprieve.

'Oh no, David, it's sweet, you mustn't change it.'

Natalia was delighted with the 'spare room' and insisted on seeing David's abode – probably assuming he occupied the master en-suite bedroom. What met her eyes was a single room with various model aircraft suspended from the ceiling and all the usual clutter of adolescent imagination adorning the walls, book shelves and cupboards. Above the fireplace was a large poster of Zachariah Lightning looking every bit the saviour of humanity.

Natalia surveyed the contents with fascination.

'This must have been your room for a long time.'

'Since I was five.'

He watched quietly as she went back in time; reading, touching, studying, absorbing – trying to visualise 'young David'. Until finally she spotted her photograph.

'So THIS is where you keep me.'

'Yes Natalia.' And with a cheeky wink he added, 'I also take you downstairs with me in the evening.'

It struck a chord.

'I meant to tell you, David — I've brought my Rockette's uniform with me. It's been let out a little to fit me and I just need to sew the two buttons back on.'

She smiled coyly, 'I might model it for you if you ask me nicely.'

For David it couldn't get any better. It would almost be as if Natalia was stepping out of the silver frame.

But as yet she was unaware of the strange journey of the heart inspired by her lovely photograph. For Natalia, the her pretty image at fourteen committed to photographic paper was simple childhood nostalgia — an event of no real consequence that briefly steamed up a bunch of limey schoolboys. And David realised she couldn't possibly be touched by the same deep emotions that inspired his search for 1958.

Fondly he acknowledged her offer.

'I'd like that very much — it really means a lot to me.'

Then came a heart-warming surprise — it was as if Natalia had been earwigging on his inner thoughts, and she turned to him wistfully.

'Oh, David, I wish I'd known you when you were young.' Slowly she cast her gaze around the room scanning again the memorabilia of a lifetime. 'This room has a lovely mystique to it — I can just see you in here reading your *BoyZo* comics and making things. Do you have any photos of you as a boy?'

Did he have any photos? Just a bureau full.

'Loads and loads — you'll be bored silly.'

When Natalia was satisfied she'd plumbed the depths of David's adolescent years, which extended into his fifties, she retired to bath, unpack and maybe sleep for an hour or so.

In the meantime David pottered and tinkered and smiled to himself, still pleasantly in denial.

Later they drove to Richmond and after a stroll in the park supped tea together in Dickens and Jones. Quickly they became a loving couple. And if they weren't arm in arm or tightly holding hands, they'd be strolling with arms curled around each other.

For simplicity David organised an Italian takeaway — which they ate in slow time in the dining room with candles, wine and the works.

By 8.00 the large Edwardian semi was getting chilly, prompting a move to the lounge and the soft hiss and 'blup blup' of gas-fired coal. In the warm glow they sat affectionately locked together on the settee. As in any love scene their lips were magnetically attracted. But when contact seemed imminent, Natalia mischievously pulled back, explaining, 'You can't kiss me, David, because you haven't won the *BoyZo* competition.'

He playfully hmm'd a few times and retrieved page 6 from its plastic cover in the bureau. Within ten minutes he'd crafted his twenty-word entry on a sheet of writing paper. On holding up the prize-winning entry to read it out loud Natalia cut in with a wicked smile, 'No David, you must fill in the coupon on page six and give it to me.'

With amusement, he obliged.

It took only a few seconds for Natalia to read the brief wording. But when she looked up at David again, her pretty cheeks were wet with tears.

'Oh David, that is so, so beautiful – oh David.'

As the coupon floated down to the carpet their lips finally met in a kiss that lasted for ever and they drifted into the timeless world of true BoyZo love.

Zachariah Lightning eased himself into an armchair and pushed the black eyepatch up to reveal a perfectly good eye. Leaning forward he retrieved the completed competition coupon and read the words that only a captive heart could scribe. They stirred emotions that were as old as the Universe, and a warm and understanding smile briefly softened his rugged countenance.

Carefully returning the coupon he reclined in the deep upholstery and for a while fondly observed his two charges as they embarked on their romantic journey back to 1958.

Then he was gone – reabsorbed into the two-dimensional world of *BoyZo* to join Fists Malone, Hoss Maguire and the rest of the crew. As now, his mission was complete.